MURDER IN THE CASTRO

A Lou Spencer Mystery

ELAINE BEALE

MURDER IN THE CASTRO

A Lou Spencer Mystery

Elaine Beale

New Victoria Publishers
Norwich, Vermont

Published by New Victoria Publishers, Inc., a feminist literary and cultural organization, PO Box 27, Norwich, VT 05055-0027

1 2 3 4 5 2001 2000 1999 1998 1997
Printed and bound in Canada

Cover Design by Claudia McKay
Photo of author by Lisa Rudman

Library of Congress Catalog-in-Publication Data

Beale, Elaine, 1962-
    Murder in the Castro / by Elaine Beale.
        p. cm.
    ISBN 0934678-87-1
    I. Title.
    PS3552.E1366M87   1997
    813' .54--dc21   97-14674
                                                         CIP

Chapter One

I felt a hard, urgent tug on my right shoulder. Without even pausing to think, I pulled back my arm, clenched my fist, and was about to jab a well-targeted elbow into the abdomen of the stranger accosting me. Luckily, I hesitated long enough to feel the hand on my shoulder drop loosely away and to hear a strained voice inquire, "Excuse me, but you work at Stop The Violence Project, don't you?"

I turned around slowly to see a stocky young woman looking at me from wide, bloodshot eyes, her complexion ashen. The line of spectacular bruises just above her collar decorated her neck like a string of purple-black pearls. And like many victims of assault I had seen in the course of my work, she wrapped her arms around her body in a protective gesture.

"Bloody hell," I muttered in shock, letting my hand drop to my side.

She took a step back. "I'm sorry, I didn't mean to startle you."

"No, no that's fine…I should be the one apologizing. You look as if you've been through enough already."

"Yeah, I guess you could say that," she agreed, running a hand self-consciously over her face, and skittishly moving her weight from one foot to the other.

I couldn't help but feel annoyed with myself. My over-reaction probably hadn't helped ease her trauma. It was my job to help victims of violence, and here I was, twelve weeks of self-defense classes under my belt and I was acting like a female version of Rambo.

"I thought maybe you'd be able to help me out. You do work at The Project, don't you?"

"Yes. I'm on my way to the office right now. Why don't you come with me? If you like I can set you up with one of our advocates."

"Thanks, I really appreciate that," she said, looking pathetically grateful. "By the way, I'm Natalie Featherstone." She reached out to grasp my hand in a damp and wavering grip.

"And I'm Lou Spencer," I replied as I squeezed her hand reassuringly, hoping she sensed my sympathy. Poor thing, she looked like yet another naive and hopeful prairie girl who had run away from small town homophobia to embrace the 'gay mecca' of San Francisco. Being gay-bashed probably wasn't the welcome she'd hoped for.

"So, you're not one of The Project's advocates?" Natalie asked as we stood at the intersection of Castro and Eighteenth, waiting for the light to change.

"No, I'm the Office Manager," I answered. "How did you know I work there?"

"I saw you give a talk at a rally once, I remember your accent—English, right? And the red hair, of course, it's pretty distinctive." I nodded. Friends and strangers alike told me my long, flame-red hair made it easy to pick me out in a crowd. After all these years, I still wasn't sure if that made it an asset or a liability.

When we reached the Project, a few doors down on Castro Street, I unlocked the door and gestured Natalie up the treacherously steep flight of stairs that led to our ramshackle second floor office. Once inside, I directed her to a chair. She sat down and let her gaze wander over the room. She took in the chaotic stacks of files covering almost every available surface, the stained carpet of now indeterminate color, and the battered metal desks.

"Can I get you a cup of tea?" I asked. "I was about to make myself one anyway." Even after years of work with clients in crisis I revert back to my cultural training. In England tea is a cure-all for every tragedy; it's been my sustenance through a great variety of personal traumas.

"Tea would be great," she answered.

"Good, then I'll put the kettle on."

A few minutes later I handed her a steaming mug of black tea and took a moment to study her features beyond the horrible signs of her injury. Under a checked shirt and jeans, her build was thick and muscular. The way she sat with both feet planted firmly on the floor, she certainly looked like someone who could take care of herself. But her face belied the tough butch image she seemed eager to cultivate—round-cheeked and wide-eyed, she had a button nose and the kind of mouth I've seen painted on the faces of cherubs fluttering around naked women in Renaissance paintings.

"Do you take sugar? It's good for shock, I think."

"Shock?" She asked, frowning.

"Yes, you're probably in shock. Looks like something pretty bad happened to you."

She took a sip of the tea. "It's fine without the sugar, thanks. But, yeah, I guess I am in shock."

"You want to talk about it? Or would you rather wait for one of our advocates?" I checked my watch, the other staff were due in the office in a matter of minutes.

"I think I'd rather wait," she said, squeezing both hands tightly around the tea mug.

I nodded. I could tell from the way she held herself that she wasn't someone who had an easy time expressing emotions. And though I was sure she'd never admit it, it had probably taken all her courage to come up to me in the street. I didn't intend to push her to talk about anything she didn't want to. So we waited in silence, Natalie studying the floor and taking occasional sips from her tea mug, while I sorted through the papers on my desk, until Mario Fuentes, my dearest friend and the Project's Education Coordinator, arrived.

"Hi, Lou," he said as he sauntered into the office, his sleek, black hair bobbing in its tight pony tail. "How's it going? Hey, I like the shirt." He gave a long and appreciative look at the black linen shirt I'd bought just last week. "Brings out your hair and emphasizes those nice broad shoulders...Very Sexy," he finished suggestively.

I rolled my eyes, pretending offense. But Mario knew he was one of the few people I'd let get away with that kind of comment. He also knew I could be a sucker for flattery—and having spent a sizable portion of my meager wages on this particular item, I needed all the flattery I could get. But I didn't let myself get distracted for too long. "Mario, this is Natalie." I said, gesturing towards her.

"Wow, you look like you went through a rough time," he said, pulling his most sympathetic smile. "When did this happen?"

"Last night." Natalie said, looking up reluctantly.

"Well, you've come to the right place, you know." He gave a reassuring nod. "One of the advocates will be in real soon and they'll definitely be able to help you. They can help file police reports, follow up with investigators and if the cops find out who attacked you, we'll help if you have to go to court and testify. We can do all kinds of stuff to make things easier."

Natalie's face brightened. "Yeah, that's right." Her voice sounded suddenly animated. "My friend Jim said you guys made sure the creep who assaulted him went to trial. The D.A. wanted to make a deal, but you stopped that happening. And he said that when his boss was giving him such a hard time for being out sick because of the attack, someone from your office called up and explained why Jim needed the time off. He said you guys were just great."

"Well, I'm sure there's a lot of ways we can help you, too."

Natalie nodded, her lips edging into a hesitant smile. "Yeah, maybe you can," she said, placing the tea mug on my desk, pushing her legs out and relaxing back into her chair.

It wasn't the first time I'd seen Mario bring about such a dramatic transformation in a client. Some days, his presence was like a ray of sunshine in our dark and dingy office. It was for this, and many other reasons, that we had become best friends. And as I watched him take his seat at the desk across from mine, I found myself once again admiring his beautiful face. With his angular jaw, soft, delicate mouth, and long, straight nose, Mario was neither pretty nor handsome, but somewhere in between, and I often joked that if he had been a girl I would have married him in a second.

"Hi, Lou. Hi, Mario." Peter Williams, one of The Project's advocates strode into the office. He stopped to lean against the door jamb where he beamed a boyish smile that quickly collapsed into a loud yawn.

"Up late last night?" Mario said acidly.

"That's none of your business," Peter sniped back, pushing a hand through his straw blond hair to finger one of the gold hoop earrings that dangled from his ears.

"Really?" Mario pushed his chair back from his desk and seemed about to march over to Peter.

Peter responded by rolling his eyes and planting his hands on his slim, angled hips. "That's right," he said defiantly. "So just get over it."

"Ah, hem." I sounded a loud, throaty cough and flashed them both my sternest look. "Peter, this is Natalie. She's here to see an advocate. Are you available right now?"

"Er, yes," he said, his eyes still on Mario, filled with what I could only describe as disdain. He let out another loud, tonsil-flashing yawn before turning to Natalie. "I can see you right now. Why don't you come with me to my office." Natalie nodded and eased herself out of her chair to follow him down the hallway.

As soon as they disappeared into Peter's office, I turned to Mario. "Jesus, Mario, you two need to calm down. Talk about tension at work. You and Peter take the bloody biscuit. And not to mention professionalism. I can't believe you started that in front of a client. And I, for one, am sick of having to listen to your little digs at one another…" My voice trailed off as I noticed a tear form in the corner of his eye and trickle slowly down his cheek.

"I'm sorry, Lou," he said, lifting the back of his hand to his face, dabbing away the solitary tear and struggling to regain his composure. "I know I need to control myself. But it's impossible. I just don't know what to do. I feel so…dumped. I know you probably think it was stupid of me to get involved with Peter in the first place." I resisted the urge to nod. It wasn't going to help if I started saying 'I told you so'—even though I was sorely tempted. "Goddamn it, Lou," he continued. "I just can't get over how Peter blew me off. I mean, three months when everything seems like it's going wonderfully and then bam, he says he can't continue to date someone he's working with. And I'm history, just like that. What a jerk!"

"You're right," I nodded, "he's behaved like a real wanker."

"A what?" Mario gave me a quizzical look.

"Sort of the British version of jerk," I replied.

"Oh." He paused thoughtfully for a moment. "But he's not all bad, you know. He does a great job with his clients." He gestured down the hall towards Peter's office. "And he's so committed to his politics. He does something with Act-Up or Queer Nation almost every night."

I shook my head. Maybe Peter was good at his job, and maybe Mario had shown bad judgment by getting involved with a co-worker. But that didn't change the fact that Peter had treated him shamefully. "Take it from me, Mario," I said, "you're better off without him."

He sighed. "I know you're right. But I still can't seem to get over him. God, it's so hard to see him every day. I'm sorry for the tension, Lou. And I know he's a …wanker. It's just going to take me a long time to get over him. You of all people should know how that goes."

I nodded. Unfortunately, after Justine, I knew far too well.

Chapter Two

"Oh my God, Lou, help!" Amanda Jensen, The Project's Executive Director, made her entry by tripping over the loose piece of carpet in the office doorway. With one broad arm laden with an overstuffed shopping bag and a black leather attaché case, the other precariously carrying a Styrofoam cup of coffee and a folded *San Francisco Chronicle*, she stumbled towards me. Seeing the sloshing coffee threaten to overturn and transform the entire surface of my desk into a coffee-splattered mess, I leapt up and deftly plucked the cup from her hand. Amanda staggered to a halt. "Thank God for that," she sighed, dropping the rest of her load onto one of the chairs before turning to me with a grim stare. "Now didn't you say you were going to fix that carpet, Lou? It's a goddamn health hazard."

"I'm sorry," I said sheepishly, handing her back her coffee. "I just didn't get around to it. It's been really busy these last few days."

"Well take care of it today, can you?" She placed the coffee on my desk and began unfastening the buttons on her heavy wool coat. "The last thing we need is a client coming in and reinjuring themselves. We can scarcely make payroll this month, never mind deal with a personal injury law suit."

"Okay," I agreed, "I'll do it as soon as I can."

"Brrrr," Amanda shivered as she opened her coat to reveal a tailored blue linen pant suit and cream silk blouse, "it's cold in here!"

"It is a little chilly," I responded.

"Chilly? It's absolutely freezing. Dressing for work these days is like setting out for an Arctic expedition."

"Well, you always have that extra set of clothes in your office you keep for press interviews and stuff. You could put them on over your outfit. You know, create a layered effect, I understand it's very trendy these days," I offered.

"Now that's a great suggestion," Amanda said, her voice filled with irony.

"Oh, come on, Amanda, you know you just got spoiled by all those perks of corporate life," Mario commented. "Climate-controlled offices, catered lunches, expense accounts. Sounds like a great life to me." He leaned back in his chair and folded his arms behind his head. "Can't imagine what made you come to The Project."

Amanda waved her hand dismissively, wafting the rich odor of her expensive perfume towards me. "I can assure you, when I came to The Project eighteen months ago I was sick up to here of corporate America. Even the pay check wasn't enough to make up for working with a bunch of money-grabbing robots. And here in San Francisco they pretend they're all so liberal and gay-friendly, but scrape below the surface and you'll find the homophobia, believe me."

"So did you get discriminated against?" Mario asked.

"As an out lesbian, I wasn't exactly invited into management with warm and welcoming arms." A cool bitterness settled across Amanda's features. "I was the best damn PR person they had, but I was never allowed to go as far as I could. And towards the end, well, I was pretty much ousted, though everything was just so subtle that I'd never win any kind of law suit. Besides, discrimination against lesbians and gays is completely legal, you know." Frosty anger blazed in Amanda's ice-gray eyes; it seemed she was still far from over whatever had befallen her at her previous job. When she'd started work at The Project, we had heard she'd left under a cloud. But being intensely suspicious of the corporate world, we didn't necessarily see that as a strike against her. "At least here," she continued, "I can reach my full potential and have some real influence." She looked thoughtful for a moment, brushing a hand over her heavily-powdered cheek. "And help the community, of course," she added in what almost seemed like an afterthought.

"Speaking of working for the community, I better get on. And I'll fix that carpet just as soon as I take the messages off the machine." I stood up, made my way to the back of the office and pushed down the play button on the blinking answering machine. The tape rewound and the first beep sounded. Then a hard, sharp voice started to speak, one I had heard before. He spoke slowly, relishing each word. "You fucking queers, you all deserve to die. If AIDS doesn't get you, we will. Count on it." There was a long pause in which I could make out his steady, rasping breaths before he hung up the phone. An involuntary shudder ran down my back. I hit the pause button.

"My God, what is wrong with these people?" Amanda placed both hands on her wide hips and let out an exasperated sigh. "Don't they have anything better to do than make threatening phone calls?"

"Apparently not," I said flatly.

"Yeah, and next time I pick up the phone and it's that creep, I'm gonna make sure I've got my whistle next to me," Mario declared. "I'm going to blow so hard I'll perforate his eardrum. That'll teach the little bigot, don't you think?"

I smiled. "Not a bad idea. But I think it's time we made a police report. I hate to take these creeps seriously, but this must be the fifth call we've had this week." In the last week we had received a hate-filled phone call every day; not only was it becoming tiresome, it was also becoming a serious cause for concern. It's not like we weren't used to phone harassment, but most callers weren't nearly so persistent, and there was something about the unadulterated hatred in that voice that really disturbed me.

"Wouldn't you just love to meet these jerks face to face?" asked Mario. "I bet they wouldn't be so brave then."

"Perhaps not," said Amanda, "but I think it's wise to treat these things seriously. Lou's right, we need to make a police report. In fact, I think we should probably have done that sooner." She gave me a disapproving glance.

I opened my mouth to reply but Amanda lifted a hand to silence me. "I know, I understand everyone's reluctance to deal with the cops these days. But I want to make sure we get these threats on record in case things escalate. Remember, despite the recent actions of the SFPD, they are still supposed to be there to protect us."

Mario raise his eyes skyward. "You'd never think so the way they're carrying on. I mean, look at those arrests at the ACT-UP demo."

Amanda nodded. "I know, but with the present city administration it hardly comes as a surprise, does it?"

"What, you mean the fact that our new mayor couldn't care less about how gay bashings are on the increase? And how he's instructing the cops to lay into us at legitimate political protests?" I was pretty angry with the way things had been going under Mayor Finch's leadership. His administration was only a matter of months old but already city policies, as part of what he called 'a drive to bring law and order to San Francisco', had taken a very drastic turn to the right. In recent weeks, many political demonstrations had been violently broken up by police and several prominent gay and lesbian activists had been arrested on the flimsiest of pretexts.

"You know," Mario said, "the weird thing about the ACT-UP action is that people were sure the cops could have no idea what they'd planned. I mean, they had to keep things pretty secret if they were going to block the Bay Bridge. But I was talking to one of the organizers and she swears that the cops must've known what was going to happen. They seemed to know every move the protesters were going to make before they even made it. She thinks there must have been a police informer involved in the planning.

Pretty disturbing, huh?"

"I know, the Community Coalition is very concerned about it," Amanda said. "It's the first thing on the agenda for our meeting this afternoon."

The Community Coalition was an alliance of the many different organizations representing lesbian and gay interests in the city, from AIDS service agencies to radical activist groups like Queer Nation and ACT-UP. In previous years these organizations had put more energy into in-fighting than in working together to confront a common foe. But during her tenure at The Project, through what seemed to me like sheer force of personality, Amanda had managed to bring them into a powerful alliance which was now solidly focused on protesting the policies of the current mayor. I couldn't help but admire her ability to get things done.

"So, can one of you make a police report?" Amanda inquired. "I'd do it myself but I'm afraid I just don't have a second today." She swept her hand up to her forehead in a melodramatic gesture.

And I have nothing but free time, I thought. That was the trouble with Amanda, she had this tendency to think that her work was so much more important than anyone else's. It was probably a holdover from her life in the rigid hierarchy of corporate America that a year and a half in an underfunded nonprofit hadn't quite cured her of yet. Still, there was plenty of time for that.

"I'll do it," I volunteered, knowing the task would probably come down to me anyway.

"Great. Thanks, Lou." Amanda gave me a bright smile and began gathering her things from the chair. "I'm heading for my office. Hold my calls for the rest of the morning, can you? I'm working on a keynote address for that city-wide conference this evening and I haven't a clue yet what I'm going to say. This afternoon I have the Coalition meeting, a working lunch with a couple of other nonprofit directors, an article to write, and somewhere in there I have to fit in an interview with *The National Gay Times*. It's going to be a long day."

I know what you mean, I thought, taking a quick glance at the piles of work awaiting me on my desk. I found myself fantasizing for a moment about expense-paid trips, business lunches, and an eager secretary to help me out. But then I shook my head and smiled. Even with all the perks, I'd be lucky if I lasted a week in corporate life. I was too much of a rebel, and besides, I had a hard time visualizing myself in a power suit and heels. Amanda was the only one around here who knew how to dress for success, and apparently it hadn't even worked that well for her.

Almost immediately after Amanda had closed her office door the power went out. "Damn and blast," I said, seeing the computer screen I had just turned on flicker then go blank. "Amanda must have put on her space heater again. I am so sick of that bloody wiring. I swear it must have been installed sometime last century."

"I have to leave for a meeting, I'll get the switches on the way out," Mario reassured me as he stood up and pulled on his jacket. The switch box was located downstairs, by the door. "You know, we really should get the wiring looked at."

"Tell me about it," I responded. In recent weeks I had been getting more aerobic exercise each day by running up and down those stairs to fix the electricity than in an entire Jane Fonda video workout. "I've tried talking to Joey Pepper, but of course that's a lost cause." Joey Pepper was our land-lord, the kind who'd rather battle starving piranhas than do any repairs to his property. "What bothers me more than the wiring is those damn dead rats, I wish we could do something about them." The whole building was rat-infested and generally they didn't bother us, but the other tenants routinely put down rat poison and it wasn't unusual for the rats to creep into our clos-ets and ceilings to die. The resulting smell from rotting rat was disgusting.

"You never know, Lou, maybe we could persuade Joey to do some repairs, you know, fix the place up a bit."

I threw my head back and laughed. "Right, and while we're at it, let's try and talk Mayor Finch into changing his anti-gay policies."

Chapter Three

It was lust at first sight. And it wasn't the uniform because I never have been turned on by them. Probably something to do with spending five traumatic years in an English girls' grammar school that required its students to wear knee-length navy blue skirts, gingham blouses, and itchy cotton underwear. But the moment I glanced up from my desk to see those brilliant brown eyes looking down at me, a half-smile across full, gently curved lips, my heart started beating faster and I could feel color rise to my face in a gentle heat. "Can I help you?" I managed to stammer while I let my eyes move down the full length of her tall, broad-shouldered body. She looked to be about my height, maybe a little taller. I guessed six feet. She wore her black curly hair short. Her skin was olive-toned, smooth and stretched over the most impressive set of cheek bones I'd seen since Mario had last dragged me along to an old Sophia Loren movie. Beneath the uniform she looked trim, sturdy. She held herself with confidence.

"I'm here to take a report. Harassment, right?" Her voice was soft, measured. I could hear a hint of what I had learned to recognize as New York in the accent.

I blinked but didn't shift my mesmerized gaze.

"Did you make the report? Are you…" She looked down at the notebook she held in her hand, "…Lou Spencer?"

I nodded.

"I'm Officer Ramon, Alex Ramon. Just started the beat earlier this week." She spoke with unguarded enthusiasm as she smiled wide, showing even white teeth and dimples at the side of her mouth.

"Hi…er, yes…I made the report." My voice came out weak, almost strangled, and my heart was thumping loud, so loud I wondered if she could hear it. I stood up. "It came in on the answering machine…er… I played it when I got in this morning. And…we've had one every day. I…er…I think it's likely they're all done by the same group or individual." Good God, Lou, pull yourself together, I berated myself silently. The last time I recalled feeling so weak-kneed and pathetic was when I was thirteen, watching Billie Jean King play at Wimbledon. Of course, since then there had been a few women I'd fallen for, but I'd always managed to keep myself a little aloof. Even with Justine it had taken a little while before I'd let my guard down. One of my more costly mistakes, as it turned out.

"Must have shaken you up, huh? Getting phone calls like that." She frowned so that two sharp creases appeared across her high forehead.

"Oh, yes. It was pretty scary," I said, giving a vigorous nod, relieved that she thought my lack of composure was due to the shock of getting those threats. I wasn't about to correct her.

"So, you still have the tape?" She looked me straight in the eyes. I found myself staring into her wide, black pupils. It made me feel a little dizzy. "Is it still in the machine?"

Quickly, I pulled my gaze away. "Er...yes." I went over to the answering machine where I played the sinister message again. It did leave me feeling a little shaky still, hearing that cold, slow voice.

"Sounds like a real creep," she said, shaking her head slowly and shaping her lips into a distasteful expression. "But probably just some crazy with nothing better to do. Ninety-nine per cent of them never act on it. They're usually the kind that get their kicks just frightening people."

"And what about the other one per cent?"

She shrugged. "Well, there's always that chance, I guess, but it's pretty negligible. Anyway, I'll take the tape with the message over to the investigators in the Hate Crimes Unit. And you should contact the phone company and get them to set a trap on your phone."

"What does that mean? Is it like a tap?"

"Kinda, they just keep a record of which numbers call you. Then, when you get a threatening call you record the exact time it came in, call the phone company, let them know and then they'll contact us and we'll follow up on it. You should probably get one of those answering machines that records the time and date a call comes in. Then if they reach the machine we can trace it."

I nodded.

"So, is there anything more I can help you with?" She reached up and ran a hand through her hair. The fingers were long and thin. "Anything else you can think of?"

"Not right now." I shook my head regretfully, the idea of keeping her in the office a little longer was extremely appealing.

"Be wary of visitors you don't know, okay? And it would be better if you could keep that door locked downstairs. Pretty easy for someone to get up here without you noticing 'til they're right on top of you. You should get an intercom or something." I thought about how excited Amanda would be to hear about all these suggested extra expenditures. "Okay, well, take it easy." She walked towards the door. Her gait was self-assured, not quite a swagger, but definitely filled with some of that butch attitude I find so appealing. Before she left she turned, once again that dazzling dimpled smile across her face. "You know, you have a very nice accent," she said, placing one hand on her hip.

"Oh…thanks," I managed to mutter.

"English, right?" She raised her dark, arching brows.

I nodded.

"Y'know, since I was a kid I always wanted to go there. Something about all that history you guys have, castles and old mansions and all that. And those double decker buses, boy, did I want to ride on one of those when I was little. You live in London?"

"For a few years," I answered.

"You miss it?"

"I suppose so."

"What do you miss most?" She looked at me expectantly, her brows knotted in an expression of keen interest.

I shrugged. "Well, it's hard to say really. There are the seasons, the way winter is really winter and spring is definitely spring. Here they just sort of blend into one another." She nodded in agreement. "And I miss all the different accents, that famous British dry sense of humor—no one ever gets my jokes here. And I miss the old buildings, my mother's roast dinners on a Sunday." It had been a while since I'd really thought about home, I was surprised to find myself so eager to talk about it. "I miss good chocolate, Branston Pickle, people who know how to make a decent cup of tea, and I suppose I just miss the way that everything is so familiar…so much like home."

"You must go back and visit a lot."

"No, I…er…haven't been back in five years," I answered. Because there was one thing I didn't miss, and that was Justine. How could I explain the relief of being this far from England on account of her?

"How come?"

I looked away from her penetrating stare. "Just too busy, I suppose," I answered vaguely.

"Really? Even for a short trip? Surely you must have one planned."

I shook my head. "No, I haven't really given it any thought. And you know, it is quite a long way."

She looked at me incredulously for a moment. "Well, I'd love to go there. Hey, maybe you could tell me more about it sometime." And with that she turned to the door and exited into the hallway.

"Hey, Lou, what's up with you? You look like you've seen a ghost or something. Anything wrong?"

"No, no." I looked up from my thoughts to see Donna Travis, the Project's second advocate, looking expectantly into my face. "I...er..I just had to make a police report. We got another one of those threatening phone calls."

"Oh," Donna shrugged and tossed her hair, which hung in thick black dreads, about her moon-shaped face. "That's a bummer. Don't expect the police will do much about it, though. It's not easy to get people for phone harassment."

"I'm a bit worried they'll carry out some of these threats."

"Oh, I don't think so, Lou. It's just some crazy person with nothing better to do. I bet it'll stop once they get bored, you'll see." I found myself wishing I shared her confidence. Something about these calls just left me feeling so uneasy. "Hey," she continued, "sorry I'm late. I overslept. They opened up this new dance club in the Haight, it was a blast. Tons of cute girls, Lou. You should check it out sometime." She winked at me. "Anyway, needless to say, I didn't get home until the early hours and I slept right through my alarm. I'm sorry."

"That's okay. You got a couple of phone calls. Here's the messages." I handed her two pink message slips and found myself wondering if I just needed to get myself out to some club and go dancing. Maybe it was all these nights spent home alone, going to bed early with a cup of hot chocolate that left me lusting so pathetically after the cop who came to take our police report. "And someone else called for you, a woman. But she wouldn't leave her name, said she'd call back later. She sounded sort of familiar, actually."

"She did?" A concerned look clouded Donna's face.

"Yes, but I've no idea who it was."

"Oh, well thanks for the messages," she smiled. "See you later, Lou." She swung around and, with her heavy boots clunking on the hardwood floor, she set off towards her office down the hall.

I called the phone company to set up the phone trap as Alex Ramon had suggested, then hastily fixed the carpet. I spent the rest of the morning dealing with payables (the usual depressing task of juggling bills so that we paid the businesses who seemed on the verge of suing us and kept aside those who could be put off for a while longer).

14

Just before one, while Mario and I were getting ready to step out for some lunch, we heard the front door open and footsteps sound on the stairs. I glanced down the hallway to see a woman come into view.

She walked into the office looking like she had just stepped off the set of Melrose Place. At first I thought she must have stumbled into the wrong office. No one who came to Stop The Violence Project, not even Amanda, ever looked this perfectly groomed. Tall and impossibly slender, she swung her lustrous blond mane down her long back with a slow, practiced gesture before walking towards my desk. She looked at Mario and me from her perfect oval face, make-up immaculate over apparently flawless skin. Her wide-spaced eyes were ocean blue, the lashes dark and long.

"I'm here to see Peter Williams. We have a lunch appointment." Her voice was husky. As she spoke she gestured with a large, gold-encrusted hand.

"I'll go and see if he's available," I offered. "Who shall I say is waiting?"

She hesitated for just a moment. "Tell him it's Julia."

When I reached Peter's office I paused before knocking. Behind the door his voice was raised. He was arguing with someone over the phone. I thought at first that he was probably talking to a difficult D.A. or some antagonistic city official. But I soon realized that this was personal business. "Look, don't try sweet-talking or guilt-tripping me out of this. And don't give me all those tired excuses, I'm just not interested. I don't care what you say, Malcolm, I've already made up my mind. You can argue with me until you're blue in the face but you're wasting your breath." I was tempted to stand outside and listen for a while longer, after all I was more than a little intrigued to find out who Malcolm was and just what he was trying to talk Peter out of. Was he a new boyfriend? That might go some way towards explaining why Peter had dropped Mario like a hot potato. I'd like to say that honorable character and good breeding are what made me cease my eavesdropping. But to tell the truth, I glanced down the hall and noticed Julia peering around the door of my office to give me a curious glance, so I quickly raised my hand to knock at Peter's door.

"Come in," he yelled. He was leaning back in his chair, feet resting on the edge of his desk, the phone cradled in his neck. In one hand he held a long-handled silver letter-opener, he gestured with it as he spoke. The sharp blade caught the light, glinting like a flashing sword as it moved. It made his obvious anger with Malcolm seem even more forceful, as if they were engaged in some over-the-phone duel.

I shivered as I approached Peter—there was something a little ominous

15

about that letter-opener, the way its blade stabbed the air. But I was probably just cold since on this chilly San Francisco morning he had his window wide open—if it had been any colder in his office The Project could've run an ice cream store on site. (Now there was a new fundraising idea for us to consider!) Like certain members of the British Royal Family, Peter was one of those fresh air freaks, he hardly ever turned on the heat and even in the middle of winter he kept his window open. Personally, I thought it was a little eccentric to actually want to be cold, but his habits didn't annoy me nearly as much as they did Amanda. At staff meetings she and Peter had a constant battle over the room temperature, with Amanda generally winning out since when it came to getting her way, she seldom had qualms about pulling rank.

"Look, I'll talk to you when I see you tonight," Peter said into the mouthpiece, his voice a harsh whisper. Then he replaced the handset, dropped the letter-opener onto his desk, pulled his feet down and turned to look at me. For a brief moment I caught this strange, almost disturbed look on his face, as if he were weighed down by some overwhelming trouble. But quickly the look was gone as he adjusted his features into an awkward smile.

"There's someone called Julia here to see you," I announced.

"Oh, good," he said distractedly. "Thanks."

I turned to leave. "Have a nice lunch," I said, then stopped and looked over at him again. "By the way, who is she? Julia, I mean."

"A good friend from school, we went to U.C. Berkeley together."

"She really is quite gorgeous." Not my type, but I could certainly appreciate her Hollywoodesque looks. "I'll bet she turned a lot of heads on campus," I added.

"Yeah, you might say that," he said as an enigmatic look flashed across his face.

I spent lunchtime in Dolores Park with Mario, then returned to the office to begin work on an overdue grant report.After a few minutes, I glanced up from my desk to see Peter and Donna simultaneously emerge from their offices and almost collide in the hall. "Jesus, watch where you're going," Donna snapped at Peter, taking a step back and staring into his face.

"Well, excuse the hell out of me," Peter responded, folding his arms across his chest and meeting her glare.

"Hmmph," Donna snorted, shoving heavily past him and knocking him against the wall before continuing down the hall. Peter looked a little stunned as he recovered, slowly shaking his head and smoothing his hands over his T-shirt before stepping back into his office. Donna approached me, her features knotted into a heavy scowl, but as soon as she noticed me looking up at her, she transformed her grimace into a beaming smile.

"Is everything all right?" I asked as she walked past me and into the kitchen area at the back of my office.

"Why?" she asked, pushing her heavy locks from her face and giving me a wary glance.

"Oh, nothing," I shrugged, "I just noticed…well, didn't you just push Peter out of your way?"

"Push? Don't be silly, Lou," she said dismissively, lifting the lid on the coffee can. "You know you must have imagined that." Her tone was light, jolly. It struck me as a little false. "Oh, shit, there's no coffee left. Maybe I'll just go out and get an espresso. You want some, Lou?"

"No, thanks," I answered, knowing I had not imagined Donna's shoving Peter and wondering what on earth could have gotten into her that she'd behave like that. It seemed so out of character.

"Well, I need some caffeine or I'm not going to make it through the rest of the day," she said, making her way towards the door. "Too many late nights, I guess."

"By the way, Donna," I called after her, "I was wondering if you feel like getting together one evening next week." I liked hanging out with Donna, she was fun to be with and it was always nice to have someone to talk through office politics with. And after what I'd just witnessed, I realized there were some office politics that might bear a little discussion between Donna and me.

"Sorry, Lou," she called back without even turning to look at me. "I'm really busy next week, maybe some other time, okay?"

Fine, I thought to myself, if Donna wanted to snub me I wasn't going to let it bother me. We used to go out at least one evening a week after work, but the last few times I'd asked her out she'd just made some vague excuse. I might have taken it personally if I was the only one she'd been cool with. Even Amanda, who was often too absorbed with her own work and community politics to take much of an interest in staff interactions, had noticed a difference in Donna.

"I'm going to do the interview with *The National Gay Times* in a few minutes," Amanda announced, leaning over my desk at a little before five. "Then I'm heading straight over to the conference. Lou, let anyone who calls know that I won't be available until Monday. Okay?"

I nodded. "Hey, good luck with the keynote. Did you manage to write something you like?"

"Oh, I just put something together at the last minute as usual," she sighed. "But I guess it will just have to do." She was being far too modest, Amanda's speeches were always outstanding. It was for good reason she was known for her ability to rouse and inspire a crowd.

"Amanda, are you leaving soon?" Peter peered from his open door.

"I'm leaving now," she said, checking her watch.

Peter strode quickly towards her. "I need to talk to you." He sounded a little breathless.

"Can't it wait 'til Monday?" she asked, "I'm already late as it is."

"No," he said firmly as the color spread from his ruddy cheeks across the whole of his face. "I really need to talk to you now, it's urgent."

"Okay," she conceded, sighing and glancing once again at her watch, "but try to make it quick could you?" She marched back down the hall and Peter scurried after her and into her office.

When Amanda emerged a few minutes later her face was set into a worried frown. "Bye, Amanda," I called as she walked to the stairs.

"Oh, er…yeah, bye, Lou," she called, looking and sounding like someone who'd received some very bad news.

"Hey, Lou, check this out." A few minutes later, Mario breezed into the office, returning from an afternoon presentation at a city-sponsored youth program. He waved a magazine at me. It was a copy of *San Francisco Freedom*. Advertising itself as the 'essential guide to what's hot and what's not in the city by the Bay,' it had been recently launched with a considerable amount of hype.

I shrugged. "I've seen it already, it's really no big deal."

"No," he said, moving towards me and flapping the magazine furiously, "look at the cover."

I steadied his hand and squinted at the bright, excessively glossy page. It showed a photograph of a tall blond woman dressed in a skin-tight black dress. She stood under a street lamp. The view behind her was the distinctive nighttime skyline of downtown San Francisco. The caption read, 'What to do when the clock strikes midnight.'

"I don't know why…" I began, then suddenly realized what he was so excited about. The cover model was Julia, the woman who had come to visit Peter at lunch time. "Well…" I shrugged, gazing at the startlingly beautiful face, "…I suppose it should come as no great surprise that she's a model."

"And just think," said Mario. "I was in the company of a real celebrity and I didn't even bother to get her autograph. You know, I should show this to Peter."

I shook my head and let out a loud sigh. Mario certainly could be a sucker for punishment sometimes.

"Hey, I'm sure he'd be interested in seeing his friend on the cover of a magazine."

"Yes, and you get an excuse to engage him in conversation. But I suppose there's no use trying to talk you out of it. Just don't put up with him being a wanker, okay?"

He moved towards me, put his arm around my shoulder and planted a wet kiss on my cheek. "Now what would I do without this big butch dyke to protect me?"

"Hey, watch out who you're calling big and butch," I answered, digging my elbow gently into his side.

At six o'clock precisely Donna emerged from her office, slammed the door behind her, calling, "See you Monday," before galloping down the stairs. Following her cue, Mario pushed his chair under his desk, and the copy of *San Francisco Freedom* under his arm, sauntered towards Peter's office. I was sure he was going to end up disappointed, but short of throwing myself bodily in his way, I knew there was no stopping him. Besides, it's my firm philosophy that everyone is at least entitled to make their own mistakes. Sure enough, a few minutes later, I heard raised and furious voices coming from Peter's office. Worried about Mario, I walked into the hallway.

"For God's sake, just get a clue. It's over, okay," Peter yelled.

"You're seeing someone else, aren't you? I know you are. Why else would you be so secretive?"

"It's none of your business," Peter countered.

"And no one else's either, it would seem. I've asked around, but everyone says you're playing your cards close to your chest these days."

"You've no right to ask people about me. What I do and who I see is my own business."

"But I don't understand what happened between us."

"Look, just accept it, it's over. We may have to work together but as far as I'm concerned there is nothing else between us. And that's the way it should be. Now do you mind leaving my office? I still have work to do."

A moment later Mario burst out of the room.

"Are you okay?" I asked.

"Not really," he answered, brushing past me and into our office. Still carrying *San Francisco Freedom* magazine, he tossed it on one of the chairs in the waiting area before striding over to his desk. I followed him.

"Do you need to talk?" I asked.

"I'm okay." He sniffed and wiped his eyes. "I guess I just need to face facts. God, it sucks to be dumped. Right now I hate him more than anyone else in the world. I wish, I wish…oh, hell, I don't know what I wish." His hands clenched and unclenched as they swung at his sides.

I rubbed my hand across his back. "I'll come home with you if you want some company."

"No, Lou. I think I just need to be alone for a while. I'd better go," he said, sighing, picking up his jacket and dashing down the stairs.

As I watched Mario leave I felt a surge of anger towards Peter, and I seriously considered marching back down the hallway to give him a piece of my mind. But I decided against it; I'm not sure that it would have done any good, and besides, Mario probably wouldn't have thanked me for it. So I turned off the lights and the photocopier, turned on the answering machine, and left Peter alone in the office.

Like many lesbians I know, I was quite the tomboy when I was a kid. While all the other girls were giggling about their latest dates, reading *Jackie* magazine, and swapping diet ideas, I spent my evenings dressed in a scruffy T-shirt and shorts, dribbling a ball up and down the pavement and trying to persuade the boys to let me join their street soccer games. It was a painful time, never really knowing why everyone regarded me as such a misfit. Thankfully, those days are far behind me, but I never did lose my love of soccer.

When I lived in London I always played on women's teams and only a few months after I came to the States I joined the SF Dynamite Dykes. I've been with them over four years now and have become good friends with several team members. During the summer we didn't have any games scheduled, but we still met for practice once a week. That evening, I ran around yelling, kicking, and sprinting after the ball until all the accumulated tension of the week seemed to fall away. By the time we finished practice it was close to nine.

"Hey, Lou, you gonna come have coffee?" My friend Terri tossed her soccer shoes into her duffel and slung it over her shoulder.

"Of course," I answered.

Terri smiled and turned to follow the rest of our teammates out of the park, her slight, four feet eleven body bouncing over the damp grass as she ran to catch up.

I made my way with everyone else over to the coffee shop in the Haight where we usually spent our evenings after practice. During the next couple of hours I listened to my teammates stories of political action, community intrigue and romantic escapades.

"So what about you, Lou?" Terri asked as she dipped a spoon into the foam on her decaf latte. "Any developments on the love front?"

"No, not really, but I did meet… " My voice trailed off as several of my teammates turned suddenly towards me, their expressions eager and expectant.

"Go on, go on," Terri said, nudging me with her elbow.

I surveyed my wide-eyed companions and kept my lips firmly closed. I wasn't sure I wanted to share my encounter with Alex Ramon, the new Castro beat cop, with the entire soccer team. And besides, the whole issue of my love life was a far too touchy subject.

"Yeah, Lou, you have a date?" Jane, the goalie, asked.

"No, it was just someone I met through work," I said, trying my best to sound nonchalant. "Nothing's going to come of it, I'm sure."

"You don't know that, Lou," Terri said softly.

"Yeah, Lou, I don't know what you're holding out for but five years is a hell of a long time to stay single." Jenny, our center forward, piped up. "Hey, did you have a girlfriend when you were in England?"

Naturally, my thoughts turned to Justine. I felt my face start to burn. "Yes," I said slowly, "and it's not necessarily an experience I care to repeat."

I was still bleary-eyed and half asleep at nine on Monday morning as I searched my pockets for my key and clumsily pushed it into the lock. As soon as I opened the door the smell hit me, sweet and sickly; it made the inside of my nostrils itch and my stomach turn over in disgust.

"Oh, sod it," I muttered to myself as I climbed the stairs, "not another bloody dead rat." I cursed Joey Pepper and his dilapidated, infested building. It wouldn't have bothered me quite so much if it didn't always come down to me to find the offending animal, somehow put it into a trash bag, and arrange for its disposal, since I was the only one on staff who wasn't terminally squeamish. The smell was pretty bad in the hallway, but when I opened my office, thankfully the air was clear. I spent a few minutes looking over the papers on my desk, noted the flashing light on the answering machine, and put on the kettle for tea. Then I ventured out into the hall. Not sure from which room the smell came, I walked first to Amanda's office and unlocked the door. Not there, it did not smell inside. Next to Donna's, but that was ratless, too. Then I started to unlock Peter's office, but there was no need, it was already unlocked.

I pushed the door. It swung open and I walked inside. I was immediately overwhelmed by the stifling heat and the cruel stink of decomposing flesh. At first my eyes followed the crazy pattern of rust-colored spatters over the dull white walls, then I looked around—at the mess of stained papers pushed across Peter's desk, his lamp knocked over and the shade battered and torn, the two-drawer file cabinet pushed at an angle, the two chairs tipped to the floor. And that's when I noticed the body.

Peter lay next to one of the portable heaters we used throughout the office, it was turned on high. He was on his back, arms splayed out, legs bent as if, before he'd died, he'd been pulling them to his body in an effort to protect himself. There was blood everywhere—on the walls (I now realized what that pattern of rust-colored spatters actually was), in dark patches on the furniture, drops had even dried on the metal surface of the heater. And Peter himself lay in a deep, liver-colored pool of congealed blood. His clothes, the same jeans and T-shirt he'd worn to work on Friday, were covered in blood stains. His T-shirt was stained dark red and his silver letter-opener was pushed into his chest. His face was partially hidden by a piece of paper, as if someone, out of respect for the dead, had tried to cover his lifeless and contorted features. But then, as I took a cautious step forward, I realized it held a crudely scrawled message in block letters that said: ALL QUEERS SHOULD DIE!

Chapter Four

I've never been very good at dealing with the sight of blood. Once, while peeling potatoes, the knife slipped and I cut my hand—my immediate response was to keel over in a dead faint. I ended up with ten stitches for the gash in my head that I got from hitting the edge of metal sink as I fell, the cut on my hand needed nothing more than a bandaid and some disinfectant cream. So I wasn't exactly the best person to deal with finding a dead and very bloody body. All I could do was just stand there for what felt like forever, shaking and trying desperately not to throw up. When I finally pulled myself together a little bit, I stumbled over to the desk and was about to pick up the phone when I thought of all those seventies detective shows I liked to watch and those men in their pale raincoats, frowning as they glanced around the murder scene. "Don't touch anything!" they'd command. I concluded that I had better go down the hall and call the cops from my office.

"Are you all right, ma'am?" the female dispatcher asked after I had given her details of the situation.

"No, not really," I answered honestly, "I think I need a cup of tea." I replaced the hand set before she could say anything else.

The electric tea kettle was still boiling on the counter by the sink at the back of the office, I put a tea bag into a mug and poured the steaming water onto it. Sipping the hot tea helped calm my stomach and distracted me from the awful smell that filled the office. But within a few minutes I started to get agitated, it seemed to take ages for the police to arrive. "Might as well make myself useful," I muttered as I walked over to the answering machine, pressed the play button and began to write down the messages.

With the benefit of hindsight I can see that I was doing what people in shock often do: minimizing trauma by pretending that nothing out of the ordinary has happened. And though the pen shook between my fingers and my handwriting leaned haphazardly over the message slips, for a few minutes I was almost able to convince myself that this was just another normal day.

There were several messages from potential clients, people who were calling to report being assaulted over the weekend. I even marked those messages 'for Donna or Peter'. A couple of people called to congratulate Amanda on an excellent keynote speech at the Friday night conference. Then there was a message for Peter from Jeff Easton, a reporter at *The City Reporter*, a gay community newspaper. I had met him several times when he came by the office to do stories on cases we were handling. "Hey, Peter," his animated voice sounded into the machine, "where were you on Friday night, man? I waited for you for almost an hour. The least you could've done was called. Think I got nothing better to do than to wait around for your so-called hot stories? Well, call me when you get this 'cause I tried you, must have been four times, at your place this weekend. You decide to leave town or something?" He left his number at the newspaper and hung up.

The final message brought me back to ugly reality. The slow, familiar snarl relishing every word: "Remember what we said, all you fucking queers should die." I slammed my finger onto the pause button of the machine, my heart pounding like an engine. At the same time, the door downstairs pulled open and heavy footfalls sounded on the stairs. Panic swept through me. There was no doubt in my mind, it had to be the author of the message come to carry out the threat I'd just listened to. Quickly, I glanced around the office searching helplessly for somewhere to hide. As the footsteps reached the hall, I breathed fast and urgent, my thoughts racing to find some way of escaping my would-be attacker. But there was nowhere to go. All I could do was keep rehearsing my repertoire of self-defense moves in my mind and hope that they didn't have a gun. I stiffened, seeing two figures approaching me from the hallway, realizing that I was almost bound to be overwhelmed. But then, as they came closer, I let out a long sigh of relief. I saw the dark uniforms and realized the two figures were SFPD officers responding to my 911 call. I never thought I'd be quite so glad to see the police.

Alex Ramon was the first to enter my office, followed by an older, heavy-set cop she introduced as Officer Riley. He looked at me from dark green eyes, giving a barely perceptible nod as he ran his hand through his thick thatch of carrot-colored hair.

"We got a call about a homicide." She sounded a little breathless.

I nodded and pointed down the hallway. "It's one of the guys I work with. I found him a few minutes ago but I think he must have been there since Friday."

"Jeez, that explains that godawful smell," Riley grimaced and pulled a wrinkled handkerchief out of his pocket. He put it over his face. "We better go take a look."

They both strode towards Peter's office. I felt my legs sway under me as I watched them push open the door. Reaching out for the nearest chair, I sank down and leaned forward to put my head between my knees. I took some slow, deep breaths.

"Hey, are you okay?" Alex Ramon had come back from Peter's office. She placed a warm hand on my shoulder and squeezed gently. Her voice was filled with compassion.

I looked up. "Yes, I think I'm all right," I answered. "It's just such a shock. It's horrible."

"I know," she said softly, "it must be awful for you finding him like that, it's a pretty ugly scene." She gestured towards his office. "Was he a friend?"

"Not really, but I worked with him every day. I didn't exactly expect to find him dead." I shook my head slowly. "This is not supposed to happen to someone I know." My voice shook, I felt hot and dizzy. But even in my state of agitation I couldn't help but notice how I found Alex Ramon's presence reassuring.

"Yeah," she said, "you're right, it stinks."

Riley strode into the room, catching the tail end of our conversation. "Stinks isn't the word. Looks like the guy's been slow-roasting in there all weekend. Must have put the heater on before he died—ended up cooking himself." He creased his round ruddy face into a tight grimace. "I called it in, Homicide are on their way," he said, looking around the office and then longingly towards the kitchen. He turned to me. "Hey, you got any coffee?"

The two homicide detectives arrived while Riley was slurping down his second cup. After examining the murder scene one of them approached me. In scuffed black shoes, he walked slowly down the hallway, eyes narrowed, head nodding as if engaged in some deep and penetrating thought. His brown suit clung to his bulky frame, it looked like it might have been quite a sharp and well-fitting outfit some ten or fifteen years ago, now, like the detective himself, it just looked drab and worn.

"So, you're the one who found the body?" he asked.

"Yes," I answered.

"And you are…?" His voice trailed into a slow slur as he waited for me to answer.

"I'm Lou Spencer, I'm the Office Manager here. And you are…?"

"Detective Cochran," he replied shortly. Apparently he was the one who was supposed to ask the questions. "And how did you come to find the body, Miss Spencer?" He patted his hand over his hair, arranged in a very creative but nonetheless vain attempt to hide his advancing baldness.

"I went into his office because of the smell, I thought maybe it was a dead rat, we get them every now and again." Some other police-type people opened the door and started up the stairs, the place was getting to feel crowded very quickly. I wondered when the rest of the staff would turn up.

"So, the victim is…"

"Peter Williams."

"And he worked here, right?"

I nodded.

"And what is it exactly you do here?" His watery blue eyes darted quickly around the office. "You're a gay organization, right?" He said the word 'gay' with all the relish of someone who'd just sucked on a lemon.

"Yes," I said steadily, trying not to react to his tone, "we work with victims of hate crimes."

"I see." He pushed his hands into the sagging pockets of his jacket. "So, when was the last time you saw this Peter Williams?"

"Friday evening, around six o'clock, that's when I left work. I think he must have been killed sometime that night because he's still wearing the same clothes."

"Maybe. But that's something we leave to the medical examiner to determine. Right now I'm just here to examine the scene, gather preliminary evidence. When the autopsy report is in, and maybe when I've had a chance to establish motive—"

"Well, it's obvious, isn't it?" I interrupted. "I mean there's that note—it's got to be a hate crime."

"I'm not in the business of jumping to conclusions, Miss Spencer. Who the murderer is and why they did it are questions that are wide open. As far as I'm concerned, it could be anyone. In fact, right now, you're my best suspect since you're the one who found the body." A smile itched at the edges of his pale lips.

I put my hands on my hips and glared at him. "Look, we got five hate calls last week and we even got a message on the machine this morning. And why would anyone leave a note like that unless it was a hate crime?"

"I didn't say it wasn't a hate crime, did I Miss Spencer?" he sneered. "So don't go getting all uptight. I'm just doing my job, that's all. Now, I'm going to need a full statement from anyone who works here. We'll also need to take your fingerprints."

"Great, so we get treated like the criminals," I huffed.

"Like I said, for now at least, the field's wide open. So maybe you want to go outside and get some fresh air. And while you're at it you can point out your co-workers to Officer Riley. Tell them to get over to the Hall of Justice sometime after eleven o'clock. I should be finished here by then."

Outside, a large crowd had assembled by the entrance to Stop The Violence Project. Some shuffled against one another, jostling for a better view, others leaned against the cluster of police cars parked haphazardly on Castro Street. As I walked out the door all eyes fixed on me, staring from excited, concerned faces. A little dazed, I glanced about looking for someone I knew. "What the hell is going on?" A familiar voice came through the crowd—Mario. I suddenly realized that I would have to break the news to him about Peter's death. It was a task I didn't relish.

"Hey Lou, what's up? I've been here fifteen minutes and they won't let me in the office. Are you okay?" He reached out to smooth a hand over my hair.

"Yeah, I'm all right," I said slowly. "It's Peter."

"What do you mean?" The muscles on his face tightened, his dark brown eyes signaled apprehension. "What's wrong with Peter?"

The image of him lying in a pool of his own sticky crimson blood came back to me. "He's dead," I managed to whisper.

"Dead?" Mario repeated, his slender face filled with incomprehension.

I put an arm around him. "Yes, somebody killed him."

"But that's ridiculous, why would anyone want to kill Peter?"

"I think it was a hate crime. There was a note on his body, something about killing queers."

"I want to go upstairs, I want to go and see him." Mario lunged forward towards the office door.

I grabbed his arm and pulled him back. "You can't, not right now. The cops won't let you." I pointed towards Riley who stood with another officer guarding the entrance to The Project. "He's dead, Mario. There's nothing you can do."

A moment later, Donna and Amanda arrived. Pushing and heaving towards us through the expanding crowd, they both looked deeply puzzled. "What the hell is this?" Donna asked, gesturing with a nod towards the office. "Some kind of police raid or something?" Briefly, I explained what had happened. Donna's mouth dropped open in what was almost a parody of shock.

Amanda turned ashen. "Oh my God," she muttered, shaking her head several times, as if trying to let the terrible news sink all the way in. Then she took my hand in hers. "How awful for you to find him, Lou," she said. "What a nightmare." Her fingers trembled against mine. Tears rolled swiftly down her cheeks, streaking her mascara and making jagged tracks through her foundation. "And poor Peter. Do they know who did it?"

As I told them about the note left on Peter's body, people in the crowd pushed against us, craning their heads to try to hear our conversation. "I spoke to one of the homicide detectives," I said. "His name's Cochran. A bit of a bloody homophobe himself, if you ask me. Even with a note right there on the body, he doesn't seem too eager to look at it as a hate crime. Prefers to think that one of us lot did Peter in. You know how the cops are." All three of them nodded.

The news of an apparently anti-gay murder at Stop The Violence Project spread rapidly around the Castro. The crowd outside the office grew so large that it began to block the street. Eager and flushed reporters descended upon us with insistent questions. Soon there was a bus stuck in the intersection of Eighteenth and Castro, cars and trucks sounding their horns from all directions. More cops arrived and began trying to push the crowd up the street. So far, they were using relatively gentle tactics.

"We're going to have to do something about this," Amanda said, gesturing vaguely towards the crowd.

"Yeah," Donna agreed, "people are getting really freaked out. I mean, it's bad enough when someone gets killed in a gay-bashing, people get real nervous. But when it's at The Project..."

"Exactly," interrupted Amanda. "The whole community's going to be stirred up. This is going to call for some really skillful leadership. I'm going to have to talk to the Coalition about this. Let's meet back here, say at two, in the restaurant across the street." I nodded and she immediately began pushing her way to the edge of the crowd, stopping to talk to people she knew as she went.

"You want to go over to the Hall of Justice together?" Mario asked. "I don't know about you, but I'd rather not deal with that alone."

Chapter Five

The corridors of The Hall of Justice at 850 Bryant Street spew forth a constant stream of people looking tired and more than a little the worse for wear from their encounters with the law. I'd been there just three times before, twice to deal with a flourishing collection of parking tickets, and once to bail out a friend arrested during a 'Homes not Bombs' demonstration. Each of those visits had yielded long waits, hostile glares from a whole range of officials who seemed to think good manners nothing more than a waste of energy, and the handing over of significant amounts of money to the City of San Francisco. Needless to say, just like Mario, I wasn't exactly thrilled to be going there again.

"Jesus, it's a zoo in here," Mario muttered after we'd made our way through the metal detectors and security check and were finally granted entry into the lobby. I nodded an agreement. People bearing confused expressions wandered about, their hands wrapped tight around pieces of crumpled, official-looking papers. There was a line by the three pay phones and a line by the plexi-glass window beyond which uniformed officers dealt with inquiries and reports. An endless flow of lawyers, plain clothes cops and city officials moved in and out of the cavernous hallways. Voices echoed off the smooth floor and the high, marble-lined walls. We made our way towards the motley crowd outside the elevators.

My interview with Cochran lasted a little more than half an hour. He sat opposite me at a scarred wooden desk, a tape recorder lay between us. The florescent lights in his office did his appearance no favors—I could make out the pattern of pockmarks over his sallow skin, and his carefully-arranged strands of hair seemed so pathetic, that I seriously thought of suggesting that he check out the Hair Club for Men. But I wasn't sure he'd appreciate the advice.

After going over when I had last seen Peter, what time I arrived at work that morning, exactly what I saw before calling the police, he asked me:

"Are you able to account for your time between about six-twenty and nine o'clock on Friday evening?"

"Why? Is that when Peter was killed?"

He gave me a stony look. "Possibly. From our preliminary investigations it would seem that he was murdered sometime Friday evening."

I wanted to tell him 'I told you so', but again, I didn't think he'd appreciate my input.

"A friend of Mr. Williams'," he continued, "has already informed us that he had a brief phone conversation with him a little before six twenty. And since he had a meeting with some reporter set for nine which he never made, that would seem to suggest that he died sometime before then. Of course, once we get the medical examiner's report we'll know a little more. So, where were you, Miss Spencer, at that time?"

"I was at my soccer practice in Golden Gate Park from about six forty. I went out for coffee afterwards. I got home after midnight."

"Witnesses?"

"I can give you names and phone numbers of the whole team if you want," I said, smiling.

"Three or four will do," he snarled.

I began to write a list on a piece of paper he pushed across the desk towards me.

"So Mr. Williams was in the office before you left?"

"Yes."

"Did you speak to him?"

"No, actually I didn't. I overheard him arguing with Mario..."

A flicker of interest showed in Cochran's eyes. "A violent argument?" At that moment I could have kicked myself. The last thing I wanted was to cast unnecessary suspicion in Mario's direction.

"Of course not," I answered tersely.

"Do you know what was it about?" As if readying to get into the meat of our interview he began to take off his jacket, struggling to pull his arms from the tight, wrinkled sleeves.

"I don't know what they were arguing about," I lied. "But Mario left the office before I did. And it seems to me that you're looking in the wrong place for a murderer. It's perfectly clear that this was anti-gay." I gave him an irate glare.

"Is that so?" he asked, smiling to show a set of drab, nicotine-yellow teeth.

"Yes."

"Well, of course you could be right. After all, Miss Spencer, you have infinitely more investigative experience than my mere twenty-seven years on the San Francisco Police Force."

"I'm just trying to say that I hope you take the issue of this being a hate crime seriously. I mean, the community will be furious if you don't."

"Is that a threat? Because a bunch of lesbians and limp-wristed so-called men screaming injustice is not going to bother me. Anyway, Mayor Finch has been showing you what we think of your protests. And about time too, if you ask me."

Incensed, I had to take a long, deep breath before I allowed myself to reply. "You know, working in San Francisco all this time, it might pay to educate yourself about anti-gay crime. And while you're at it you should take some time to get rid of your own homophobia."

"My what?"

"Your fear of gay people," I stated slowly.

"Fear?" He tossed his head back in a loud and obviously nervous laugh. "That's ridiculous. What have I got to be afraid of?" He shifted in his seat. "Anyway, this is wasting my time. If you don't mind, I have a few more questions to ask."

I folded my arms in front of me and said nothing, feeling increasingly pessimistic about Cochran's ability to investigate this murder.

"When you left the office, did you lock the front door?"

"Er…" I tried to visualize leaving the office that Friday evening. "Yes, I always do after hours."

"And as far as you know, did Peter have any plans to see anyone at the office that night."

"No."

"Now, Miss Spencer, do you know of anyone who might have had a motive to kill Peter?"

"You mean other than some bigot who hated him because he was a fag-got? No, I don't know anyone."

Mario looked even angrier than I had when he emerged from his inter-view with Cochran. "God, can you believe that guy, Lou? What a creep, huh?"

I nodded.

"He spent most of the time grilling me about my relationship with Peter. Apparently someone had told him that things were troubled between the two of us." Inside I winced, I should never have mentioned Mario to Cochran. Maybe it was the shock of Peter's murder that was making me so slow-wit-ted, or at least that was my excuse. "And Jesus, he must have asked me ten times to tell him what I was doing on Friday night."

"What did you tell him?" I asked.

"The truth—that I was home by myself. You remember how upset I was after that stupid argument with Peter. I just climbed into bed and stared at the ceiling until I fell asleep."

We took the elevator down to the first floor and left the building. "Maybe we should go back to my place for a while," I suggested. "Amanda and Donna haven't even arrived to make their statements. It could be a couple of hours before they're done. And anyway, I feel like going home to check on Hairy Boy. For some reason this whole thing makes me anxious and I want to check that he's okay."

Hairy Boy was my nine month-old Border Collie. Needless to say, he was delighted by our unexpected visit home. When I opened the door, he pounced first on me, then Mario, his face nuzzling against us, his tail swinging crazily, like a bushy black and white propeller.

"Hi, sweetheart," I ran my hands over his face and ruffled his curly and profuse (hence the name) coat.

Mario had given me Hairy Boy. Earlier that year, on the morning of my birthday, he had arrived at my door holding a blinking ball of fur in his hands. "Happy birthday," he had announced, thrusting the bewildered puppy towards me.

My initial reaction was guarded, to say the least. "But Mario," I protested, shoving my hands into my pockets and refusing to take the dog from his outstretched hands. "I can't have an animal, my landlord—"

"I checked with your landlord and he said a dog is fine, so you can't use that excuse, Lou."

"But I can't take on the responsibility of looking after a dog. I mean, I have a hard enough time taking care of myself!"

"Exactly!" he declared. "And that's why I got you a dog. First of all, you spend far too much time alone and a dog will be company for you. Secondly, dogs are great protection. And thirdly, this is not just a dog—he's a Border Collie. So not only is he the most intelligent breed of dogs around, but this puppy here can trace his ancestry back to dogs in England who herded sheep in the very town in which you were born!" Mario nodded and gave me a wide smile. I had never seen him looking quite so pleased with himself.

"You're kidding me," I said, casting him a very skeptical look.

"No, I'm serious, the woman I got him from told me his grandparents come from the town of Ambleside in Cumbria. Now will you take this poor dog? He's already starting to feel profoundly rejected and if you're not careful he may need psychological counseling. And you know how expensive those animal therapists can be."

I let out a heavy sigh before reluctantly taking the puppy into my arms. That, of course, was my first mistake. Within seconds I was oohing and aahing over his huge black eyes, cute little nose, and the way he curled his tiny body close to mine. It was all downhill from there. Surprising though it may seem, especially to me, since of all the people I know I have been the most impervious to the charms of small children and animals, (and before receiving Hairy Boy I had never considered acquiring even so much as a hamster), I quickly became a shamelessly devoted and doting dog owner.

After arriving at my apartment, my irrational anxiety about Hairy Boy quelled, I set about making two large mugs of tea. We took them into the living room, Mario slouched on the sofa while I sat on the floor.

"Y'know, I feel so bad that I fought with Peter just before he died," Mario said breaking what had been many minutes of silence. "Jesus, Lou, I just can't seem to take it in. I know you think he was a jerk to me. And you're right, he was. But when things were good they were…well, they were wonderful. Sometimes it was hard for me to realize that the jerky Peter who was mean to me and the good Peter who loved me were really the same person."

I nodded, remembering that I had felt exactly the same way about Justine. She had been capable of similar transformations, though hers had been quite a bit more extreme.

"I hate that I had to fight with him the last time I saw him," Mario continued. "Not just because it's a horrible way to have things end, but because I really got this feeling that he needed to talk to someone." He pursed his lips together for a moment, straining hard, it seemed, to hold back tears. "I've never seen him look quite so troubled, like he was really upset about something and he wanted to reach out for help."

"Did he say what it was?"

Mario shook his head. "No. All he said was he needed to work late but he was feeling distracted. He said he had to make a difficult decision and it was hard to know what was the right thing to do. And just when it seemed like he was going to tell me what was bothering him, I stupidly said something about us getting back together again. And that's when he went off the deep end. You know, I feel guilty that he's dead."

"What on earth for?"

"Well, maybe if we hadn't argued I would've stuck around that night at the office. Maybe I would've been able to help him with whatever was bothering him. Maybe he wouldn't have been at the office alone. And maybe he wouldn't have been killed." Mario finally succumbed to tears. They rolled silently down his cheeks, dripping from his chin to make dark splashes on his gray sweatshirt.

I went over to sit beside him, placing my arm around his shoulder. "Look, Mario," I said firmly, "you have no reason to feel guilty. The only person responsible for Peter's death is his murderer, right?"

"Yeah, I guess so," he sniffed. "But with the way that idiot Cochran is dealing with things, we may never find out who that is."

I nodded an agreement, since, at least about that issue, I couldn't help but think that Mario might be right.

"Well, things seemed to have calmed down a bit," I commented as I strode with Mario along Castro Street.

"Yeah, I was afraid it was going to get ugly earlier outside the office with all those cops and that crowd."

The gathering outside The Project had dispersed, but the mood on the street still seemed uneasy. Despite the bright afternoon sun, the Castro lacked its normal summer exuberance. The faces we passed were solemn and anxious. Small groups gathered outside the shops and by the bus stops. As we walked I caught snippets of nervous, angry conversations. Even the wandering tourists seemed infected by the tension.

On the corner of Eighteenth, outside the drug store, the early edition of *The Examiner* was on sale. I bought a copy before we crossed the street. 'Gays claim hate motive in activist murder,' it said. Below it was a recent photograph of Peter at a demonstration, his face contorted, mouth open as he yelled something at the line of blue uniforms in front of him.

Inside the restaurant we took a table by the window. As we sat, the smell of frying bacon filled my nostrils. My stomach groaned in yearning appreciation and I reached for the sticky, coffee-stained menu. Since living in California I'd suffered under the pressure to eat low-fat, cholesterol-free food (not an easy experience for someone brought up in England where anything fried in lard or baked with plenty of butter and sugar is considered a national delicacy). But the fad for healthy cuisine seemed to have passed by this particular establishment completely. So I ordered a Swiss cheese omelet, fries, bacon, and buttered toast without the guilt of overlooking all those healthy, heart-friendly alternatives. I tried to persuade Mario to join me, as he was tired and pale and looked like he could use a good meal inside him.

But he shook his head. "I just can't eat right now."

While we waited I spread the newspaper out over the table. The article about Peter's murder was brief, merely stating that 'the body of gay activist, Peter Williams, was found this morning at the offices of the well-known gay organization, Stop The Violence Project. He had been stabbed and some reports indicate that there was a note left on the body which included anti-gay epithets. The Project's Executive Director, Amanda Jensen, stated that "there is undoubtedly a hate motive in this crime. Stop The Violence Project and its staff are obvious targets for bigots."' The article went on to give personal details about Peter and background on the work of The Project. The final quote, which I couldn't help but roll my eyes at, was from Inspector Cochran who promised a 'thorough investigation into the murder.'

Moments later Amanda arrived, breezing past the hostess and over to our table. "Oh, so it made the afternoon edition," she said, pointing to the folded *Examiner* and dropping into the seat across from me. "I spoke to one of their reporters this morning. He wasn't sure if it would get in." She placed her bulging attaché case on the floor and eyed my omelet. "Mmm, that looks good. I think I'll order one myself."

I tucked into my food with relish and glanced out the window to see Donna marching solemnly toward the restaurant. I could tell by the grim frown across her face and the way she swung her arms heavily at her sides that she was not in a good mood.

"I can't eat anything, I'm so goddamn pissed," she said as she pulled out the chair next to me, its legs scraping noisily against the tile floor. "I can't believe the way that asshole Cochran treated me down at the Hall of Injustice. Anyone would think that we were suspects in this damn murder."

"I think that's exactly how they see us," I commented, my mouth full with a half-chewed piece of toast. "In fact, that's what Cochran told me."

"But that's ridiculous." Donna slammed her hand down so hard that the plates and knives jumped and clattered on the table. "I've never heard anything so ridiculous in my life. I don't see why I should be under suspicion," she said, her normally steady voice becoming tight and high. "Why would one of us kill Peter?" She looked around the table and each of us shrugged. "And anyway, it's obvious it's a hate crime. I mean, how much more evidence do they want?"

"Did he want to know what you were doing on Friday night?" Amanda asked, taking a sip from the glass of ice water in front of her.

"Yeah. And like I told him I spent the evening soaking in my bathtub and watching TV before going out dancing sometime after eleven. If I'm supposed to come up with an alibi, I guess that's not much of one." Donna pulled a brief, nervous smile. "What about you, Amanda, did he ask you?"

Amanda's omelet arrived and she waited for the waiter to slide the plate in front of her before she replied. "Yes. I left the office to do an interview with *The Gay Times* and then I had to go to that conference. The interview went way over—we didn't finish until after six-thirty. I dashed straight over to the conference and I was there from around seven or so until past eleven o'clock. So there's no way I should be considered a suspect. I mean, hundreds of people saw me there." She picked up her napkin and squeezed it tightly in her palm. "What about you two?" She asked looking at me and Mario.

We both shared what we had told Cochran.

"Well, I guess that leaves Amanda and Lou in the clear while you and me, Mario, are still suspects," Donna huffed, looking anxiously over at Mario. "What a joke! But I suppose we can't expect much more from the likes of dear Inspector Cochran. God, what an idiot! He wouldn't know a hate crime if it hit him in the face—which of course it wouldn't, him being the epitome of everything straight, white and male. What does he think? That we make up all this anti-gay violence just for fun?"

"Probably," sighed Amanda. "And unless we put pressure on the police department and on the city government, I'm sure they're going to let Cochran investigate for a couple of days at most, announce that they cannot find the killer and we'll be left with some murderous bigot running around town. And I don't know about you all, but that doesn't make me feel too safe."

Mario and Donna shook their heads. I looked down at my plate and realized I didn't really have an appetite any longer. As was my normal habit, I'd covered my fries in generous dabs of tomato ketchup. Suddenly, I was reminded of the horrific scene in Peter's office. I flinched and pushed my plate away.

"Anyway, I've been thinking about how to respond to what's happened, and we need to be organized if the community is going to have its say." Amanda stabbed one of her fries. As she continued to talk she gesticulated with her fork, the french fry dancing hypnotically in the air. "I talked with the Coalition this morning and the first thing that's clear to me is we need to have a press conference. Tomorrow afternoon seems like a good time. I want the media to hear our perspective before this becomes old news. We need to let people know how the lesbian and gay community feels about this murder. And we need to let the police department know that we won't put up with some shoddy, half-hearted investigation. I'm even going to try to get the mayor to make an appearance. If we can get him to make some kind of statement condemning hate crime then it will really help our case. I'll work on pressuring him this afternoon. After all, if he has such a strong stance on law and order, surely making a comment on hate-motivated murder won't be too far from his agenda." She paused as she finally popped the french fry into her mouth, chewed it, then swallowed quickly. "We should also have some kind of memorial service for Peter. His family is from the Midwest, they're going to make arrangements to have his body sent back home. But we really should have some kind of community recognition of him and the work that he contributed."

Mario nodded a firm agreement. "Yes, that's a good idea. It'll give people a chance to come together not only to acknowledge Peter, but also to make a statement about the murder. Make them feel like they're doing something constructive."

"Actually, I figured that you'd be the person to organize that, Mario. I thought Wednesday evening would be a good time."

"It's a little soon…" he said cautiously, "but, yeah, I think we can pull it together by then."

Amanda gulped down another mouthful of food. "And Lou, I'm relying on you to make sure the office keeps functioning. Once we're allowed back in, which according to Cochran will be tomorrow morning, we're going to be swamped with calls. Maybe you could get in a volunteer?"

"Yeah, I'm sure that'll be no problem," I said, already thinking of a particularly eager young woman activist I could recruit.

"I don't know about you all," said Donna, her tone reflecting our gloomy attempts at action, "but I'm just weirded out about this whole thing. I mean, it makes everything seem so crazy, so random. In a way Peter was just unlucky—it could have been anyone of us alone up there in the office."

We all looked around the table, each of us letting out a heavy, pensive sigh.

Chapter Six

I was woken early the next morning. I glanced over to my bedside alarm, the glowing red digits read five forty-five. From the apartment above I could hear the sound of loud, taut violins. It wasn't the first time I'd woken to The Blue Danube. Trust my luck to have an upstairs neighbor who was a Johann Strauss freak.

It never ceases to amaze me how people assume everyone around them is just dying to hear their music—twenty-four hours a day, at extremely high volumes. I read somewhere that it's the modern-day way for people to mark out their territory. If that's true, and with that Viennese racket rattling through my ceiling, I was beginning to think that dogs had a lot to teach us.

I pushed aside my comforter and struggled out of bed, bleary-eyed and not in my best of moods. A hot shower and a strong cup of tea left me feeling in somewhat better shape, but I couldn't shake the profound anxiety that the events of the previous day had left me with. I needed to take a walk, and so, of course, did Hairy Boy.

I grew up in a town in the Lake District of North West England, surrounded by some of the most breathtaking landscape I have ever known. My mother was an avid hiker and a true lover of natural beauty. Almost every weekend, come rain or shine (and believe me, in that part of the world there's a lot more rain than shine), the whole family was taken on a hike onto the fells or along the nearby coast. Sometimes it was just annoying, being forced out on a Saturday afternoon into the cold and the drizzle on what I regarded as the English equivalent of Mao's Long March. And it was even more annoying to have my mother sit atop some hillside, pull out her pocket collection of Wordsworth and recite nineteenth century poetry extolling the landscape we gazed down upon. As a teenager, I just thought she was weird. But when I left to live in London, I found I felt trapped in a city where escape involved long drives through dreary sprawling suburbs, and I slowly began to appreciate the admiration of nature she had taught me. So, when I came to San Francisco and discovered the acres of surrounding parkland, trails and beaches, in a way it was almost like coming home.

That morning I clambered down the cliff side to descend into a still, empty world. The drive along Highway One had been through dense, swirling fog and here at Montara State Beach it lay even thicker, like a wash of gray paint covering land and water. The sand lay in front of me, dark and smooth as freshly-laid concrete, marred only by the zig-zag pattern of Hairy Boy's paw prints. I followed him down to the shore where I watched the waves unfurl in foamy white banners, and let my mind wander over the events of the last twenty-four hours.

Walking through the Pacific's ethereal mist, everything felt unreal. After all, who would have thought I'd get up to go to work on a Monday morning only to discover my co-worker murdered in his office? 'Only in America,' my friends back in Britain would probably say. But hate crimes happened everywhere—racist murders in East London, gay-bashings even in the tiny town in which I grew up. It was all so ugly, and even uglier when you saw it for yourself. As much as I tried to let the fresh ocean air clear out my mind, I just couldn't stop thinking about that horrible scene I had walked in on. And I couldn't get rid of the feeling that something just did not make sense. Call it intuition, call it whatever you like, there was a part of me that knew that there was something I was missing. But like a word on the tip of my tongue, I was unable to say what it was.

"Hey, Lou, Mario, how's it going?" Jasmine, the volunteer I had recruited to help out at The Project, greeted me later that morning. Sporting a sleek cap of close-cropped hair and a fascinating assortment of facial piercings, she perched her petite frame on the edge of my desk, her fine-boned Filipina features breaking into a wide smile. Over excruciatingly tight black jeans, she wore a T-shirt that bore the phrase, 'Read My Lips,' and a picture of two women engaged in a passionate kiss. A touching tribute, I thought, to the famous words of former President Bush.

"God, it's just awful what happened," she said making her velvet brown eyes wide. "I heard you found Peter's body. Man, you must be really weird-ed out."

Yes, you might say that, I thought to myself, and I might have been amused at Jasmine's apparent gift for understatement if I wasn't feeling quite so disturbed.

"You know, I kinda knew Peter," she continued as Mario glanced up at her from his desk with a look of both irritation and reluctant curiosity. "Yeah, he was there at that blockade of the Federal Building when I got arrested. I've never known anybody who was murdered before."

Just then there was a loud knock at the front door. "I'll get it," Jasmine announced, bouncing off my desk and running towards the stairs.

"Ask who it is first!" I warned.

A few moments later Inspector Cochran strode into the office. Gruffly, he acknowledged my presence before looking past me to Mario who was sitting at his desk busily writing. "Could I have a word, Mr. Fuentes?" Cochran moved towards him.

"I guess so," Mario said, making clear from his tone that he looked forward to a conversation with Cochran with about as much enthusiasm as he reserved for getting a root canal.

"Well, good, if we could go somewhere a little more private… " Cochran glanced hopefully around the office.

"Not really, this is it."

Cochran turned around and gave Jasmine and me a fierce and meaningful glare.

"Er, I guess I'll go out and get some coffee," Jasmine said, looking a little confused.

"Actually, why don't you go pick up these supplies we need," I said, handing her a list and a twenty dollar bill from petty cash. She quickly obliged by dashing down the stairs.

I had far too much work to do to be forced out of the office so I turned my back to Cochran, sat down at my desk and began my search through the yellow pages for someone to put in a new lock downstairs and install an intercom. I had already decided that my priority that day was to make sure Peter's murderer wouldn't be able to pay us a second visit. As I skimmed the phone book, however, I kept one ear on the conversation between Mario and Cochran.

"Now let me get this clear, Mr. Fuentes," Cochran began, "you and Mr. Williams were…lovers." He muttered the last word with particular distaste.

"Yeah, that's right." Mario's tone was defiant.

"And I have already established that things were not exactly…harmonious between the two of you."

"We broke up, if that's what you mean."

"Well, it was a little more than that, wasn't it? You were angry with him because he tossed you aside. You had several arguments with him."

"Yes, but we've already been over this once and I still don't see what you're trying to get at. Even if I was angry with Peter, that has nothing to do with his death."

"It doesn't?"

"No, it doesn't."

"Well, what if I told you, Mr. Fuentes, that we found your fingerprints on the letter-opener that killed Peter Williams?" There was an edge of cruel satisfaction in Cochran's tone.

"His letter-opener? But that's impossible, I didn't kill Peter."

"Then could you explain how your fingerprints got on it?"

"I don't know," Mario muttered softly. "Maybe I used it to open letters. Maybe I just picked it up off his desk."

"When you killed him?"

"No, I didn't kill Peter!" Mario suddenly stood up, pushing his chair back so that it clattered to the floor.

"Now, now, Mr. Fuentes. Don't go losing control. Isn't that a trait of you...Latin types?"

I turned around to see Mario's face flushed with rage, his brows pressed into a deep, angry scowl. He squeezed his hands into tight fists, taking a long breath before answering. "You know what, Inspector Cochran," he said slowly, "if you're going to charge me with murder because you don't like Mexicans, maybe you should go ahead and do it now."

Cochran spat out a hard laugh. "Now, now, I don't know why all you people have to be so goddamn sensitive...first I hate gays, now I'm racially prejudiced. Maybe you're being so touchy because you've got something to hide. Is that it?"

Mario responded with stony silence.

"Not feeling talkative right now? Oh, well, don't worry, I'm sure me and you will have plenty more time to talk." With that Cochran turned and strolled out of the office, murmuring a cheerful, "Good Morning, Miss Spencer," at me before he headed for the stairs.

"I don't remember how my fingerprints got on Peter's letter-opener, Lou, I really don't." Mario turned to me once Cochran had left the building. "I can't believe that I'm being accused. There's no way in hell I could even think of murdering Peter, but I'll tell you something, I could end up killing that racist pig if he doesn't leave me alone. And you know what, I wouldn't feel in the least bit guilty."

I thought back to when I had last seen Peter's letter-opener in his chest, left, like the note on his face, for almost theatrical effect. Was it possible, with its smooth, long handle that Mario could have left his prints on it before the murder had actually taken place? And even after all that blood and carnage, they might still be left intact? Anything was possible, I supposed. But right now, at least in Cochran's eyes, Mario's prospects didn't look too good at all.

A few minutes later Amanda strode into the office, a copy of the morning paper under her arm. "Have either of you seen today's *Chronicle*?"

"I did see the headline, something about that supervisor's seat, right?" Mario commented, looking up from his desk.

"Yep, it's finally official. Supervisor Jones is stepping down in a month. You know what this means, don't you?"

We both nodded. With her contacts in city government, Amanda had known that Patricia Jones' departure from the city's Board of Supervisors was imminent. Patricia's young daughter had recently been diagnosed with a terminal illness, and Patricia wanted to give up her duties so she could take care of her.

"It's going to be a disaster." Amanda shook her head slowly, the overhead light catching the highlights in her bobbed chestnut hair. "It makes me pine for the days when we had a progressive board with a couple of openly gay supervisors. Those days seem pretty much over now. With Patricia gone, we'll have no one to challenge the right-wing craziness of Mayor Finch. I mean, at least she was pretty liberal, and not one of his damn lackeys! And now she's leaving, well, Finch can just appoint who he damn well pleases. This whole thing makes me crazy." She spoke through gritted teeth. "Just think who we'll end up with if Finch has his way. You think things are bad now, they're going to get way worse. I mean, listen to what he says in this damn article." She unfurled her copy of the *Chronicle* and began skimming through the offending article. "Talking garbage about the importance of law and order, teaching the radicals not to disrupt the everyday lives of law-abiding people. Doesn't it occur to him that the radicals might want to get on with their everyday lives if they weren't dying of AIDS or being beaten up on the streets by gay-bashers?" She slammed the paper down on my desk. "God, and I'm going to have to stand next to him at the press conference this afternoon." She shuddered and pulled an expression of utter distaste. "I'm beginning to wish we hadn't asked him to speak, he's such a right-wing bigot."

"Things do look pretty bad," I commented, looking over the crumpled newspaper.

"Bad doesn't even begin to describe it," she huffed. "It's so damned depressing. Now, if you gave me a chance at the reins of power in this city…" She shook her head, her round, hazel eyes showing a wistful glint.

"Man, now that's an idea, isn't it?" Mario commented. "If I was mayor I'd fire all those stupid bureaucrats up at City Hall, I'd get rid of the supervisors altogether and I'd send the entire police force into early retirement. I'd make homosexuality compulsory within the city of San Francisco and I'd…"

"You know Mario," I laughed, "you should stand for election, you might even get into office—but I think you might have to reconsider the compulsory homosexuality thing."

"Okay, well in that case I'll just make it compulsory for cute guys. How's that sound? Hey, at least I'd be guaranteed the gay male vote. Right?" He flashed me a mischievous grin and let his tongue peek out over his upper lip. I was glad to see that he'd made such a quick recovery from his encounter with Cochran. But then that was Mario, he never let himself stay upset for very long.

Amanda creased her meticulously plucked brows and cast us both a scornful glance. "This is serious, you know. I'm really worried what this is going to mean for the community. If someone with decent politics and some skill were able to get that supervisorial seat it could make all the difference."

"Yeah," agreed Mario, "but there's not much chance of that."

"You never know," said Amanda. "Maybe there's still someone or something that can make a difference. We have to make sure that Finch doesn't get his way on this…if he does, well, we're in for a very rough and ugly ride. I'm pushing the Community Coalition to really fight this one, we have to."

Chapter Seven

"Stop The Violence Project, can you hold?… Stop The Violence Project, can you hold?…" By mid-morning, I was beginning to feel like a well-trained parrot. I'd never known the phones could ring so relentlessly. And with all the running up and down the stairs to let in the scores of visitors, I was beginning to think I might have a shot at winning the San Francisco Marathon. Fortunately, I was able to get a new lock and intercom installed by midday, which meant we could now buzz people in from upstairs. Jasmine was able to help out with the phones and she was a godsend—without her, I'd have checked into the local psych ward by about ten o'clock. There was one caller, however, who she didn't have much success with, and when I noticed her holding the phone at arm's length, her normally placid features straining to contain her frustration, I signaled her to hand me the phone. Even from several feet away I could recognize the familiar rantings of Patrick Tanner.

I lifted the phone to my ear.

"…and I don't care who the hell you are, volunteer, lackey or just plain slave. I want to see a goddamn advocate today…"

"Mr. Tanner," I interrupted, "is there something I can help you with?" I used my most soothing tone.

"I know you, I recognize your accent, you're that Australian woman. I've talked to you before and a lot of good it did me. Put that other one back on the phone she was a lot more helpful than you ever were."

"I'm sorry, she's no longer available." I smiled as I looked over at Jasmine, she rolled her eyes. "But let me see if I can help."

"I don't want to talk to you, I want to see a fucking advocate." I pulled the phone away from my ear; listening to Patrick Tanner was as much fun as standing next to the speakers at a Sex Pistols concert. "If you fucking people would just do your fucking job and help me get the justice I deserve then I wouldn't be in this goddamn mess. I need to talk to someone right now, you hear me? I'm sick of being pushed around by you goddamn assholes."

This wasn't the first of Patrick's outbursts, nor, I was sure, would it be his last. Over the last few weeks he had become a regular caller, and so beloved by The Project staff that we'd unanimously voted him 'the client from hell.' Despite that, I was still able to sympathize with him. A few weeks ago, he had been riding a bus home late at night when a group of youths began taunting him, calling him faggot and leering into his face. The bus was full of people but no one said anything and when he complained to the driver he was told that he was 'nothing but a faggot trouble-maker.' The driver set Tanner, and the group of youths, out on the sidewalk in a deserted and badly-lit part of the city. Of course, they'd beaten him up. He received broken fingers, cracked ribs, lost a few teeth and spent several days in the hospital under observation for a severe concussion. Since then he had lost his job, was having terrible nightmares and was often too afraid to go out of his house.

"Can you tell me what's happened, Patrick?" I asked, during the lull in his ravings.

He took a breath and seemed about to launch further into his harangue but his voice came out quiet and strained, as if he was trying to hold back tears. "I just need to see someone. I got this letter from the bus company. God, I just can't believe those SOBs. Peter told me to write and ask them what they were going to do to discipline that driver, you know, the bastard that left me to get beat up. And all they can tell me is that all disciplinary procedures are closed per union contract, or some other such bullshit. I want someone to help me out. I just want to get some justice, y'know."

"Yeah, that's really too bad that they won't let you know what's going on. Maybe I can have Donna call you back, she's our other advocate, I don't know if you've heard about what happened to Peter." I spoke gently, I was afraid the news would upset him more.

"Yeah, I know, it's been all over the papers." I was surprised at his tone, it was dismissive, like he didn't seem to think it was a big deal.

"Oh, well, then you wouldn't mind talking to Donna?"

"Not if she's better than Peter, that's for sure."

"Okay, let me see if I can put you through."

"No," he shouted. Again I jerked the receiver away from my ear. "I don't want to talk about this on the phone, I'm too upset. I need to see someone in person."

"Well, Donna is really busy. She wouldn't be able to see you until…" I looked through the staff appointment calendar that I kept on my desk. "Would tomorrow morning be okay?"

"Don't you have anything in the evening? Say around six-thirty?"

45

"No, I'm sorry, but advocates are only available until six."

"That's not true!" He yelled at me again. "Peter saw me last Friday at six-twenty. He didn't have a problem making an appointment with me then."

"What do you mean?" I asked quickly. "Were you here last Friday evening? Were you here the night Peter was killed?"

He hesitated. "I wasn't there that long, only ten minutes or so. And anyway, what if I was?" He sounded nervous, like a little boy caught in a lie.

"Mr. Tanner, if you were at the office last Friday night you really should talk to the police. You may be able to help with the investigation of Peter's murder."

"I wouldn't talk to those assholes if you paid me. They never lifted a goddamned finger to help me. Now can you just tell me what time I can see Donna tomorrow?"

"Mr. Tanner, I really think you should tell—"

"Don't tell me what to do," he interrupted. "Just give me an appointment, okay?"

"How about eleven o'clock?"

"That's fine," he said and hung up the phone.

As I penciled in Patrick Tanner's name, I found myself wondering if he had witnessed anything on Friday night that might help find the murderer, after all, if he had seen Peter at six-twenty then he could be the last person—apart from the killer—to have seen Peter alive. But I wasn't too hopeful that he'd help the police out with their inquiries. For one thing, his experiences after the assault left him hating the cops with a vengeance, and for another, as a long-term client of Peter's, he seemed strangely unaffected by his death. He seemed far more interested in his own problems than in bringing a murderer to justice. I toyed with the idea of telling Cochran myself what Patrick Tanner had just blurted out. But we had a very strict policy at The Project and at least for the time being, I didn't feel I could break client confidentiality.

"Who was that?" Jasmine asked, shaking her head as I closed the appointment book.

"Just one of the clients," I answered, "I'm sorry if he was rude."

"Oh it's okay," she said as she played with the thin silver ring that pierced the skin near her eyebrow. "Jeez, but I wouldn't want to be his advocate, that guy sounds kinda scary."

Almost everyone who had come by the office that day was there to see Amanda. They all traipsed down the hall to her office where some intense strategizing about that afternoon's press conference was taking place. But close to midday, someone arrived to see me. It was Alex Ramon.

"Hi, just came by to see how you're doing. You seemed pretty shaken up yesterday." I looked up to see her long body leaning across the doorway. Her lips were shaped in a broad, warm smile.

"Yeah, I'm doing okay," I said, doing my best to appear poised and unflustered while inside my pulse galloped like a racehorse on amphetamines.

"Good," she said, frowning as she looked past me. "Mario?" she said, staring towards him.

Mario glanced up from his work. Suddenly his face lit up. "Alex. Como estas?"

"Muy bien, y tu?"

"Asi asi," he answered, gesturing with his hand.

"Hold on a minute, I didn't know you two knew each other," I interrupted.

"Sure," answered Alex, "Mario and I share a couple of the same hangouts, right?"

Mario nodded.

"I knew he worked for a nonprofit, but I didn't realize it was The Project."

"So, what are you doing here?" Mario asked.

"I'm working the Castro beat, took the call from Lou about the homicide."

"I didn't see you," Mario commented. "But then it was probably easy to miss you in that crowd. It felt like the entire San Francisco Police Force had descended upon us."

"Yeah, I guess there were quite a few of us around." I noticed a slight rosy blush ease over her olive complexion. She glanced at her feet and then over at me. "I…er…I just felt bad for being a little dismissive about that complaint you made about the hate call the other day. I didn't realize it was going to end up in murder. I hope I didn't offend you or anything."

I shrugged. "No, not at all, you couldn't know what would happen."

"Well, I was just wondering if I could make it up to you by buying you dinner sometime?"

Immediately a thousand reasons for not taking up her invitation flooded my brain. I was too busy. There were more important things to do. She'd pick a bad restaurant. I hated going out for dinner anyway. It would be awkward and a waste of time. And besides, we were far too different, we'd have absolutely nothing to talk about.

"But if you'd rather not, I…"

"No… I mean yes…I mean I'd like to." The words came out before I could even stop them.

"Good," she said, smiling, "how about tonight?"

"Tonight?"

"Yeah, I could meet you at that Italian place down the street at, say eight?"

"Er……sure…that's fine."

"See you at eight, then," she concluded as she turned to leave.

When I looked over at Mario he had a grin on his face that stretched from ear to ear. "So, I guess that's a date then," he said, giving me an exaggerated wink.

"Finch is late, goddamn it." Amanda stood on the steps of San Francisco City Hall, huffing as she glanced once again at her watch. "But I'm sure he has far more important things to do than this. After all, we're only discussing a murder here!"

I stood beside her, next to the make-shift podium, looking down across the assembled crowd which shifted impatiently, waiting for the mayor's arrival so the press conference could begin. It was a mixed gathering. There was a large contingent of allies from the Coalition, representatives from all kinds of gay organizations, and a smattering of weather-worn homeless people who'd made their way over from nearby Civic Center Plaza with shopping carts in tow to check out what was going on. In the very front, right below us, a rowdy group of brightly-clad young activists waved placards which read, "Finch is the biggest gay basher of them all!" and "Finch hates queers!"

Meanwhile, the media dashed about the crowd like sharks at a feeding frenzy. Men hauling news cameras trailed after microphone-toting reporters who approached just about everyone there to ask them what they knew about the murder. I had narrowly escaped being ensnared by a reporter from *Hard News,* the notorious tabloid show. In her powder pink suit and teased blond hair, she'd chased me, grabbing at my sleeve as I made my way to City Hall steps. Fortunately for me, one of the heels on her stilettos broke, leaving her to shriek and stagger to a halt. Once again, I thanked my mother for indoctrinating me at a very early age in the virtues of sensible shoes.

At two-fifteen the mayor finally arrived. Making his entrance through the revolving doors of City Hall, he strode towards the assembly, a suitably solemn expression fixed on his pale and jowly face. He was escorted by a group of aides, a bland collection of white men in tailored suits who eyed all around them with a smug air of self-satisfaction.

"Good afternoon Mayor Finch, I'm so glad you could make it," Amanda shaped her face into a smile, there was no hint in her voice of her earlier irritation. "Your presence means a lot to us here today. I'm pleased you're willing to speak out against such a terrible crime." As they shook hands the mayor faced the crowd, pulling his thin lips into a tight smile for the busily snapping photographers. A chorus of boos and hisses emanated from the activists in front as they waved their painted placards with furious energy. The mayor acknowledged their presence with nothing more than a contemptuous movement of an eyebrow before moving confidently towards the podium.

He read from a prepared statement, "It is with great sadness that I speak to you today about the death of a young man in our city." The group at the front groaned and muttered. "We San Franciscans pride ourselves on our appreciation of diversity, our tolerance of differences."

"Yeah, right, that's why you have the police beat us up on the streets," someone heckled from the back of the crowd.

The mayor closed his eyes and shook his head in a brief gesture of disdain before continuing. "I can only say that I share the grief of the gay community at this untimely death. And I offer everyone who knew Peter Williams my sincerest condolences."

"You can shove them up your ass," a voice shouted out.

The color rose abruptly into Mayor Finch's face, he took a deep breath, inflating himself like an aggravated puffer fish. As the anger quivered in his face I wondered if his polished cool was about to desert him. But in an instant he seemed to regain composure, raising his hand to cover a muted cough before going on. "I have already spoken to Amanda Jensen, Executive Director of Stop The Violence Project," he continued, turning to give Amanda a swift smile, "and I have given her my firm commitment that the police department will do their utmost to see that this murderer is apprehended. As mayor I will ensure that no one has to be afraid of despicable criminals like the person who took the life of Peter Williams. To this end I pledge to continue my war against crime and violence here in San Francisco." Ignoring the questions yelled out by reporters, he turned quickly from the podium. No longer facing the cameras, his expression disintegrated into one of annoyance and disdain. And muttering unhappily under his breath, he gestured his entourage to follow him back into City Hall.

Amanda looked a little disconcerted as she watched Finch make his swift exit, but it was now her turn to speak, so clearing her throat with a loud cough, she approached the podium. "There is no doubt," she began "that the murder of Peter Williams was a hate crime." A few mutterings of agreement sounded in the crowd. "We in the San Francisco lesbian and gay community are tired of being the targets of violence. In the last year assaults reported to The Project increased by almost forty per cent. So far nothing has been done to stem this terrible tide."

When her speech was over Amanda proceeded to answer reporters' questions. "It sounds like there's lot of anger among gays about this murder. Can we expect a repeat of the riots after the death of Harvey Milk?" A reporter from KRON news pointed a microphone at Amanda. He referred to what are known as the White Night Riots which occurred when Dan White, murderer of the first openly gay San Francisco supervisor, was given a ridiculously lenient sentence for his crime. When the verdict was announced many lesbians and gay men protested by running through the streets, setting fire to police cars and causing thousands of dollars worth of property damage.

"I should remind you that the White Night Riots happened only after our community had been let down by the judicial system in this city. I would like to hope that such a travesty of justice will not happen again."

"Do you think, Miss Jensen," a reporter from KCBS asked, "that Peter Williams was the target of a random hate crime? Or do you have reason to believe he was deliberately targeted?"

Amanda looked thoughtful before answering. "Well…that's hard to say. Of course, because of our work at Stop The Violence Project we make prime targets for anti-gay violence. It is also true that Peter worked on some high profile cases and helped make sure that some particularly vicious criminals were prosecuted. There could always be a revenge motive…but I can only speculate about that."

The questions continued for twenty minutes. There were a few representatives from gay and lesbian publications who asked what I considered the more sensitive, thoughtful questions. But most of the media, as usual, were obviously trying for the most sensational angle they could muster.

Suddenly I felt depressed. The press conference began to seem like a silly, useless spectacle. The mayor was there only because he thought it would benefit his political image; the small pack of demonstrators were there just to heckle the mayor. And the media, the people for whom this whole thing had been organized, would spin out the story of Peter's death for only as long as their ratings and sales could justify. Tomorrow would bring along another tragedy that would make headline news and Peter would just end up another statistic. If I thought about the whole thing for too long I could become more jaded than I already was. I decided to leave and make my way back to the office where at least I would be of more use.

As I eased my way through the crowd towards Civic Center I was approached by another reporter. "Hi, Lou Spencer, right?" He extended a large, thin-fingered hand towards me.

"Yeah, that's right," I answered, taking a step back and meeting his gaze. There was something familiar about his anxious dark eyes, the way they darted about behind his heavy-framed spectacles. "Do I know you?"

He pulled an amused smile. "It's Jeff Easton, I'm with *The City Reporter*. I think we've met a couple of times before."

"Oh, yes, I remember now," I said, finally shaking his hand. "You've worked on a few articles about cases we were handling. I knew I'd seen you somewhere before but you know how busy The Project can get. I'm sorry, I'm just a little suspicious of reporters these days. They're like vultures around carrion, this lot." I gestured towards the crowd of journalists still questioning Amanda.

"Well, I guess we have to make a living," he said, still smiling.

"Oh, I didn't mean to include you. I mean, you've done some great work on *The Reporter*. I like your stuff a lot." And I meant it. Jeff was a good journalist whose investigative pieces made the otherwise badly-written and gossip-filled pages of *The City Reporter* worth reading. Over the years I'd enjoyed the way he'd uncovered stories on everything from city officials who spent money meant for AIDS services on personal expenses, to homophobia in the San Francisco Fire Department.

"I'm sorry about Peter," he said. "You're the one that found him, right?"

I nodded.

"Man, was I shocked when I heard. I've worked with him more than once, you know, stories on his cases. Nice guy, real nice. And real committed to his work. I know you've probably been asked this already by all the vultures over there, but I was wondering if you wouldn't mind talking about finding the body. Y'know, just what the office was like, what the time was, those kinds of things."

"Haven't the police told you?" I asked.

"Oh, yeah, but it's always better to get things first hand." He looked at me eagerly, his finger itching at the button of his hand-held tape recorder.

"To tell you the truth, I don't really feel like talking about it right now. Maybe some other time."

"I guess it must be kinda hard finding a body and all…But I was hoping since I've done so much work with the Project that you might make an exception…"

"Sorry," I said flatly. "It's still pretty upsetting. Try talking to Amanda, she's the official spokesperson for The Project."

"Okay," he shrugged, "but if you change your mind…"

"I'll let you know," I said, turning away and hoping this was my last encounter with the press for a while. But then I remembered the message Jeff had left on the office answering machine and curiosity got the better of me. I turned back again. "Didn't you have a meeting, scheduled with Peter on Friday night?" I asked.

"Yeah, yeah," he frowned as he nodded. "That's strange, isn't it, that he died that night? Made me feel real weird when I thought about it afterwards. I mean, there I was waiting for him and there he was probably already dead. The whole thing was pretty weird really. He had me wait for him in some straight bar in the Outer Mission. God knows why he picked there."

"It was probably about one of his cases."

He shook his head. "I don't think so. We usually met during his work time at the office. And from what he said, I got the impression that this was something different. He told me he had this really hot story, said he wanted to expose someone for what they were. It didn't sound like a client case to me, more like it was someone he knew personally. He just sounded pretty angry, I guess."

"Did he say who it was he wanted to expose?" I was intrigued.

"Uh-uh. He called me Friday morning around eight. I remember because I'd been working real late the night before and his call got me outta bed. I was still half asleep so I agreed to meet him and didn't ask a lot of questions. I didn't feel the need to, Peter always came through with good stuff. And it sounded like it was pretty good because he told me I wasn't to tell anyone about our meeting, that it was to be completely confidential. Now I guess I'll never find out what it was he wanted to tell me." He got a wistful look in his eyes. "Though I guess I did get my hot story. But who knew it would be Peter's murder. Funny the way things work out, huh?"

Chapter Eight

The Italian restaurant at which I was to meet Alex Ramon was a popular evening hang-out in the Castro. On warmer days they opened the big wood-framed windows at the front and diners leaned out to absorb the street's atmosphere as they ate their tortellini and sipped from delicate cups of syrupy espresso. The fog had held the city in its dismal thrall all that day and by evening a cold wind gusted through the streets, sending litter and dust capering across the sidewalk. That night the windows were tightly closed.

As I approached I glanced through the glass at the restaurant's interior. Bathed in warm yellow light, several couples sat murmuring conversation across wooden tables. Waiters moved swiftly and smoothly around them, sweeping plates of steaming pasta from the kitchen onto the crisp linen tablecloths. Wine glasses glinted as they were held aloft in cheerful toasts. It all looked so romantic—down to the single red roses in vases on the tables, the beautiful candelabra on the marble-topped bar.

As I watched it all I couldn't help ask myself what the hell was I doing, letting myself be invited out on a date? I couldn't remember the last time I'd had a date; it had to be almost a year ago at least. And I was sure, that like that last encounter, this evening was also bound to end in disaster. Indeed, dating was something I hadn't done much of in the last five years. On my arrival in San Francisco, I'd sworn off relationships, and up until now, I'd had no problem remaining single.

It was never easy to explain my reasons. In fact, I had confided only in Terri and Mario about the relationship that had caused me to flee my home and make a new start in a strange and distant land. Justine—she had started out as the love of my life and ended up the bane of my existence. A charismatic and moderately successful playwright, I'd met her at a party. We got along well immediately and after she'd broken through my initial reserve, I had fallen for her hard. I was twenty-three, naive and besotted, and imagined us riding off together into a glowing sunset of lesbian romance—alas, nothing could have been further from the truth. Because within a matter of months, she became abusive—oh, nothing too serious at first, just nasty, humiliating comments I tried to brush off after we made up. But gradually, by tiny, incremental steps, things got worse and worse. Until she started to hit me, at first with an open palm, then with a fist, and finally with anything she could get her hands on. People always wonder why battered women stay (and, as far as I'm concerned, that's just what I was—a lesbian, a feminist, and a battered woman). It's not easy to explain. I stayed because I loved her, because she always said she was sorry and that she'd never do it again, because when she wasn't violent she was kind and attentive and sweet, and because, for the final year of the relationship, I was just too damn afraid to leave. But finally, when she lost her temper one last time and literally tried to strangle me, I knew I had to go. So, to cut a long (and not too pretty) story short, I bought a ticket to San Francisco, and set about the hard and painful process of making a new life for myself.

I stared into the window of the restaurant, reflected on that nightmarish experience, and I felt an almost irresistible urge to turn around and go home. I must have been nuts to accept Alex's invitation. First of all, what was I thinking when I agreed to have dinner with a San Francisco cop? Surely everything I'd learned in my work should tell me to stay well away from the SFPD? Secondly, I had no inclination to get romantically involved. And thirdly, well thirdly, I just didn't let anyone get that close. I'd learned my lesson about that. In fact, I was just about to spin on my heels and head back to my apartment when I noticed someone waving to me from inside the restaurant; it was Alex. Sitting alone at one of the tables and looking stunning in a cream shirt and black pants, she gestured me inside. I returned her wave, took a deep breath, shaped my face into a smile and walked rather reluctantly to the door.

Inside, the air was warm, heady with the rich aroma of red wine. The strident, twangy sounds of flamenco guitar overlaid the conversation and clatter of plates. "Madam?" The waiter was young, his hair silky blond, skin tanned to an even copper brown and his shirt just tight enough to reveal the impressive contours of his muscular torso. "Do you have a reservation?" When he smiled he revealed a set of perfectly capped, bright white teeth. Tips must be pretty good, I couldn't help speculating, to allow for such a high maintenance look.

"I'm meeting a friend," I said, making my way towards Alex.

"Hey," she said, dimples showing as she smiled. "Glad you made it. You looked like you were having second thoughts out there by the window."

"Me? No, I was just er…just trying to work out if I was in the right place." Only ten seconds in her presence and again I felt the color rise to my face.

"So how's it going?" she asked, as I pulled out the chair and sat down.

"Oh, not too bad, considering." I nodded.

"Yeah, I bet these last couple of days have been a bit of a roller coaster."

This close I could see the creases at the edges of her eyes, fine lines across her forehead, and the beginnings of salt and pepper streaks through her glossy hair. She looked like a woman who would age well, experience enriching rather than ravaging her features.

"It must be awful having one of your co-workers murdered like that. I guess the guy who left those messages is probably the one who did it."

"That's not what your friends down at homicide seem to think," I said sharply.

"Really?" She seemed surprised.

"Yeah, that Inspector Cochran is a real bonehead. But that's no surprise, with my job I've seen enough of the police to know what to expect. Of course, it goes without saying that most cops are jerks." It wasn't until I'd finished that I fully realized what I'd said. Congratulations, Lou, I thought to myself, you told yourself the evening was bound to end in disaster and here you are making it happen. Talk about self-fulfilling prophecy. If Alex had gotten up and stalked off in a temper at my anti-police outburst, I would hardly have been surprised.

But I was surprised when Alex nodded calmly. "Yeah, I tend to agree with you, most cops are jerks. Of course, I also like to think that there are some exceptions, most notably yours truly." A smile played across her lips as she picked up her menu. "You want to order? I'm starving, forgot to eat lunch and though Riley was offering me donuts all afternoon, I'm proud to say I held out for dinner."

I decided on spaghetti al pesto while Alex ordered the lasagna. And since what I know about wine can be written in very large letters on a very small piece of paper, I let her pick one out. She requested a bottle of something that sounded Italian.

When the waiter left there were a few seconds of awkward silence. I shuffled uncomfortably in my seat and let my gaze wander everywhere but Alex's face.

"Look," she said, interrupting the silence, "I know that with your job you've probably heard enough stories about attitudes in the department, seen enough people making complaints that you think we're all a bunch of thugs. And you know what, in a lot of cases you'd be right. But I hate those kinds of people as much as you do."

"Yeah, but how much can you do when you work in the police force? I mean, you have to follow orders, right?" I rested my elbows on the table.

"True, yeah, I do have to follow orders. But it's not the military. If I don't like it, I can quit. But so far I think what I do is important. There's not that many out Latina lesbians in the San Francisco Police Department, you know."

"I know, it must be hard for you sometimes."

"Hey, it could be a lot worse. At least I have a good career with a decent pay check. A lot of the girls I grew up with got pregnant before they got near graduating high school and never had a chance from there on. The only restaurant most of them ever see the inside of is MacDonalds, and the best they can hope for someday is that they find themselves a steady, reliable, boring guy." Her voice was still soft but it had an angry edge, the kind that comes from harsh experiences and witnessing too much pain. "There may be things I don't like about being in the police department but at least it means I get a little respect. For that I don't mind making compromises every now and then."

"But you must have heard about how the cops behaved at the recent ACT-UP and Queer Nation demonstrations, doesn't that bother you?"

"Of course it does. I might not support some of their opinions, but I do support their right to demonstrate. And I don't like what the mayor's doing right now. He seems to think he's doing us a favor by encouraging the use of strong arm tactics. But you know what?—I think in the long run it does more harm than good. There's enough people who don't like the police as it is without us making even more enemies. I know you don't have a high opinion of cops, but just because I wear the uniform it doesn't make me a fascist pig, right?"

"No, I…"

"Yeah, I know, that's not what you said. After all, you can't think that I'm like those types because you wouldn't be having dinner with me, right?"

"Yes, I suppose so. It's just that it's really getting to me, the way they're conducting this investigation. Cochran seems to think his strongest suspect is Mario, for God's sake."

"That's ridiculous," Alex retorted. "Mario wouldn't hurt a fly."

"Try telling Cochran that," I answered.

The waiter arrived, and we sank into silence as he made a flamboyant display of uncorking the wine and pouring it into Alex's glass. She winked over at me as she obliged him by sniffing the cork, swirling the wine around in her glass, and taking a sip that she swished around her mouth before swallowing and giving an appreciative nod. "Don't worry," she continued after the waiter left, "I'm sure they'll find a suspect other than Mario soon." She set her glass back down on the table and ran her tongue over her lips.

"They found his fingerprints on the letter-opener that was used to kill Peter."

"Hmmm." She looked suddenly concerned. "I'm not sure that proves anything…I mean, he could've touched it another time, right? They do work together. Cochran will need more than that to charge him."

"Yeah, I suppose you're right," I said and glanced around the restaurant. A few tables away from us someone was celebrating a birthday. A small cake bearing a single candle sat at the center of the table and above the flamenco music several friends were engaged in a tuneless rendition of 'Happy Birthday.'

When I turned back, Alex had placed both elbows on the edge of the table and was leaning towards me. As I played nervously with my fork she brushed my hand with the barest touch of her fingertips. Immediately I felt a jolt of electricity move through my body. My first impulse was jump up and run away, my second was to reach out, grab her hand and take it in mine. I did neither and merely tried to hide the turmoil blustering through my mind behind a cool, impassive expression.

"Do you mind if I change the subject?" she asked.

"No," I answered warily.

"Well…it's about why I asked you to dinner. I know I said it was to apologize, and it is. But I also want you to know that I don't do this with everyone I take a police report from." A slight grin edged across her lips. "I…well…I wanted to ask you out because I'm attracted to you." She kept eye contact for a second before looking down at the table and making an intense study of her napkin.

Well, this is a woman who cuts right to the chase, I thought to myself. An admirable quality, I supposed, but right at that moment I was too busy feeling tense to be much impressed. So tense that the muscles in the back of my neck knotted tight, and panic fluttered in my chest like a trapped bird. Suddenly my throat felt very dry. I picked up my wine and played for time.

"Well," I said after draining almost the entire glass, "I'm flattered."

She looked up to meet my gaze and immediately I looked away to concentrate on rearranging my silverware, all the while praying that the floor beneath me would open and discreetly swallow me up.

This was not my idea of a good time. In fact, right at that moment I would rather have been spectator to a five to zero German victory over England in the World Cup (the most awful experience for any dedicated English soccer fan) than sitting opposite Alex Ramon. I would rather have been anywhere. Unfortunately, it didn't look like I was going to be rescued by a hole suddenly opening up in the ground or any other act of God. I was going to have to talk my way out of this situation.

"I…er…I…" There was no doubt about it, I just didn't know what to say. And yet, I did. Or at least I knew how I felt. I knew I was attracted to her. I was wary, even afraid, perhaps, but so far I liked her company, and surely someone who could risk being so honest only deserved the same treatment back. So I did my best. "I'm really attracted to you, too," I said, speaking so fast that the sentence sounded like one many-syllabled word. "I…er…I was glad when you asked me out." I felt a little giddy—and no wonder—my stomach was not only doing somersaults, but a whole gymnastic routine that could qualify it for a place in the Olympics.

Thankfully, at that moment the waiter arrived with two steaming plates of pasta. We sat back while he ground black pepper over our food. When he left I gathered a few strands of spaghetti onto my fork and pushed it into my mouth. I was far too anxious to have much of an appetite but eating provided a welcome distraction. The food was delicious, and for a few moments I let myself focus on its fresh, subtle flavors. At the same time I began to feel the effects of the wine spreading through my body; a warm relaxant, it eased the brittle tension in my muscles. I reached over, poured myself another glass and gulped back a mouthful. "I'm not really sure what to say now," I said, dabbing my mouth with my napkin. "I mean I'm not used to being so frank about my feelings. It's a little strange."

Alex nodded, letting a bite of lasagna cool on her fork. "Well, I think it's good to be honest. I like to get things out in the open as much as I can. But listen, just because we've admitted that we're attracted to one another doesn't mean we have to do anything. No pressure, where things go from here, well, we'll just have to see. I've been single for almost two years now and I know that you haven't been involved for quite a while…"

"Hang on a minute," I waved my fork at her, "how do you know that? What is this, you did a background check?" I was only half-joking.

"Well, not exactly, but I called Mario after I saw him at your office this afternoon, and I just asked a few questions. Y'know, just wanted to find out if you were already committed—"

"Just wait 'til I get hold of him." I kept my tone light but I felt suddenly guarded. I didn't like the idea of people discussing my relationship history. As far as I was concerned that was my own affair.

"Hey, he said absolutely nothing but nice things about you."

"That's not the point…" I knew I could trust Mario, it was Alex I was unsure of.

She shrugged. "I didn't want to end up making a fool of myself. And since Mario's such a mine of information, I figured he'd know if I should back off. All he told me was that you hadn't been involved for a few years."

"Well, I suppose that's okay, but you know we British are very touchy about preserving our privacy. Surely you've heard about the famous British reserve?" I quipped.

"Well, I guess you managed to overcome it a little tonight," she replied and I felt the blush rise into my cheeks yet again.

When we had finished eating we ordered coffee. There was still some wine left in the bottle, but after polishing off my second glass I was feeling just this side of tipsy. The waiter took away our plates and Alex rested her chin on her hand and gazed over at me. "So, tell me about yourself," she said.

"Not too much to tell," I answered, shrugging.

"Aw, come on, or is that the famous British reserve getting in the way again? I tell you what, I'll give you my life history and then you can give me yours, okay?" She looked at me with a mischievous glint in her eye.

"Okay," I nodded.

"Well, I was born in Puerto Rico," she began, and continued by describing how her parents had immigrated to the United States when she was two. She grew up in the Bronx and came to California when she was in her early twenties. "I was sick of New York and to be honest it was hard to be so near my family. We were real close, but they're pretty strong Catholics and they didn't take well to me being a lesbian. I came out when I was eighteen. My father reacted by giving me the silent treatment for two long years and my mother spent a lot of time praying. God, she used to cry hysterically every time she heard about someone else's daughter getting married or having a baby." Alex shook her head and let out a long sigh. "The guilt was killing me so I felt I needed to make a break. The best thing I've ever done, as far as I'm concerned. Now, after all these years I guess they've gotten used to it." She pulled an amused smile. "Yeah, last time I was back there I even heard my mother bragging to my Aunt Carmen about how I was the first Puerto Rican lesbian on the SFPD." We both laughed.

"So, what made you decide to join the force then?" I asked.

She looked embarrassed. "Well, it probably sounds corny but I really wanted to do something to help people, and y'know help my community."

I was thoughtful for a moment. "I suppose that's pretty much the reason I do the work I do. Maybe we have more in common than I thought."

She nodded and signaled the waiter to bring more coffee. "Okay, now your turn."

"Well, as I told you, there's not very much to tell. I'm thirty-one, came here when I was twenty-six. Started out by working jobs under the table, you know, bar work, waitressing, that kind of thing. I was lucky, though. Applied for the Office Manager position at The Project, they offered me the job and agreed to sponsor me. I got my green card and never looked back."

"Hold on a second, what about life before the States?"

"Oh, that...well, I lived in London, in Notting Hill. Worked as a school administrator."

"Did you like it?"

"Yes, I did actually."

"So what made you give it up and come here?"

"I wasn't happy...I wasn't happy and I needed a change," I said, looking down to stir a cube of sugar into my coffee. I knew I was being vague, but telling someone that you were beaten up by your ex-girlfriend isn't exactly what I consider first date material. I preferred to keep the conversation a little more upbeat.

"Well, that's pretty drastic, just upping and moving continents. It was hard enough just moving from the East Coast. You must have needed a change pretty bad."

"Yes, I did," I replied.

When we left the restaurant and stepped into the cold night air, the last effects of the wine began to dull. I shivered and wrapped my arms tight around my body as we made our way up Castro Street. "Let me give you a ride home," Alex suggested. "My car's just a couple of blocks away."

"Okay," I nodded.

During the short drive I sat beside her, looking ahead but stealing sly glances at her face. She had a strong profile—high forehead, a long, straight nose and a firm jawline that suggested a determined stubbornness. As the passing street lamps sent shadows scurrying over her face, I found myself feeling restless, fidgeting in the soft upholstered seat and resisting a powerful urge to reach over and touch her.

When she pulled up in front of my apartment building, I could resist no longer. I turned towards her and put my hand up to her cheek. My palm brushed smooth and surprisingly cool flesh. She shifted to face me, in the dull half-darkness our eyes met. I could make out her pupils, deep black circles that seemed to pull me towards her. I felt like I was standing on the edge of a precipice, staring down into its dizzying depths. "Can I kiss you?" she asked, her voice a thin, throaty whisper. I nodded.

Our lips met and a charge of heat and energy rushed though me. My whole body seemed to liquefy as she pressed herself closer and her tongue pushed against mine. She tasted of wine and sweetness. I could smell her hair, the musk of her body, the warm scent of her clothes. I kissed her and I felt like I was diving down, fast, with no knowledge of what lay below. It was fierce, exhilarating and just on the edge of fear. Suddenly I saw the ground loom into sight. I pulled away.

"I'd better go," I said, breathless as I reached for the door handle.

Alex sat back, frowning. "Are you okay?"

I nodded quickly. "Yes, I'm fine," I answered, opening the door to let in a blast of cold night air.

"Was it something I did—or said?" She asked, her expression bewildered.

"No...it's not you," I answered, gripping the car door and placing one foot on the sidewalk. As much as I wanted to lean back and relax into her embrace, I needed to break away. "I just...I just need to get home, that's all. So...er...goodnight, and thanks for a nice evening." Before she could say anything I stepped out of the car and ran across Dolores Street. Without looking back, I entered my apartment building and closed the door behind me.

Chapter Nine

For the first time in ages, I dreamed about Justine that night. It wasn't exactly a nightmare, more like one of those vague dreams that shakes you from sleep leaving you disturbed and awake. And as I lay wide-eyed and tense at three o'clock, I couldn't help but feel resentful that even after all this time, her violence still had an impact on me. She was the main reason I had decided to take a self-defense class—I was determined to fight back if someone ever hit me again, and I knew that it was because of her that I was so scared of even letting myself think about getting involved. Of course, since I'd come to California I'd done therapy (doesn't everyone?), and I'd talked about the whole damn relationship until I was sick of hearing about it myself (and sick of paying someone fifty dollars an hour to listen to me!). But the fall-out didn't go away that easily. If I was going to let myself get close to Alex, I knew it was going to be a slow and difficult process, one I really didn't know if I was up to.

I fell asleep again sometime around six and when the alarm went off at its usual time, I rolled over, turned it off and went right back to sleep. It wasn't until a car alarm going off on Dolores Street brought me to an indignant consciousness that I realized I'd overslept. I peered at the clock, it was nine forty-five.

"Damn!" I leapt out of bed, doused myself under the shower, took Hairy Boy for a run around the park in record time before dashing out the door for work. On my way I picked up a copy of *The San Francisco Chronicle,* scanning its pages as I strode down Eighteenth Street. Peter's murder still made the front page although it was no longer the banner headline. The lead story was an article speculating who the candidates might be to fill the soon-to-be vacant supervisorial seat. Apparently some rumors were coming out of City Hall that Supervisor Patricia Jones was trying hard to influence the mayor in his choice of successor. So far Mayor Finch had refused to comment on the subject.

The piece on Peter's death continued onto one of the inside pages. As well as quoting the mayor and Amanda from the press conference the previous day, it included information released by the police. They stated that as yet no witnesses had been found who might have seen a suspect entering or leaving Stop The Violence Project offices. This was thought surprising since the murderer would probably have been quite conspicuous—whoever killed Peter had engaged in quite a struggle and they would have left with a lot of blood on their clothing. They also mentioned that Peter's keys, which included those to his apartment and The Project, had been taken. I breathed a sigh of relief that I'd already changed the lock at the office.

When I finished the article I folded the newspaper under my arm and quickened my pace. It was almost twenty past ten and I was sure, given the recent chaos at The Project, that my absence in the office would be keenly noticed. I walked with my head down, watching my feet make fast steps over the pavement. I had almost reached Castro Street when I looked up to find myself suddenly face to face with Donna. She had just bounded down the steps of one of the apartment houses that lined Eighteenth Street.

"Hi, Lou, er…a little late for you to be going into work, huh?" Her lips shaped a lethargic smile and her eyes darted quickly back up the stairs. I followed her gaze to see a figure standing in the shadowy doorway. Before I had a chance to make out anything beyond a broad-shouldered outline the door was slammed shut.

"I was just visiting a…friend. We like to meet in the early morning and have breakfast together." Donna made her smile broader and brighter, but it could not quite hide her discomfort. I nodded, but I knew Donna was no early riser, and by the sleepy look in her eyes I wasn't sure she'd had coffee, never mind breakfast. I would have been willing to bet that Donna had only just got out of bed.

"So, how come you're so late?" She asked, taking my arm and turning to walk towards the office.

"Oh, I just overslept," I said absently, gazing back at the house and wondering why Donna felt the need to lie to me.

When we arrived at the office Amanda had already left for a meeting and Mario was out making final arrangements for Peter's memorial service. Poor Jasmine was completely overwhelmed. The phone rang constantly, and from the blinking lights in front of her it looked like she had at least three people on hold. I sat down at my desk and immediately began helping her field calls. I gave out information to several callers about Peter's memorial service, and talked to the victim of a bashing the previous night. The next call, however, made me wish I hadn't bothered to drag myself out of bed.

"Just called to tell you that we're glad he's dead. One more fucking

dead little queer, just a few thousand more to go. All queers should die."
They hung up and I was left holding the receiver, listening to dull silence at
the end of the line.

"You all right, Lou?" Jasmine asked as I slammed the phone down on
the receiver.

"Yeah," I answered uncertainly. "I suppose so."

"What's up?"

"Oh, just another bloody hate call."

"What did they say?"

I described the malicious message.

"Jesus, these people are so sick. I guess this creep is just gonna keep
calling. You think it's the murderer?" She asked.

I shrugged. "I really don't know. But I don't think it's the same person
that called before. Not the one who left those messages, this one sounded
different. The voice was a little higher." I thought for a moment. "You
know, it could even have been a woman, but it's hard to tell."

"Well, the murder's been splashed all over the papers. I mean, it
wouldn't be a surprise if someone got the idea to just do some kind of copy-
cat call. There's plenty of sickos might think it's kinda fun." Jasmine shook
her head derisively.

"I know. But this caller used a lot of the same words that were in the
previous calls and in the note that was left on Peter."

"Well, you know there could be more than one of them involved, like it
could be a hate group that's responsible. They could be orchestrating the
calls and the murder. This could just be another of their members."

"God, that makes me feel great," I sighed, "a whole organization out
there ready to kill us."

I took a couple of minutes to recover my composure, then I called the
phone company. With the trap in place they should be able to make a trace.
Then I made a call to Cochran. He was unavailable, so I left a message letting him know the exact words of the call. Maybe after this he would take
the idea of a hate murder seriously.

At five to eleven I looked up to see Patrick Tanner standing at the door,
surveying the room with bright, darting eyes. His long skinny body bristled
with anxiety.

"Donna's still with a client, Mr. Tanner, would you like to take a seat?"

He responded by muttering under his breath and loping over to the waiting area, his shoulders hunched so high they threatened to touch his ears.
"She gonna be long?" he asked, running a hand through his greasy,

uncombed hair. "I haven't got all day, you know."

"She'll be with you just as soon as she can," I assured him. "She's expecting you."

When Patrick Tanner had first stepped into The Project, just a few weeks ago, he looked like he'd been through hell. With his face swollen in a ghastly pattern of cuts and bruises, he walked with the stilted stiffness of someone whose every movement brought excruciating pain. And though, over the course of his frequent visits, his injuries had faded, it was obvious from his nervous agitation that he was suffering terribly in the aftermath of the attack. He was so jittery that just being around him made me feel tense.

Tanner sank into one of the chairs and picked a magazine. I was entertaining the idea of quizzing him about the conversation we'd had the previous day and his mention of seeing Peter the night he died, when he suddenly burst out, "She was here!" He turned towards me waving the copy of *San Francisco Freedom* that Mario had tossed there after his argument with Peter. "This woman, the one in this photo, she was here at this office," he exclaimed, pushing his index finger into the glossy cover.

"Yes," I nodded, "she was a friend of Peter's, she came to meet him for lunch on Friday."

He shook his head. "No, she was here on Friday night, when I was leaving the office. She told me she was Peter's client."

"Hold on a minute. Are you telling me that she was here the night Peter was killed?"

"Sure. You think I'm making this up or something?" He looked at me through narrowed eyes. "She came right up to me when I was leaving. Wanted to know if Peter was still in the office. She said something about being a client of his."

I thought for a moment. "You know, Patrick, you really should go to the police with this information. It's important. It could help find Peter's killer."

He folded his scrawny arms tight around his stomach, squeezed his lips together and said nothing. After a few seconds he began rocking very slowly back and forth as he stared at the wall on the other side of the room. "I ain't talking to those goddamn sons of bitches. Not after the way they treated me. I don't care what you say. And anyway, why the hell should I care about finding Peter's killer, nobody helped me when I needed it."

"But, Patrick—"

He shot me a fiery glare and stamped his foot down on the floor. "Don't tell me what to do. Nobody tells me what to do. I'm sick of being pushed around by you people...bureaucrats, cops, goddamn counselors. You all think you know what's best. Well, you don't. You hear?" He pushed out his lower lip in a childish pout.

"Patrick," I said softly, "I'm only trying to suggest that you let the police know what you saw. You don't have to do anything more than that. It could help find the person who killed Peter, you know, someone who hates gays…just like the people who attacked you."

A flicker of interest flashed across his face, but just as quickly it disappeared and Tanner sat silent, staring studiously at the wall. It seemed, as far as he was concerned, that our conversation was over.

"Mr. Tanner?" Donna sauntered into the office. "I'm Donna Travis. Would you like to step into my office?"

Tanner tossed the copy of *San Francisco Freedom* onto the chair beside him, leapt up and followed Donna. I was left to stare over at the photograph of Julia. As if, by studying her likeness, I might figure out why she had been outside The Project on Friday night, pretending to be a client.

When I made my second call to Inspector Cochran that day, I got him live and in-person. "What do you want?" he asked. I got the impression he wasn't exactly over the moon to hear from me.

"I have some information that could be important for your investigation," I said. "I thought I'd better let you know."

I'd spent my lunch hour pondering what I should do about what Patrick Tanner had told me, weighing the pros and cons of sharing it with Cochran. Though I hated informing the police of anything a client had told me in the offices of The Project, in the circumstances it seemed I didn't have much choice. Either Julia or Tanner could have vital information that might lead to the apprehension of the murderer. And I didn't like to think that some maniac might still be out there roaming the streets just because I'd had qualms about client confidentiality. I decided on a compromise and called Cochran, telling him merely that I had reason to believe that a friend of Peter's called Julia had been at The Project on Friday night. He listened to me coolly. "Thank you for your information, Miss Spencer. Could you tell me where you obtained it?"

I hesitated. "Er…no, not really."

"I see." There was more than a hint of derision in his voice. "Well, if this is your attempt to turn suspicion away from your friend, Mr. Fuentes, it's a very nice gesture. But not the kind of thing," he continued, raising his voice, "that helps me solve a murder. Now stop wasting my time, or I'll have you arrested for obstruction of a police investigation." With that, he slammed down the phone.

I sat staring at the handset, understanding for the first time the full meaning of the phrase 'caught between a rock and a hard place.' I couldn't tell Cochran everything I knew without jeopardizing the trust of The Project's clients, but if I wasn't completely honest with him, he'd never follow up on what I had told him. And even if he did, it wasn't as if I had complete confidence in his investigative abilities.

I was far too busy the rest of the afternoon to think much about the implications of my conversation with Cochran. Amanda and Mario returned briefly around three but left early to supervise last-minute arrangements for the memorial service. Just after six I closed up the office and made my way to the Metropolitan Community Church a couple of blocks away on Eureka Street. Once inside, I took a seat near the front of the high-ceilinged chapel and tried to get comfortable on the hard wooden pew.

The church was filled to capacity. There were members of ACT-UP and Queer Nation; people with whom Peter had had professional relationships, including some gay City Hall employees, several people from the D.A.'s office, and even a couple of cops. And, of course, many of his clients were present, although I saw no sign of Patrick Tanner.

When the pastor had finished speaking, she invited people who had known Peter to share their feelings about him and his death. There were many who wanted to speak. One of them was Bob Marlow, who happened to live in my apartment building. Bob had become a client of Peter's after he had been chased by a group of teenagers, wielding baseball bats, down a Castro sidestreet. He kept his comments brief. "All I know is that Peter was there when I really needed someone. If it hadn't been for him I don't know what I would have done. He was a really nice guy and I'm real sorry that he was killed." Others spoke of Peter's commitment to the community, his energy for political activism. A couple of friends shared touching stories of relying on Peter through hard times. I realized that, as Peter's co-worker, there had been many aspects of his life and character that I had not known.

"Hey, Lou." As I was leaving the church I turned to see Mario. He was with someone I didn't recognize, a tall man in a dark suit and black tie—and probably the only person at the entire service who'd bothered to dress formally. "This is Daryl, Daryl Banks," Mario said. "He was a good friend of Peter's, they went to school together."

Daryl gave me a thin-lipped smile, regarding me from deep-set blue eyes. "Nice to meet you," he said, holding out his hand which felt soft and clammy when I shook it. "Although I wish it could have been in different circumstances."

"Me too. So, you were a friend of Peter's?" I asked.

"Yeah, we met through the Gay and Lesbian Association at Berkeley," Daryl answered, biting his lip and lowering his head as though the memory of meeting Peter were too much for him. Mario placed a comforting hand on Daryl's arm. I found myself less sympathetic. There was something about his gestures that seemed a little calculated. After a few moments he looked up. "You know, Peter mentioned you to me. He talked about everyone he worked with a lot."

"Really? He never mentioned you to me," I said, "though we were never really close. But I expect Peter talked to you about Daryl, right Mario?"

"Actually, we just met tonight," Mario said. "Daryl came over and introduced himself after the service."

"Yes," Daryl said nodding, "since we were both so close to Peter I thought it would be nice to make the connection. Of course, I've known Peter a lot longer since we did go to school together." He spoke as if he were in some kind of playground popularity competition.

"You know, I met someone else who knew Peter at Berkeley just the other day," I commented. "I'm surprised I didn't see her here at the ceremony. Julia, maybe you know her?"

"Julia?" Daryl looked puzzled.

"Yes, Julia. She came to visit Peter at The Project the day he was killed. Peter said that he met her at Berkeley, said they were good friends at school."

"Well I don't remember anyone from school by that name." He sounded indignant.

"Maybe Peter just never introduced you," I suggested.

"No," Daryl said firmly. "I knew all of Peter's friends and I never even heard of anyone called Julia. You see, Peter and I went everywhere together," he said beaming proudly.

"Well, I'm sure Peter said he met her at Berkeley, but maybe I'm mistaken," I said, knowing that my memory was perfectly accurate, but not feeling like it was worth getting into an argument over.

"Yes, you probably were mistaken," he nodded. "But anyway, that's not important, what's most important…is that Peter is no longer with us." He sniffed and pulled out a handkerchief to dab at the edges of his eyes, though from what I could tell, there were no tears there. "Oh, well," he sighed, stuffing the crumpled handkerchief into his jacket pocket, "I guess I'd better be getting along. But, hey, let me give you guys my phone number. A friend of Peter's is always a friend of mine. Let's stay in touch, okay?" Before either of us could answer he handed both Mario and me a business card. I looked it over quickly, apparently Daryl was self-employed, at Daryl's Designs. A home and business number were listed.

"Poor guy seems to be taking it pretty hard." Mario said as we watched Daryl walk away.

"Maybe," I replied, "and then again, maybe not. I'm not sure what it is, but there's just something about that bloke that I don't like."

Chapter Ten

I had only been in the office a matter of seconds the next morning when I picked up the phone to hear an urgent voice at the other end of the line. "Is this Lou, Lou Spencer?"

"Yes," I answered.

"This is Stevie Levinson from Gay Legal Advocates."

"Oh, hi, Stevie." Gay Legal Advocates was a member organization of the Community Coalition. A nonprofit group of lawyers, they provided free and low-cost representation to gay and lesbian clients. Most recently they had been occupied helping the people arrested during the ACT-UP and Queer Nation demonstrations that the police had so brutally broken-up. Stevie had become a regular visitor to our office.

"Hi, Lou. Listen, I have some bad news…" He spoke hesitantly.

"Oh, no, not more arrests of demonstrators."

"No, it's Mario. He's been charged with Peter's murder."

My first reaction was to laugh, it was ridiculous, incredible. It couldn't be true. "Is this some kind of a joke?" I asked.

"No, I wish it were. He called me early this morning to let me know they had taken him into custody…"

"Where is he? When can I go and see him?"

"They're holding him at the Hall of Justice, I'm not sure when he'll be allowed visitors."

"Well, I'm going over there right away."

"But they may not let you see him, Lou."

"I don't care. I'll wait. And anyway, I want to give that boneheaded detective a piece of my mind."

Cochran was looking particularly pleased with himself when he stepped away from his desk to greet my arrival at the Homicide Unit of the SFPD. His smile was undeniably smug and he walked with the swagger of a man who felt he had accomplished something meriting admiration. "Hello, Miss

Spencer," he said, offering me his hand.

I ignored the gesture and instead glared directly at him. "You know this is ridiculous, don't you? Mario is incapable of any kind of violence. And while the real killer is still on the loose, maybe plotting his next queer murder, you're strutting around your office like a balding John Wayne."

The smile on his face transformed into an ugly grimace. "I do not appreciate your humor, Miss Spencer."

"I wasn't trying to be funny. I'm trying to get you to see that you're making a big mistake."

"Well, thank you for your concern. But for your information, I am convinced that we have the right man. We do have witnesses, you know."

"What do you mean?"

"I'm not at liberty to give you any details. Suffice to say, their accounts of what they saw contradict that of Mr. Fuentes'."

"I'm sure there must be some explanation," I blurted out.

"If there is, Mr. Fuentes hasn't yet offered one."

"But that doesn't give you grounds to charge Mario with murder," I protested.

"I'm afraid the D.A. doesn't agree with you there."

"Why? What else do you have?"

"Now, now, Miss Spencer, I can't go giving all my secrets away, can I?" He thrust his hands deep into the pockets of his pants and gazed absently around the room.

"But it's a hate crime!" I protested.

Cochran shrugged. "Let's just say you have your theory and I have mine. Only difference is that I'm in charge of this investigation and I happen to be damn sure that I have the right man."

"But what about Julia?"

Cochran pulled a thin, cynical smile. "Might I suggest, once again Miss Spencer, that you perhaps imagined this Julia person in a pathetic attempt to focus attention away from your friend Mario. After all, you were aware that he was being considered as a suspect."

"Don't be ridiculous," I huffed. "It's true that I don't want to see Mario blamed for something he didn't do. But I only told you about Julia to ensure that you had all the information for a thorough investigation."

"Well, I can assure you that we have that already. Now if you don't mind, I have other things to do." Abruptly, he pulled his jacket from its hanger by his desk and pushed past me into the corridor.

I followed Cochran out of the door, watching as he marched towards the elevators. He turned the corner and I shuffled to a halt, slumping back against the wall. I felt terrible. First I find my co-worker murdered, then my best friend is charged with the crime. And the man heading the investigation seemed determined to look no further than the end of his nose. Cochran wasn't engaged in an investigation, he was taking the easiest and quickest way out. The whole thing made me feel sick to my stomach. I found myself fantasizing blowing up what I considered the rather inappropriately named Hall of Justice, once I had rescued Mario, of course. Instead, in a pathetic gesture of anger, I kicked my heel against the hard marble wall behind me and let out a frustrated groan.

It was a few minutes before I was calm enough to make my way down to the first floor where I phoned The Project to let them know what had happened. Jasmine quickly put me through to Amanda.

"We cannot let them get away with this!" Amanda exclaimed. "This is outrageous. What on earth do they think they are doing? I'm so tired of the police department pretending that anti-gay violence doesn't happen, but this has gone too far. We need to react immediately. I'm going to call the mayor and the police chief right away. Then I'm going to call an emergency meeting of the Coalition. Do you know when you'll get a chance to talk to Mario?"

"Well, Stevie's acting as Mario's lawyer and he says I might get to visit him later today. But I want to hang out here and wait. I don't want to miss my chance to talk to him."

"Yeah, I think that's the right thing for you to do, Lou. Call me if you find out anything further. And when you do see Mario tell him that we're doing everything we can to protest the way he's being treated. I'm going to make sure the whole community mobilizes on this."

I put down the phone feeling profoundly despondent. I had the distinct feeling that it was going to take more than a few protests to get Mario out of this situation.

It wasn't until much later that I got to see Mario. He was being detained in one of the interview rooms. Following a thick-set uniformed cop, I entered, searching for Mario behind a screen of thick, malignant-smelling blue smoke. "Looks like you took up smoking again," I said, coughing as I wafted a hand in front of me. He was seated at a wooden table, a burned-down cigarette held between thumb and forefinger, a battered pack of Camels by his elbow.

"Yeah, I guess so," he answered, attempting to shape his tired and worried face into a smile. "It's pretty much the only vice they let you indulge in here. Well, that and telling lies so you'll confess to a murder you didn't commit."

"You didn't confess, did you?"

Mario sucked hard on the cigarette. I noticed his hand was shaking. He let the smoke out in a long breath. "No, of course I didn't confess. But these guys sure would love me to." He glanced over at the cop who stood stock still a few feet away from us.

I took the chair opposite Mario and reached out to touch his hand. "You'll be out of here soon, this is all a stupid mistake. A few days from now you'll look back on this and laugh."

He put out his cigarette and immediately shook another from the pack. "I sure hope you're right, Lou. They seem to think they've got enough evidence to convict me, the way they've been talking."

"What exactly do they have?" I asked.

Mario lit his cigarette and took a drag, he blew the smoke out hard.

I coughed again. "Jesus, Mario, can you ease up on that? The smoke's about as thick in here as in an English pub! The rate you're going you'll die of lung cancer before the night is out. And you'll be taking me with you if you're not careful."

He shrugged. "Sorry, Lou. I guess it's the stress that's getting to me. You know what they say, once a smoker always a smoker. I might have given up three years ago, but I feel like I'm right back in the habit. But I'll try and cut it out while you're here." He crushed the cigarette in the overflowing ashtray. "So, you asked about the evidence."

I nodded. "Cochran mentioned something about witnesses."

"Yeah, they have witnesses," he said solemnly. "Two who say they saw me at The Project around seven-thirty, and one who saw me at Peter's apartment later."

"But I thought you said you stayed at home that night."

Mario looked away. "I lied."

"Why?" I asked, puzzled.

He rested his chin in his cupped palms. "Oh, I don't know, Lou. I guess I thought it was the best thing to do. I was afraid. The cops scare me and I just didn't want to have to get involved in any investigation. Now I can see how stupid that was. I guess I'm in it up to my neck."

"So you went back to the office?"

"After me and Peter argued I was really upset. I did go home but I felt bad. I kept thinking how bothered Peter had seemed by whatever was on his mind. And I knew it was my fault that we had argued. He'd told me he was working late so I went back to the office hoping that he'd talk to me."

"Did you see him?"

"No. The downstairs door was locked. I had forgotten my key so I

73

knocked and knocked, but Peter didn't come down. I figured he must have already left. So I went over to his apartment to see if he'd gone home. But he wasn't there either. Now I realize how stupid I've been. Lying only makes me look worse."

"Yeah, but I understand why you were afraid. Don't blame yourself too much, okay?"

He nodded, tapping his fingers on the edge of the table and eyeing the pack of Camels.

"Cochran mentioned something else too, some other piece of evidence…"

Mario sighed. "Yeah. They came to my house last night with a search warrant. Assholes got me out of bed and turned my place upside down. They found these letters that I wrote to Peter. Cochran is really fixated on them. I wrote them to Peter right after he dumped me, but I never sent them. Never even intended to send them, in fact. I think in one I said I hated him so much I could kill him, or something like that. In the other I wrote that I was so angry I wanted to hurt him. I only wrote them to get the feelings out of my system."

I nodded; it wasn't hard for me to relate. For months after I had broken up with Justine I had written similar unsent missives myself.

"Cochran doesn't believe me when I say I didn't send them," Mario continued. "He thinks I killed Peter, and then afterwards went back to his apartment so I could retrieve the letters. Apparently whoever killed Peter took his apartment keys and searched through his stuff. Of course Cochran thinks that must have been me because of the witness…I told him if I'd been so smart to have retrieved the letters surely I would have burned the damn things so no one would ever find them. He doesn't seem very convinced by that." Mario's fingers edged towards the cigarette pack.

"What about your fingerprints on the letter-opener?" I asked. "Have you managed to remember when they got there?"

He frowned. "I'm not sure, but I think I remember picking it up when I went into Peter's office on Friday evening. I handed him that *San Francisco Freedom* magazine, you know, the one with his friend on the cover. And while he was looking at it I think I picked up the letter-opener and just sort of played with it. I remember twirling it around, you know, kind of like a baton in my fingers. I suppose, since I was holding it in the middle that even after someone used it to kill Peter my prints could've stayed there. I mean, I was touching it all over. Of course, Cochran thinks I've made this up. I keep telling him, don't you think that if I killed Peter with it I'd have enough sense to wipe my prints off afterwards? But of course, there's no convincing him. In fact the only thing Cochran seems convinced of is that I murdered Peter. He's determined to pin this on me, Lou."

I nodded slowly. "Yeah, I think you're right."

"He's even convinced I made that damn phone call to the office yesterday. You know, that hate call that you reported. Apparently they traced it to a pay phone in the Castro and after I said I was out of the office preparing for the memorial service, well, Cochran is sure I made the call just to keep up some kind of illusion that Peter's murder was a hate crime. Just like he thinks I wrote the note that was left on Peter's body."

I shook my head. "It's ridiculous, it has to be a hate crime. I mean, I know you didn't kill Peter, and why would anyone else unless it was anti-gay?"

Mario looked thoughtful. "You know, that's the only thing Cochran talks about that makes any sense to me."

I waved my hand dismissively.

"No, I'm serious, Lou. He seems to have actually given this some real consideration. First of all he says it's unlikely it was a hate crime because the front door was locked and whoever came in either had a key or was let in by Peter, so it probably wasn't a stranger. Of course he thinks that means it was me..."

I thought about what Patrick Tanner had told me of his visit to the Project on Friday night. There was always the possibility that after he departed the door had been left open but I didn't want to mention anything to Mario with the silent and apparently vigilant cop still staring over at us.

"...And then there's what Cochran says about the murder weapon," Mario continued.

"What do you mean?" I asked.

"Well, Cochran says the fact that the murderer used a letter-opener suggests that the person who killed Peter didn't go there with the plan of murdering him. His theory is that Peter and I got involved in a nasty little lover's fight, I lost my temper—being the unpredictable, fiery Latin that I am—picked up the first weapon that came to hand and stabbed him to death in a fit of rage."

"But that's not what happened," I said.

"Yeah, I know, you don't have to tell me," Mario said, picking up the cigarette pack and squeezing it in his hand. "But it's an interesting theory, don't you think? I mean, if you were a gay basher planning to murder someone, wouldn't you go armed with a weapon—say a gun, or a knife, or the ever popular baseball bat? A letter-opener isn't exactly a reliable weapon. Cochran says there was one hell of a fight before Peter was killed. It could easily have turned out different. But they managed to slash his throat." Mario paused, his eyes moistening noticeably. "The letter-opener was only left in his chest for show or something, that's not how he was killed. Anyway, a basher wouldn't just arrive on the scene in the hopes that they'd find something they could use. You know what they're like, Lou, they're usually cowards who either roam around in gangs or make sure they're so heavily armed that they can easily overcome their victim."

"Usually," I answered, "but there are exceptions to every rule."

Apparently without thinking, Mario took out a cigarette and placed it between his lips. He had picked up his matches and was about to strike a light before he became conscious of my disapproving stare. "Sorry, Lou, but I'm desperate. It's the only thing that stops me exploding in this goddamn place."

I nodded and watched as he struck the match and his shaking hand brought the flame to the tip of his cigarette. He inhaled deep and seemed to relax a little.

I wasn't allowed to stay much longer, after ten minutes or so the cop behind me gave me a tap on the shoulder and I was told I had to go. Before I left I gave Mario a hug. "Keep your chin up," I whispered, "you'll be out of here soon, I know you will." As he pulled away he gave me a weak smile. Considering the circumstances I thought he was doing pretty well, but he had been in custody less than a day. There was no telling how long he could end up in jail. I shuddered as I considered the possibilities.

It was after midnight when I finally fell exhausted into bed. But sleep did not come easily. Of course, I was thinking about Mario.

Peter's death had caused him enough suffering as it was without now being charged with the murder. Of all the ridiculous, stupid, outrageous things the police had done, this took the bloody biscuit. There was absolutely no way he was guilty. I was sure of it. Or was I?

I sat up in bed and pulled the quilt up to my shoulders as I thought about the murder. I shuddered as I remembered Peter's body, lifeless on his office floor. The spatters of blood across the walls, the letter-opener... And it was then that I began to wonder, how well did I actually know Mario? Was it possible there was a side to him that I had never seen? A violent side that was capable of stabbing Peter to death? After all, most people are murdered by people they know, husbands, fathers, mothers, lovers. And after Justine I was only too well aware that people who seemed nice, sweet, and charming to the outside world could be hiding an ugly violent side that they only showed to a select and unfortunate few. Could Mario be one of those people? Was there a chance that he was guilty? He had admitted that he had been at the office and then at Peter's apartment that Friday night. His fingerprints were on the weapon. He had written what were possibly threatening letters and I only had his word that he had never sent them. He had been out of the office when that hate call had come in. Could it be possible that he and Peter had had another fight but this time Mario had lost his temper, grabbed the letter-opener and in a fit of anger stabbed Peter to death? After all, he could have been overcome by rage and probably hadn't intended to kill him. And later, when he found himself panicking, afraid, and desperate to point suspicion away from himself, he had quickly scribbled a note and thrust it onto Peter's inert body.

I got out of bed and headed for the kitchen, where I put on the kettle and made myself a cup of Cadbury's Hot Chocolate from a package my mother had sent me from home just the other week. It was what she used to give me as a kid when I couldn't sleep. I'd sit with her in my pajamas by the stove in the kitchen, sipping the sweet, milky liquid as she held her arm around me and stroked my hair. It was like being given a sleep-inducing magical formula and I was always ready to go back to bed before I'd drained the cup. Now, I sat in my own kitchen in San Francisco, drinking the same drink, but somehow it didn't give me the same comfort as it had as a child. In a way it just served to make me feel even more melancholy as I listened to the stray noises of the city in the dead of night. I heard the rhythmic patter of high heels over the pavement, a car sped by, in the distance a drunk was singing loud and out of key. The noises echoed through the empty streets below and I found myself feeling dismal and alone. And at the same time I knew the person I felt closest to at that moment, the person whose company would have most comforted me, was Mario. Since we'd become friends, I had learned to trust him more than anyone else I knew. I had confided in him my innermost secrets, he had been my support through some very difficult times. And I had watched him go through some pretty severe crises and never, not once, had I ever seen him lose his temper or even threaten violence. He was one of the nicest, sweetest, kindest men I had ever met. How could I possibly imagine that he could have killed Peter? Not only should I have more sense, but Mario deserved nothing but my trust and my loyalty. I should be ashamed of myself even having such thoughts. Even if there were mountains of evidence stacked against him, I should know that he was innocent. The Mario I knew could not be a murderer, that's all there was to it. I had to resolve to rely on my intuition and trust him.

But I knew that trust alone wasn't going to make a difference. Of course Mario needed his friends to stand by him, and the support that Amanda seemed to be mustering in the lesbian and gay community would certainly go a long way. But that alone wouldn't get him out of jail. He needed someone to take action. If Cochran was determined to pin this murder on him, then someone else would have to find out who had really killed Peter. And since, in my chilly two a.m. kitchen, there didn't seem to be any other takers, I decided that someone had better be me.

Chapter Eleven

It was after four when I finally went back to bed. I woke again at eight dazzled by the yellow stripes of sunlight that streamed through my venetian blinds. I slung a limp arm across my face to cover my eyes and tried to work up the energy to get out of bed. When the shrill blast of yet another car alarm going off on Dolores Street made even dozing impossible, I pushed aside the covers, muttering that if I ever became mayor, I'd not only make car alarms illegal, but possession of them punishable by several years hard labor. I sat up and was about to make my way to the bathroom when I suddenly recalled my earlier decision to investigate Peter's murder. I fell back onto the bed, pushed my face into the pillow and let out a painful groan. I was definitely not happy to be awake.

The only thing I could recall having investigated before were the causes of the Second World War for an essay in my secondary school history class. At the time I thought I'd done a pretty good job of it. I'd read every book on the subject in the school library and stayed up late writing my final draft in my very best handwriting. Brimming over with confidence, I'd thought I was a shoe-in for an A. But Mrs. Pearson, my elderly and bespectacled history teacher, seemed to think otherwise and gave me only a B minus, along with the comment, "You could do better." I wondered how much faith Mrs. Pearson would have in my ability to investigate a murder, because I had very little. And I was far from sure this was a challenge I was cut out to meet. But what choice did I have? I already knew the alternatives and none of them promised Mario freedom in the foreseeable future. With considerable effort I pushed myself up from the bed again, and determined to start my investigation right away. But before I could do anything else, I needed to shake the thick, soupy mist enveloping my brain; and tea just wouldn't do it —today I needed espresso.

I made my way to the coffee shop on Sixteenth Street, Hairy Boy straining at his leash to pull me along the stained and gritty sidewalk. He stopped every now and again to sniff at discarded food wrappers and lift his leg on the forlorn trees planted along the pavement, but otherwise he kept us going at quite a pace—which was just as well because I wasn't exactly brimming over with energy, and left to my own devices, the short walk would have taken me a good part of the day. We walked down Valencia Street, by the taquerias and the new, yuppie-style restaurants, past doorways ripe with the smell of urine, and alongside a gaggle of pre-schoolers waiting outside the doors of the local Head Start Program who waved excitedly as Hairy Boy trotted by. On the corner of Sixteenth Street a couple of homeless men sat on vacant doorsteps, sipping from bottles hidden in brown paper bags and holding their free hands open for spare change. Sometimes an excursion into my neighborhood was the only thing I needed to stop feeling sorry for myself.

Sipping my coffee as I walked towards Dolores Park, I began to consider my course of action. I decided that the best thing was to start with what I already knew. And what was that? Well, I knew that Peter had been murdered in his office last Friday night. The police estimated the time of death between six-twenty and nine o'clock. I had an idea that I could narrow that window considerably. After all, if Mario had been at the office at seven-thirty and Peter had not answered his knock at the front door, then it seemed very likely that Peter was already dead. I also knew that Peter's body had been left with a note on it, containing language very similar to that used in the hate calls that we had received. If Peter's murder was the work of an anti-gay bigot maybe there were some obvious suspects. There were several organized hate groups active in the Bay Area, I wondered if I could find out something about their recent activities. And I knew there had been bashers whose prosecution had been ensured by Peter's lobbying and hard work. Amanda had alluded to the possibility of a revenge motive at the press conference, maybe she was right and one of those bashers, nurturing a grudge, had decided to kill the person they considered responsible for them being made answerable for their crimes.

I couldn't help thinking, also, about what Mario had told me about Cochran and his reasons for not thinking Peter's murder was a hate crime. I had to admit I was left wondering. It was hard to imagine that anyone could have another motive strong enough to make them kill Peter, but if I remained open-minded (and if I was going to do a good job of this investigating thing then I should at least try to be), then I shouldn't rule out the possibility that this might not be a hate crime. What other motives should I consider? Jealousy? Fear? Anger? Mario had said that Peter had seemed uneasy that evening, that something was bothering him. Was that connected with his death? I tried to remember that Friday and how Peter had behaved. And now, come to think about it, he had seemed tired and distracted. I remembered how he and Donna had clashed in the hall, and the urgent meeting he had demanded with Amanda. I should talk to both of them and see if they could help me piece some clues together. And I thought about the meeting Peter had set up with Jeff Easton, a meeting which Peter did not make but in which he had intended to 'expose' someone. Did that have something to do with his murder?

How was I going to find the answers to all these questions? Were there clues at the murder scene I was missing? I tried to visualize every detail of the grizzly spectacle I had walked in upon. Once again, I found myself feeling uneasy that something didn't fit... .

I let out a sigh as I unclipped Hairy Boy's leash and he dashed across the open space of Dolores Park. You're going to have to do better than that, I thought to myself. An uneasy feeling about the murder scene certainly wasn't going to get me very far. I had to start with the concrete. I resolved to begin by talking to everyone who had seen Peter that evening, or might have seen him. One of them might provide me with a clue that would help find the murderer, or perhaps, if Cochran's theory was anywhere near correct, they could even prove to be the murderer themselves. Patrick Tanner had already admitted to seeing Peter that evening, I would have to talk to him again. And if he had told the truth about Peter's friend Julia being at the scene, then I would have to talk to her. Then there was Malcolm. I remembered the tense phone conversation I had overheard and recalled Peter saying that he would see Malcolm later that evening. Perhaps they got a chance to get together, perhaps they didn't. There was only one way to find out.

I did have one teeny, weeny little problem, though—as far as Malcolm and Julia were concerned, I had no last name, no phone number and no address. Right now Malcolm was just someone at the other end of a phone line, and Julia was supposed to have gone to school with Peter but his other school friend, Daryl, denied even knowing her. That did not leave me with very much to go on. If I was going to find them I was going to have to use a little ingenuity and a lot of determination. But then, I shrugged, isn't that what investigation is all about anyway? And smiling, I thought that by the time this was over I would do an investigation that would leave even my demanding old history teacher, Mrs. Pearson, proud.

At nine-thirty I stood outside the front door of The Project, searching my pockets for the key, when I heard someone call my name. I recognized the voice and immediately my pulse quickened. I hesitated before turning around. When I did I found myself looking into the calm, thoughtful eyes of

Alex Ramon. As she shaped her lips into a concerned smile, it crossed my mind that the only advantage to Mario's arrest was that it had made me almost entirely forget the embarrassing exit I had made after my date on Tuesday night.

"Hi," I said, pushing a wind-blown strand of hair from my face. "How are you?"

"Okay," she nodded. "I heard about Mario."

"Yeah, you can be really proud this time of the great work of the San Francisco police department." As soon as the words were out of my mouth I wanted to take them back. I seemed, once again, determined to get our meeting off to a bad start.

"Hey," she said, frowning, "I think it's totally messed up. There's no way Mario could murder anyone, I know that."

"Me, too," I said despondently. "But you try convincing Inspector Cochran…"

"I know, the guy's completely pigheaded. After I talked to you the other night I made some inquiries about him and seems he's notorious for his blinkered approach to cases. But he has a good arrest and conviction record and that's what counts, I guess."

"And I wonder how many of the people he's put behind bars are actually guilty," I speculated.

Alex gave a swift shrug. "Listen, Lou, I really am sorry about Mario. He's a nice guy and he's the last person that deserves anything like this to happen to him. If there's anything I can do, just let me know."

It suddenly crossed my mind that an ally in the SFPD might not be at all harmful to my investigation. "Actually, there is something you could do to help…if you really want to."

"Yeah," she nodded, "Mario's a friend of mine, too. What can I do?"

I didn't exactly reveal my intention to conduct an investigation to find Peter's murderer but I did explain that I was trying to find out if anyone else might have a motive to kill him. I asked if she might be able get more information about hate group activity in the city.

"I have a friend working in the Hate Crimes Unit, let me have a word with her."

"I'm also trying to follow up on anyone that Peter helped get prosecuted. I thought they might at least have reason to see him dead."

"Get me their names and as much information about their cases as you can and I'll see what I can do. Okay?"

"Okay," I answered, a grin edging its way across my face. "Thanks a lot."

"Sure. This must be a hard time for you. I know that you and Mario are pretty close. I guess I'm concerned about you, too."

I gave an embarrassed nod. We both lapsed into an awkward silence during which I concentrated on searching once again for my key and Alex let her gaze wander the length of Castro Street. When she looked back at me she pursed her lips before speaking. "Listen, Lou, I'm sorry if I…er…came on too strong or something the other night. I hope I didn't offend you."

I shook my head. "No, no, you didn't offend me." Now I found myself looking away down the street. "I just…I was…I suppose I was just a bit nervous, that's all. I'm sorry."

"Hey, that's okay," she said softly. "I just thought maybe I was a little too pushy."

I shook my head.

"Well, good." She pulled her broad, dimpled smile. "So I thought maybe we could get together again. Maybe tomorrow night?"

"Er…well, I…" I was assailed by a barrage of conflicting thoughts and emotions, none of which I seemed able to articulate. After my disastrous exit I had almost made up my mind that things between the two of us could never go far, but standing there next to her in the street I found myself feeling the same overwhelming attraction I'd felt before.

"Are you busy?" She frowned. "Because we could always make it another night."

"No, no, Saturday's fine."

"How about I come round your apartment around eight. We can figure out what we want to do from there. And maybe I'll have some of the information you asked for by then."

As I watched her turn and walk away I felt happy that already I had made some small progress in tracking down the murderer. With Alex's help I might be able to find some real suspects in this case and persuade Cochran that Mario was not guilty.

The idea of a second date with her, however, was another matter altogether. I just didn't know what to feel about that.

"Oh, Lou, am I glad to see you," Amanda skirted past a huddled group of Community Coalition members in The Project's hallway to greet me at the top of the stairs. Shrill phone-rings resounded everywhere. I peered into my office to see people standing purposefully around the photocopier and fax machine. "It's been hell here, but people are definitely pulling together on this. We've been inundated with offers of help, everyone wants to support Mario. I spoke to Stevie this morning. He says Mario's still holding up and Legal Advocates are doing what they can for him, but to tell you the truth, I don't think they can do that much. I've a feeling this is going to be a long and drawn out process. His bail's been set very high, there's no way it can be met right away."

"Shit," I said, punching the air. "So that means he's spending the week-end in jail?"

Amanda nodded. "Yes, and perhaps a lot longer."

"I know his family doesn't have any money. Do you think we can start a fund to raise bail? With all this support I really think we'd be able to do it."

"I don't see why not. I'll talk to some people in the Coalition."

"Good."

"But what I think is most important right now, Lou, is keeping up the pressure, letting the powers that be know that we won't shut up until we see justice done. I called the mayor and police chief more times than I can count yesterday, but neither of them has the guts to take my calls. Anyway, we're going to make them listen. The Coalition decided to organize a march for Sunday." She lowered her voice to a whisper. "And Queer Nation are planning on doing a direct action—of course it's better if I don't tell you the details. They want to be able to surprise the police for a change—don't want any repeats of the last fiascoes."

I nodded in agreement.

"We're not going to let those jerks pin this on Mario." She said, setting her lipsticked mouth into a determined crimson line across her face.

"When's the march scheduled?" I asked.

"We're going to assemble in Dolores Park at noon, march through the Castro, down Market Street, then on to Bryant Street and The Hall of Justice. We'll hold a rally outside."

"That should be interesting," I commented, picturing the legions of cops who make their way in and out of the building every day.

"Well, we wouldn't want them to be able to ignore us, now would we?" she said, smiling.

"No, I guess not," I answered, about to turn towards my desk and get to work. Then I remembered what I wanted to ask her. "By the way," I began, "do you know if Peter had any appointments with anyone on Friday night?"

"Not as far as I know," she answered.

"Mario mentioned that he thought Peter seemed upset on Friday, I was wondering if you knew why."

Amanda looked thoughtful for a moment then shook her head. "I've no idea," she said firmly.

"He seemed pretty upset when he asked for that meeting with you on

Friday afternoon. Was something bothering him then?"

Amanda folded her arms across her chest and looked at me hard. "Lou, what is this about?"

I shrugged. "Oh, I'm just trying to help out Mario, you know, try and find out any information that might convince the police that he didn't do it." I was deliberately vague. I had already decided that if I was to be effective I needed to keep my investigation as secret as possible—even from other staff at The Project.

Amanda stepped back, frowning. "But what does that have to do with my meeting with Peter?"

"Probably nothing. Mario seems to think there's a possibility this isn't a hate crime, so I was thinking that maybe whatever was bothering Peter could have something to do with his death."

She frowned and reached over to place her hand on my shoulder. "Lou, there's no doubt in my mind this was a hate crime. I'm sure Mario's just confused, after all, he is under a lot of stress. You took those phone calls, you even saw the body. I know it's hard to believe sometimes, but there are people out there who hate us enough to kill us. And that's what happened here."

"But how can you be so sure?" I asked.

"I just am."

"You could be wrong."

"Well, I can at least assure you that Peter's murder had nothing to do with his meeting with me. Unfortunately, I can't tell you what it was we discussed. It was a confidential personnel matter, and that's all I can really say."

"Was it about one of his cases?"

Amanda looked down to examine her carefully manicured nails and let out an impatient sigh. "Look, Lou, I've already told you that we discussed a confidential personnel matter and as director here I am not at liberty to disclose…"

"Even now that Peter's dead?"

"Yes, even now that Peter's dead."

"Okay," I shrugged.

When I sat down at my desk I found myself unable to focus. In fact, I felt almost itchy with curiosity. It seemed that Peter's meeting with Amanda had nothing to do with his murder, but I was still aching to know what they had discussed. After all, in an overcrowded office of only five people no one manages to keep anything secret for very long. What was it that was so private that it had to be treated as a "confidential personnel matter" even after Peter's death? If it wouldn't have been such a tasteless choice of words considering the circumstances, I would have said I was dying to know.

Chapter Twelve

The office swarmed with people who came to help out with planning the protest march. As I sat at my desk, surrounded by busy volunteers, I felt like Santa Claus watching the elves prepare for Christmas. They ran around faxing out press releases, making calls to journalists, TV reporters and editors, contacting all the activist groups in the Bay Area, and drinking more coffee than I ever thought humanly possible. In one day The Project had probably single-handedly remedied the problem of the glut in the coffee market. The entire country of Columbia would be forever in our debt.

It wasn't until close to five, when some of the activists began to depart and the buzz of activity abated, that I had a chance to continue my inquiries into the murder. First I made a call to Patrick Tanner's home, he answered on the second ring.

"Hello, Patrick, this is Lou Spencer from Stop The Violence Project. How are you?"

"How the hell do you think I am?" he bellowed. "If all of you over there would only do your jobs and help me out, I'd be a lot damn better. Nothing's happened with my case and I'm sick of feeling like this."

"I'm sorry."

"Don't tell me sorry! You have no idea what I have to go through. No idea how I feel. So don't tell me sorry."

"Well," I said cautiously, "I wasn't actually calling you about your case but what you told me about that woman Julia who you saw on Friday night."

"I have no idea what you're talking about."

"But Mr. Tanner…"

"If you're not calling with news on my case, I don't want to talk to you."

I could see this call was going nowhere fast. I wondered if there was a way that I could get Patrick to talk to me. All I had was a couple of questions. "Look, Patrick, how about I come over and see you at your place? I may be able to give you a little help with your case…and maybe you could just tell me what happened on Friday night—all that you know."

"You'll help me with my case?"

"Sure. If I can take on some of the work we could see some results quicker, at least make sure that the bus driver who left you to get beaten up gets his proper punishment."

"Only suitable punishment for that asshole is the capital punishment. And if I ever see him again I'll kill him myself." From the anger in his voice, I was prepared to believe him.

"Look, what do you say, Patrick?" I asked cautiously. "I could come over and see you sometime this weekend. How about Sunday?"

He was silent for a moment. "Yeah, okay, I guess."

After my successful negotiations with Tanner, I went on to make a second call. I had taken the copy of *San Francisco Freedom* and looked up the magazine's telephone number on the inside cover. I dialed, only to be put on hold by four different people until I was finally connected to the person who could answer my question.

"Hi, I'm with *Ladies Pictorial* in London," I said in my best imitation of a Princess Di accent. "I'm visiting San Francisco and I just saw the cover of your August issue. I was most impressed with the model you used on your front cover. Tell me, do you happen to know which agency she's working with?"

"Sure, I think I can help you out there, honey." I heard the sound of fingers on a computer keyboard. "Well, honey, you're in luck. She's with an agency here in San Francisco, though with the way that girl's career is going I'd like to bet she'll be joining an east coast operation very soon. Anyway, the agency is City Models." She was able to provide me with an address and phone number.

"Thanks so much, you've been so very helpful," I said.

"Oh, no problem. And by the way, you have a gorgeous accent. You know, I just love the English, you all really are so refined."

I pulled an amused smile. I suppose everyone has their stereotypes. But if she wanted to see exactly how refined the English can be she should attend a Chelsea v. Liverpool soccer match. Mixing with the fans might correct her somewhat skewed view of our national character.

When I tried calling the number for City Models, an answering machine picked up. Apparently their office was already closed for the day. Any further research I had to do on Julia would have to wait until Monday.

At six o'clock precisely, Donna locked her office and strode up to my door. "'Bye then, Lou," she said, leaning her hip into the doorjamb. "I'll see you at the march on Sunday."

"Actually," I said, looking up from my work, "I was wondering if you'd like to have a cup of coffee before you take off tonight. It'd be nice to get together and chat, don't you think?"

She glanced down at her watch. "Well…I kind of have an appointment…"

"Just for half an hour or so, I don't know about you but I could use a friend to talk to. This week's been pretty overwhelming."

She pulled a sympathetic smile. "Yeah, I guess you have had the worst of it, what with finding Peter and then Mario being hauled off like that. Sure, I can spare a few minutes. Why don't you finish up and we'll go over to the cafe across the street. Okay?"

"Okay," I answered, attempting to put the papers on my desk into some kind of order. "I'll be ready in a few seconds."

The cafe was crowded, filled mostly with men fresh off of work. They relaxed by leaning into the soft leatherette seats, sipping tall glasses of espresso coffee and cruising their fellow customers. As Donna and I walked to a table in the back we interrupted several longingly lustful glances. We ordered and it took only a few moments for the waiter to return with our drinks. I stirred the foam on my cappuccino and Donna used a long-handled spoon to lick the whipped cream that crowned her mocha as we both railed about the homophobia and racism of a system that locked up Mario while the real killer was still free.

"It's the goddamn police, they're the worst culprits of all," she finally announced, balling up her napkin and tossing it onto the table.

"Yeah, I suppose you're right," I sighed, "they're pretty despicable."

"Uh-huh," she nodded.

I thought for a moment. "Donna, what would you say to someone who was dating a cop?"

She tossed her hair back from her face and gave me a questioning glance.

"I mean, what would you say if I said I was dating a cop?"

Donna took a gulp of her coffee before speaking. "Listen, Lou, who you go out with is your business and nobody else's."

"But, with the way things are right now, with the cops being so out of control and Mario locked up, don't you think…well, don't you think it sort of looks bad?"

Donna let out a sharp laugh. "Why'd you want to waste time and energy worrying about what other people think? You need to follow your own path. I don't care if you date a cop, if that's what you're wondering. And yeah, it might not help you make your way up the scale of political correctness, but I can't say I've ever thought of you as someone who worried too much about that. As far as I'm concerned, I think who people choose to have relationships with is their own damn business." She began to speak louder, raising her voice high enough so that a couple of men at another table shot us curious glances. "And if someone wants to control what you do," she continued, her coal-dark eyes glistening with what seemed to be stored up anger, "well it's them that's at fault. We're all entitled to make our own decisions in life. Nobody has a right to tell you what you should do." As Donna became even more animated, knocking over the salt shaker with a furious gesture, I began to wonder exactly whose predicament she was talking about.

"Yeah, I guess you're right," I answered.

"I know I am," she said, her tone full of outraged confidence. "The way I figure it is if you want to be with someone then you don't let what other people think stop you. Of course, if it's more than that, if it's because there's something about her that you don't feel good about…or if you're afraid to get involved for other reasons…"

Donna's words struck a chord. I hated to admit it but I wasn't just afraid, I was terrified. I felt that pull towards Alex and at the same time all I wanted to do was run away. And if I was really honest with myself, I wasn't sure it even had anything to do with her. What I did know was that it had everything to do with me and what I'd been running away from ever since I left England.

Donna continued to expound on the importance of making your own decisions about relationships, punctuating her words with abrupt gestures and fervent frowns until she glanced at her watch and announced that she had to go.

"Before you leave, there's just one thing I want to ask you," I said.

"Yeah?"

"Well, I'm trying to help out Mario, y'know, get some information so the police will realize there could be other suspects. I was just wondering if you know whether Peter had plans to see anyone on Friday evening."

She shrugged. "I don't think so."

"And I was also wondering…well, I remember that there seemed to be some tension between you and Peter on Friday. I know when I asked, you said it was nothing. But now he's dead I just wondered…"

"Look, Lou," she interrupted, "there was no tension between me and Peter, everything was fine. If you did see something, well, you must have imagined it. And anyway, what has that got to do with anything? Peter's death was a hate crime, how could that possibly have anything to do with me?"

"Well, I just thought you might know something…"

"I don't know anything," she said, suddenly pushing her chair back from the table and rising to her feet. "Now if you don't mind, I gotta go." She turned briskly and headed towards the door.

Chapter Thirteen

By the time Donna departed it was already too late to make my Friday night soccer practice. Maybe later I could head over to the Haight and join the team for coffee afterwards, but right then I had a more pressing task to attend to.

First, I made a brief visit home to Hairy Boy where I made a call to Stevie from Gay Legal Advocates.

"Yeah, Mario's doing okay," he told me. "Had quite a few visitors today and that helps keep his spirits up. He's not too happy, of course, at the prospect of spending the next few days in jail. But Amanda talked to me about raising bail and we're starting a fund. With the kind of support he has I'm sure we can have him out in a few days." Even a few days seemed like far too long to me, but at least we were making progress.

At eight-thirty I left my apartment and headed back to the Castro. I soon found myself moving through thick crowds of drag queens, butch-femme couples, Castro clones, baby dykes, and dazed teenagers making what was possibly their first trip into the heart of gay San Francisco. On the corner a guy was selling an assortment of leather regalia, a gathering of giggling tourists looked on as he strutted around his stall cracking a whip into the bristling night air.

When I reached the office I unlocked the door to make my way up the darkened stairs, stumbling once or twice over the uneven steps. Upstairs everything was still and dark. The phones no longer shrilled, the fax machine stood quiet. The activists and Coalition members were all gone. Even Amanda, who was sometimes known to work past midnight, had left for the day. I turned on the light in the hall and made my way to Peter's office, only recently released from the police tape which had kept it off limits as a crime scene.

When I opened the door I held my breath, fully expecting to encounter the same terrible smell that had assaulted my senses when I'd found the body on Monday. But when I turned on the light I could see that someone had left the window open, and a breeze filled the room with cool evening air—just how Peter would have liked it. I walked to the window and stared out, but as I had thought, it looked over a bare, deserted backyard, shielded from the buildings behind us by a high brick wall. Unfortunately, there was no chance that someone outside could have witnessed the events that led to Peter's death.

It wasn't easy being back in Peter's office; if I'd had the option I think I would have avoided going in there for the rest of my life. I shuddered when I looked down to see the chalk outline that showed the shape of his prone body and the dark patch of dried blood soaked into the bare boards. Some of the blood had been scrubbed away; otherwise, it was all as I had discovered it on Monday, even the portable heater was still in the same place, close to his client chair. I stepped around the outline and moved towards the desk.

I began by thumbing through the client files that Peter kept in a cabinet by his desk. It didn't take me long to find what I was searching for: the two cases on which Peter had worked so hard to gain prosecution of the perpetrators. Both were pretty standard bashings. One had occurred not far from a bar on Polk Street where the victim had been drinking before running into his attacker as he tried to hail a taxi home. The second had happened in the Castro after the Halloween celebration the previous year. The victim, dressed in full drag, had been cornered in a side street and beaten unconscious. I put the files to one side, I would look them over more carefully at home.

Next, I embarked on the second stage of my search. First, I flicked through the cards in Peter's over-stuffed rolodex. There were addresses and phone numbers for everyone from the D.A. to the head of the city's sanitation department, but not the listing I wanted. Over the surface of his desk a luxuriant array of papers lay scattered in no apparent order. I sifted through client reports, letters, time sheets, and legal pads covered with notes and doodles. But they held nothing of interest to me. Then I searched his drawers, beginning with the large bottom ones that held his information files and ending with the two at the top which were filled with a jumble of staples, pencils, tape, pens and unused post-it notes. Still I found nothing and I was beginning to feel despondent. I had been certain I would discover something to help me here, but by now I was beginning to doubt my own instincts. Only the credenza in the corner of the room remained. It too was stacked with unruly papers and files. I spent almost an hour looking through everything there, until the only item left was a heavily-thumbed hard back publication, *A Guide to Services in San Francisco*. I picked it up and began to leaf through its pages, coming across numerous underlinings and notes made by

Peter to highlight the resources offered by various San Francisco agencies. There was no question that Peter had been thorough in seeking support for the clients with whom he dealt, but in this publication at least, he had left no clues for me. Resigned to defeat, I sighed and dropped the book back onto the credenza. I had been careless, however, and for a moment it balanced precariously on the edge before falling to the floor with a thud. I was so frustrated that I almost left it there, but I decided it was probably best to leave things as I had found them. Lifting the book by its spine, I let the pages flap loose, and as I did so a business card fell out and fluttered to the ground. I bent down and peeled it from wooden floor. Printed on heavy, textured stock, it bore letters embossed in black and gold. In a fancy, swirling script they read, Malcolm Devreaux, Office of the Mayor.

"Malcolm," I said aloud to myself. At last, I thought I had found the information I needed. An office phone and fax number was printed on the front, and on the back someone had handwritten another number. I had high hopes that it was Malcolm Devreaux's number at home. I also hoped this was the Malcolm Peter had spoken with the day he'd been killed. There was only one way to find out.

I punched the number into the phone on Peter's desk. "Hello." The voice was deep and self-assured.

"Is this Malcolm Devreaux?" I asked.

"Yes, this is he."

"Hello, I'm Lou Spencer, I work at Stop The Violence Project."

"Yes…and how might I help you?" I noticed that some of his assurance had faded, replaced by a cold and efficient caution.

I hadn't really thought of how to approach the conversation since I had picked up the phone so quickly. I decided to jump right in. "I understand that you knew Peter Williams."

He answered with several seconds of silence, I took that to mean I had hit upon something. I decided to take a gamble and continued. "In fact, I understand that you and Peter were lovers."

The same silent reply followed until he suddenly burst out, "What do you want? What is it you want?" The deep tones of his voice were now strained sharp, scarcely disguising panic.

I hadn't anticipated such a strong reaction. The man was obviously afraid. "Well, I just wanted to talk…"

"Not here, not over the phone," he interrupted, spitting out the words.

"Okay. Well, maybe we could meet?"

"Yes…yes, that's fine."

"What about tomorrow?" I suggested.

"Tomorrow's okay."

He suggested a place called The Hotsy Totsy, a bar in North Beach. I had never heard of it before, and with a name like that I wasn't sure I was sorry. Malcolm gave me directions. It sounded like a little hole-in-the-wall place on a side street, the kind of spot you go when you don't want to be seen by anyone you know.

"How's five-thirty for you?"

"Five-thirty's fine. How will I recognize you?" he asked.

"I'll be the tall lesbian with the bright red hair in a denim jacket and jeans." I answered.

"Oh," he replied, apparently not thrilled at the prospect of our meeting.

On Saturday morning I lay in bed, sipping tea and reading over the extensive notes in the two files I had taken from Peter's office. It was very rare for any of Stop The Violence Project's cases to end in prosecution—as far as hate crime is concerned, the wheels of justice roll excruciatingly slowly and sometimes are at a downright standstill. Perusing the information Peter had left behind about these two cases, I soon realized that they would probably have gone nowhere if it weren't for his work. He had agitated with the police and the D.A., written letters on behalf of his clients to politicians at the local and state level, and spoken to numerous reporters. In one case his work had paid off with the conviction of the perpetrator who, according to Peter's notes, was now serving seven years in San Quentin. The second case, however, did not have quite such a satisfactory ending. The attacker, a twenty year old named Frank Frederickson who hailed from the exclusive Marin community of Ross, had parents wealthy enough to hire a very successful attorney who put up what has become known as 'the homosexual panic defense'. The argument goes like this: the accused was solicited for sex by a gay man; being a full-blooded, normal, heterosexual male, the accused naturally went into a panic and in order to escape these perverted advances beat the gay man. 'Homosexual panic' has been the ticket to freedom in several cases for men who freely admitted they brutally beat homosexuals. In one case in Florida the beating resulted in death. But Florida and San Francisco are many miles apart—and not just in the physical sense. No one expected the argument to wash here—certainly not Peter who dismissed the fast-talking lawyer with a few derisive notes in his files. But juries are nothing if not unpredictable and after the four day trial they deliberated for just two hours before returning with a verdict of not guilty. So, Frank Frederickson, an admitted gaybasher , left the court a free man.

In addition to his notes, Peter had kept a few press cuttings about the case. One that caught my eye was a post-trial interview with Mr. Frederickson in *The Chronicle*. He expressed relief that the trial was over. "I can finally get on with my life," he said, adding a lot of sickening platitudes about how justice is always done in America. "Of course," he continued, "none of this sordid affair would have happened if it weren't for the agitation of all those gay organizations like the so-called Stop The Violence Project. All those people want is special privileges for their sort and I think that's wrong. Those places do nothing but corrupt young people and threaten the American family. They took a damn good shot at ruining my life. Someone should close down places like that for good."

It seemed like Frank Frederickson was holding a grudge. I wondered if it were big enough to make him kill.

I'd planned to spend the afternoon cleaning my extremely messy apartment before leaving for my meeting at five-thirty with Malcolm, but after reading through Peter's files I felt thoroughly depressed. It was so frustrating to realize that even now, even here in San Francisco, gay bashers like Frederickson got off scot free while Mario was stuck in jail accused of a murder he so obviously did not commit. And I didn't relish the idea of Mario having to take his chances in a jury trial—with twelve people like the ones who'd come up with the Frederickson verdict, Mario could well end up in the gas chamber. I shook the thought away with an involuntary shiver, hauled back the comforter and got out of bed.

"Come on, you," I said to Hairy Boy who had been snoozing at my side, "we both need some fresh air."

Thirty minutes later I was at the wheel of my Datsun, driving over the crimson span of the Golden Gate Bridge. Its sidewalk was crowded with tourists who braved the bracing winds off the Pacific to saunter along the sidewalk and snap innumerable photographs of the spectacular view. They looked down on the azure waters of the bay, across Angel Island, Alcatraz and over to the steep, glimmering buildings of downtown San Francisco. The tufts of white cloud that skidded across the sky served only to accent the radiance of the day. As I glanced out of my window I could clearly see the Bay Bridge and the distant outlines of the parched East Bay hills.

Once over the bridge, I took the exit for Highway One and followed the long string of day trippers already clogging the narrow road. It was almost twelve when I pulled into the parking lot at Muir Beach. For a couple of hours I hiked the Marin coastal trail, stopping periodically to take in the bright vistas across the cliffs and ocean, and keeping a careful eye out for the poison oak which grows along the trail-side in profusion. As I knew it would, the solitude, the startling coastline beauty, and the boisterous air off the ocean took away the edge of my depression. When I began to walk back there was a definite bounce in my step.

We stopped at the beach before leaving. I took out a sandwich from my rucksack while I sat and watched Hairy Boy run riot through the shallow waves as he pursued a gathering of seagulls. The birds were having a good time, too, teasing him by dipping dangerously close, almost within his reach, before they soared upwards to leave him hopelessly behind. But Hairy Boy did not give up easily, he ignored the attention of several other dogs, zig-zagged past children playing in the frothing water, and ran almost the entire length of the beach and back in his relentless chase. He was having so much fun that when I realized it was time to leave and I called him over, he ignored my shouts. So I stood up and began making my way towards him, calling his name as I walked. Before I reached him, however, I glanced across the sand to see two women. One of them was dark-skinned with long dreadlocks hanging about her face. She wore baggy shorts and a bright T-shirt over her petite frame. The other woman was taller, with a squarer, wider build. Her skin was several shades paler and her hair was cropped close to her scalp. Hand-in-hand, gazes fixed firmly upon one another, they sauntered slowly towards me.

"Hey, Donna." I waved over. "Donna, how's it going?"

Both of them looked over at me and I carried on waving. But instead of waving back, Donna and her companion exchanged glances and turned abruptly away. Feeling a little bewildered, I dropped my hand and watched them make a hasty retreat towards the parking lot. Just before they were out of sight, the woman accompanying Donna turned her head, giving me a swift backwards glance. And as they disappeared beyond the bushes at the edge of the beach I couldn't help thinking that she looked familiar.

Driving back in the thick traffic that edged its way over the bridge into San Francisco, I kept wondering why Donna had given me the cold shoulder. Was she angry after our conversation on Friday after work? If so, why? And if it wasn't that, then why would she ignore me? The more I thought about it, the more it seemed she'd been behaving really oddly lately.

Chapter Fourteen

I found the Hotsy Totsy under a flickering neon sign on a grubby narrow side street. Pushing open the shabby, well-kicked door, I stepped into a dismal bar room filled with sour-tasting air. Beneath a clattering ceiling fan cigarette smoke moved in thick gray ribbons, and the ceiling itself, which sometime in the last thirty years had probably sported a coat of fresh white paint, was now a dismal nicotine orange. The floor was covered in cheap linoleum and the sole decorations on the fake wood panel walls were posters of half-naked women advertising various brands of beer. Malcolm needn't have been worried about not being able to recognize me, apart from the bikini-clad Budweiser Girls, there were no other females in the whole place. I, on the other hand, had to peer through the cheerless room and scan the faces of the men who sat hunched over the rickety tables or leaned on the formica-topped bar.

Fortunately Malcolm wasn't difficult to spot since he looked so completely out of place. The middle-aged customers wore dirty T-shirts over jeans or polyester pants. Malcolm was the only guy who didn't have what looked like half a tub of Brylcream in his hair or a carefully nurtured beer belly. Sitting at the bar with his head tilted towards the door, even in the bad light I could tell that his suit probably cost as much as I spent on clothes in a couple of years. His shirt was bright white and he wore a skinny red silk tie. Probably in his early forties, he was built like an ex-rugby player who still worked hard to stay in shape.

At five-thirty the Hotsy Totsy was a surprisingly popular place, though for the life of me I couldn't imagine why. Every one turned to study me as I walked across the bar room floor, letting their eyes run the length of my body and mouthing inaudible words. Even when I had walked inadvertently into one of the all-male leather bars in the Castro, I hadn't experienced this level of hostility. If Malcolm was trying to put me at a disadvantage, he was certainly succeeding.

When I reached the bar, however, it was obvious that he was far more uncomfortable than me. His gaze moved skittishly around the room and he shuffled uneasily on his bar stool.

"Malcolm Devreaux?" I asked.

"Miss Spencer?" His voice was shaky and his skin was covered with a damp sheen. I was dying to know why I made him so nervous.

"Jesus, this place is a dive. I take it this isn't your local?"

He made a swift nod and reached down to lift a glass from the bar; it contained a copper-colored liquid. "Actually I've never been here before. I didn't want to go anywhere I'd be…I just thought it would be a good place for us to meet."

"It's like all the worse pubs I've ever been in rolled into one. Sort of like an alcoholic twilight zone, don't you think?"

"Er…can I get you a drink?" he asked, tipping back his glass to take a long gulp.

"Just a mineral water," I answered.

Malcolm signaled the bartender, a short, stocky guy with the sleeves of his flannel shirt rolled up to reveal a veritable gallery of tattoos. An unfiltered cigarette drooping lazily from his mouth, he sauntered slowly towards us.

"I'll have another of these, and a mineral water for the young lady," Malcolm said.

The bartender breathed out a slow stream of smoke from his veiny nose and gave me a disdainful stare. Apparently my choice of beverage did not impress him. I returned his glare with an exaggerated smile, and slipped onto one of the vinyl barstools to watch Malcolm swig back the last of what was left in his glass.

Good-looking in the masculine, rugged mode, he had a firm jaw, straight nose, and fierce blue eyes. His dark brown hair was streaked with strands of bright blond and his skin had the deep tan of someone who spends a considerable amount of time lying around in the sun, or at least on a sun bed. Despite his nervousness it was apparent that he was a man whose appearance was carefully groomed to exude an air of power and influence. I found myself wondering what position he held at the mayor's office when I had a sudden flash of recognition.

"Hey, you were with the mayor on Tuesday, at the press conference," I said. "You're one of his aides, right?"

"His chief aide, actually," he said with some pride as he placed his empty glass back on the counter. The bartender grunted and slid two newly-filled glasses over to us. Malcolm pulled out a bulky leather wallet and deposited a ten dollar bill on the bar.

I couldn't help wondering how Peter had become involved with someone so high up in the city's administration. They would definitely make a strange couple. It would be interesting to discover how they had met and what on earth they had in common. Reluctantly I decided to keep my questions to more pressing matters. "I want to talk to you about Peter's murder," I began.

Malcolm's body visibly jolted. With both hands he grasped the edge of the bar as if in an effort to steady himself. "I don't know what you mean…?" He spoke in a harsh whisper.

"I know you knew him, but you didn't look as though you did when you were at the press conference and the mayor made his statement about Peter's death." I took a sip of my mineral water as someone dropped a quarter into the battered juke box at the other end of the room. A scratched up version of 'I Fall to Pieces' started to play and a couple of guys started crooning right along with Patsy Cline. It was not a pretty sight, nor was it what you might call easy listening.

Malcolm leaned closer to me, I could smell his musky aftershave and the whiskey on his breath. He spoke loud to make himself heard over the record and the accompanying out-of-tune voices. "Look, just tell me how much you want," he hissed.

I gave him a puzzled look as he reached towards the inside pocket of his jacket, then realization dawned. He thought I had come here to extort money from him, although what for, I wasn't really sure.

"I don't want your money," I answered, pushing his hand back down to the bar. "I just want to know if you saw Peter the night he was killed."

Malcolm picked up his drink in a grip so tight that his knuckles turned white. "No, I didn't see him, in fact I didn't speak to him all that day."

"Are you sure?" I asked.

"Yes, of course I'm sure," he said, downing almost the whole glass and then slamming it on the bar.

"Well, I overheard an argument that Peter had with you that day on the phone. I heard him say he would see you later that night. Did he?"

"No. And I don't know what argument you're talking about. Like I said, I did not speak to Peter on Friday." He stared straight ahead, into the scratched-up mirror that hung over the assorted bottles at the back of the bar. I caught his distorted gaze in the warped glass. Immediately he looked away.

"Look, Mr. Devreaux, I might not want any money out of you, but I do want the truth. Maybe I should go to the police and tell them what I know…"

"No!" He turned towards me, reaching out to grasp my arm. His strong, thick fingers tensed like a vise around my flesh.

"Get off," I said firmly as I tensed in readiness to use my newly-learned self-defense skills. I wasn't about to put up with some man laying hands on me.

He hesitated for a moment then loosed his grip and let his hand slide to his side. "I'm sorry," he muttered.

"Look, do you know something about Peter's murder? Did you have something to do with it?"

"No," he answered again, and reached again for his glass.

"Well, what the bloody hell are you so scared of?" The twangy guitar of the Patsy Cline's song abruptly ended and I suddenly found myself bellowing over the gentle murmur of conversation. I noticed several of my fellow patrons glaring over at me. From the other end of the bar the bartender leered as he tossed another cigarette into his mouth. I felt like pausing to give them all a little lecture on the virtues of friendliness and good manners, but I couldn't help thinking that I'd probably be wasting my time. So instead, I shifted a little closer to Malcolm and lowered my voice. "What is it you are so afraid of?"

He paused for a few seconds, looking thoughtful as he bit down on his lower lip. Either he was trying to manufacture a lie or debating whether to share a secret with me. When he finally spoke his voice was close to a whisper. "I'm gay," he said, giving a furtive glance around the bar.

"Yes, I know. Call me a genius, but I managed to work out that a man having an affair with Peter would be."

He chose to ignore my sarcasm. "Nobody knows. Well, only a very small number of people. But no one else. Not my family, my job, my basketball team, no one." His face held a meek, almost apologetic expression, as if his carefully constructed facade of status and authority was made suddenly irrelevant by this revelation. "Nobody knows I'm gay." When he said the word gay he lowered his voice to a whisper, and again gave a shifty look around the room.

"So, you're in the closet, so what?"

"Do you know what it would do to my life if it became public that I'm gay?" He whispered the word and glanced around again. He was being so furtive that I couldn't help wondering if he was certifiably paranoid, laboring under the illusion that the Sexual Orientation Police were about to bust him for being queer. In fact he was so jittery I was beginning to feel a little jumpy myself, like there could be a chance I'd get picked up, too.

"This isn't the nineteen-fifties, for God's sake. And you're living in San Francisco, not Little Rock, Arkansas."

His face stiffened. "Look around this bar, Miss Spencer, and then tell me that it's safe to come out in San Francisco. You think I'm a fool? I know how people think, even here, even today. I'm the chief aide to Mayor Finch, if it came out that I was having an affair with the guy who was murdered at Stop The Violence Project, I could kiss my career good-bye."

"But that's ridiculous, there are tons of gays and lesbians working at City Hall. You'd just be one more. I don't get it."

"You think the mayor would want to be so closely associated with a fag? Look, I respect the mayor, he's an astute politician who knows where he wants to take the city. But on a personal level he's not exactly fond of gay people. If he found out about me I know I'd lose my job. I have to be very careful. The only time I can go to a gay place is when I'm out of town and I don't have to worry about bumping into someone who might recognize me."

"So instead you spend your time in lovely joints like this?" I gestured about the room.

"If it means I keep my reputation and my job, then yes. You have to admit there's not much chance of my being recognized by the guys who frequent this place." A smile tugged at the corners of his mouth. "And I've worked hard to be where I am now, I don't want to throw it away."

"As far as I'm concerned there could be worse things than losing a job as aide to Mayor Finch."

"I became well-acquainted with that attitude from Peter. I don't need to know any more of what you radicals think."

"Oh, so politics was a tension between the two of you?"

He clenched his jaw and flashed me an angry glare. It seemed I had hit a nerve. "You could say that, yes. If Peter had been more reasonable, less impetuous and eager to alienate people, well he wouldn't have..." His voice trailed off.

"He wouldn't have what?"

Malcolm sighed and slowly pushed a hand through his well-coifed hair. "He wouldn't have been so intolerable sometimes."

"Yes," I said, nodding, "I can see that the two of you would have had differences." The irony of the understatement was not lost on Malcolm. He shaped his mouth into an irritated grimace. "Anyway, let me ask you again, did you see Peter on Friday night?"

"No, I didn't." He spoke slowly, firmly. "We were supposed to meet late. I was accompanying the mayor to a party that night so I couldn't meet Peter until afterwards, but he never turned up. To be frank with you I just assumed things were over between us. We did have rather a nasty fight that day."

"Oh, so now you admit you argued?"

"Well...yes."

"What about?"

He hesitated. "Oh, just another of our disagreements about politics, that's all."

"And when he didn't contact you, you didn't think to call or to try to find him?"

He shook his head. "Look, I cared for Peter, he was a wonderful young man. I was terribly upset when I found out he had been murdered. But you just don't understand. I don't feel...comfortable with the way I am. I don't want to go shouting it out from rooftops, be seen kissing a man in public."

"You know, there is some middle ground."

"Not as far as I'm concerned," he said sullenly as he lifted his glass to gulp back the last of his drink. When he replaced the glass on the bar he turned to look at me. His expression was needy, beseeching. "Look, please don't say anything to the police about me. I don't know anything about Peter's murder. Or are you really one of those political activists wanting to...what do they call it...'out' someone to produce some tawdry little scandal? I don't see any advantage to your exposing me, do you?"

Suddenly I thought of Peter's meeting with Jeff Easton, of his intent to 'expose' someone in the gay press. Was Malcolm to be the subject of that article? And could that be a motive for murder? "What do you know about a meeting Peter had planned to have on Friday evening?" I asked.

"I have no idea what you're talking about." He turned quickly to avoid my eyes and I could tell he knew more than he was letting on.

"Do you know what that meeting was about?" I persisted.

"No." His tone was insistent but I couldn't shake the impression he was hiding something.

He pulled back the sleeve of his jacket to glance at a very expensive-looking watch. "I have to be somewhere very shortly, I have a dinner to attend. I know nothing more than I told you already and if you have no further reason to waste my time..."

"I don't have any other questions, except to inquire what you were doing from around six-thirty to seven-thirty on Friday evening."

"That's really none of your business. But since I already told you I was at a party with the mayor, I see no harm in telling you again. We left City Hall at six, or thereabouts and stayed until close to eleven. It was interminably long and filled with some very boring personalities. Unfortunately they also happen to be some of the most influential people in the city, so I had to spend my time working the room. You know, flattering ugly women, listening to tedious golf anecdotes, laughing at ridiculous jokes, and making sure that support for the mayor's policies continues in the upper echelons of

San Francisco society." He pulled a tight smile.

"Where was the party?"

"Somewhere on Van Ness. I forget the exact address."

"Can someone account for your whereabouts throughout the party?"

He snorted. "Don't be ridiculous, you think I have a baby-sitter or something?"

"Well, it just strikes me that it's a short hop from Van Ness up to the Castro. Perhaps if you were away from the party for less than an hour no one would really notice…"

"Are you suggesting that I killed Peter?" His voice was outraged, or at least that was how he was hoping it would sound. "Why on earth would I do a thing like that?"

I shrugged. "You tell me."

"I can assure you that I had nothing to do with Peter's death, absolutely nothing. Now, if you don't mind I do have to go. But I would appreciate it if you promise me you will not share with anyone what you have learned of my relationship with Peter. I mean, there's no sense in dragging me through the mud is there?"

"For now," I replied, "I won't say anything, but I can't promise to keep quiet. A friend of mine is charged with the murder and I am trying to help him. If telling the police about you and Peter will help his case, then I'm afraid I will have to do that."

"I see," he said tersely as he rose to leave.

I followed close behind, as eager to leave the Hotsy Totsy as Malcolm seemed to be. While I walked to the door, another record came on the juke box, this time Tammy Wynette singing 'Stand By Your Man'. At least Malcolm knew how to time his exits, I thought to myself as I stepped out onto the street and Tammy's ode to patriarchy faded behind the swinging door.

As Malcolm drove away in the shiny red Mercedes he had parked across the street I was surprised to find myself feeling sorry for him. I'd never, not in a million years, want to live a life like his. Always being on guard, forever having to pretend, sneaking around, lying, and to top it all off, working for a mayor who hated gays.

I'm under no illusions, I know it's not always easy to be out of the closet. Coming out wasn't exactly a piece of cake for me. I spent years nurturing unrequited crushes on a series of friends who, when push came to shove, always seemed too ready to abandon me for the company of some pimply, greasy-haired boy. When, at twelve, I first came across the word 'homosexual' in a biology textbook I knew that's what I was. But it wasn't until my flat mate at college, with whom I was madly in love, leaned across the dinner table to plant an unexpected kiss on my eager and tingling lips, that I finally admitted I was a lesbian. After that things became a lot easier. Now I worked in a job where not only was it okay for me to be a lesbian, but virtually everyone assumed I was queer. I was lucky, I knew everyone didn't have the same freedom. And Malcolm was just a real life illustration of that fact.

But he made me angry too. Here was someone who reaped the privileges of power, and by working for Mayor Finch, used that very power against other gay people. Many activists would see every reason to drag him out of the closet, they had already done it with movie stars and officials who espoused homophobic attitudes but were themselves secretly gay. What on earth was Peter doing with someone like Malcolm?

Maybe it had been a relationship based on lust and when the attraction had worn thin, the difference in outlook and politics had become too much—it was clear from Malcolm's comments that it had been a source of great tension between them. I thought back to last Friday and tried to recall the words Peter had used on the phone to Malcolm, it went something like: "I don't care what you say…it's out of your hands…I've already made up my mind." Was Peter talking about outing Malcolm in an article written by Jeff Easton? Now that would certainly make a hot story. And if Malcolm was as desperate as he seemed to protect his hidden identity and his political career, then there was no doubt that he had a clear motive for murder.

Chapter Fifteen

I returned home at seven-fifteen to an apartment in total turmoil. Dried-up dirty dishes spilled out of my sink to occupy most of my kitchen counters, a tumbling pile of unopened junk mail covered the table, magazines and books were strewn across my living room. Shoes, socks, T-shirts and even, I'm ashamed to say, several days' worth of dirty underwear lay scattered all over my bedroom floor. Not to mention Hairy Boy in the middle of it all, unbrushed and chewing on a soggy piece of raw hide. My terminally house-proud mother would have been outraged; I could picture her glancing around my apartment, giving me one of her meaningful looks then delivering one of her hour-long lectures. Fortunately, she wasn't going to get a chance to berate me since she lived over five thousand miles away (sometimes there are some definite advantages to living so far away from your family!). Alex Ramon, however, was to arrive shortly, and even I, someone who has the closest thing you can get to a medically diagnosed allergy to housecleaning, would be embarrassed for her to witness this mess. So I raced around the place like a maniac tossing paper into the recycling, pushing clothes into my overflowing hamper, and doing my best to make the kitchen look as if it might have the barest chance of passing a health inspection. Miraculously, at five past eight, when the door bell rang and Hairy Boy leapt up to begin his barking chorus, the place was almost presentable. I thought I didn't look too bad myself having showered, changed into a clean pair of jeans, and put on an emerald silk shirt that Terri had persuaded me to buy because, according to her, it accented my green eyes and, as she put it, 'makes the most of that blazing red hair.'

"Hey, you look great," Alex said, giving me a radiant smile as she leaned down to pet Hairy Boy who, after greeting her with an initial wary growl, responded to her attentions by wagging his tail furiously.

She looked pretty good herself, dressed in pale jeans and a black T-shirt that hugged her broad, well-muscled shoulders and revealed the curve of her biceps. As she followed me down the short hall into the living room I became aware of a flutter in my stomach, the scattered racing of my thoughts. I just hated how nervous she made me feel.

"Nice place," she commented as she let her gaze wander the cramped room to take in the sofa and armchairs, the array of plants which, despite my ongoing neglect, seemed to hold a surprisingly healthy grip on survival, my overstacked bookshelves, and the selection of framed political posters that decorated the white walls. "Cozy," she concluded with an appreciative nod.

"Some people might call it overcrowded," I said, "but interior decoration was never my strong point."

Alex shrugged. "Mine neither, I guess I've always thought there were more important things in life."

"Yes," I agreed as I met her gaze and then let my eyes drop to the floor. "Er…why don't you sit down? Would you like something to drink? I have er…tea, coffee, sodas, maybe even a couple of beers if I can find them."

"Soda's fine," she said, taking a seat on the sofa, and petting Hairy Boy.

"Great…well, er, I'll get you a soda then," I said, making a bee-line for the kitchen. As I poured a couple of cokes I resolved to pull myself together. I was going to have to stop letting Alex have this effect on me. I was behaving like a love-struck teenager, and I hadn't been this way since I'd let myself fall in love with Justine—all the more reason, as far as I was concerned, to keep my feelings under control.

"So," I asked as I handed her a glass and took a seat at the other end of the sofa, "were you able to find out anything about hate groups from your friend in the Hate Crimes Unit?" I thought talking about 'business' would at least distract me from my nervousness, as well as providing me with information for my investigation.

Alex frowned. "Not that much, actually. What she told me was pretty vague. Over the years there've been reports of hate group activity all over the Bay Area—most of it in the more suburban communities outside San Francisco. Inside the city it seems like most hate crime is the work of bigoted individuals who don't seem to have any organizational ties—you know, some racist punk who decides to pick a fight with an elderly black woman, or a group of kids who go down to the Castro just to gay bash for fun. But there is one group, American People for Freedom, who seem to have developed some kind of following here. They've done a lot of organizing around anti-immigration stuff, y'know, a lot of messed-up rhetoric about keeping the country safe for white people. And they may be connected to a couple of attacks—one on a young Latino who was jumped by a group of white guys wearing ski masks, and another assault on a Chinese woman—but so far there hasn't been enough evidence to take any action. They've been known to spout some pretty anti-gay stuff, too, but it seems their focus is really immigrants. Of course, there could be other groups that the people in the Hate Crimes Unit just aren't aware of—they're not exactly over staffed down there." She heaved a sigh. "I'm sorry, Lou, I know this probably isn't that helpful."

"That's okay, it's not like I expected you to come up with a prime suspect that we could take to Inspector Cochran. I just thought it was an avenue worth pursuing."

Alex shook her head, her expression pensive as she took a sip of her soda. "Well, let me know if there's anything else I can help you with."

She replaced the glass on the coffee table in front of her and I found myself admiring her long, slim-fingered hands. I remembered the way her touch had felt the night she had kissed me, how my whole body had felt like liquid in her embrace. I glanced up to meet her eyes.

"You okay?" She frowned.

Inside I winced. Why couldn't I keep my thoughts focused in her presence? Again I resolved to stop letting her have this effect on me. "I'm fine, I was just thinking about what you said," I lied, hoping she hadn't noticed the color that I knew had risen to my face. "And there is something more you can do. Remember I told you that Peter's work had ensured the prosecution of two hate crimes cases?" Alex nodded. "Well, there's a possibility that one of them could be connected to Peter's murder." I told her what I had learned about Frank Frederickson and the reason I thought he could be a suspect in the case.

When I had finished Alex rolled her eyes. "If Cochran is doing his job properly he should have looked into this already. And he may have done so and eliminated Frederickson as a suspect. But from what you've told me about the investigation so far that seems highly unlikely. I'll make some discreet inquiries into Mr. Frederickson and let you know what I find. But I just want to let you know, Lou, that if I come up with anything that indicates he could be involved I'm going to have to take this to Cochran, okay?"

"Okay," I nodded. "And thanks, Alex, I really appreciate this."

"No problem," she said, brightly. "I'm just glad that Mario has someone like you on his side."

We lapsed into silence for a few seconds. I looked down to take an intense interest in brushing some dried-up biscuit crumbs from the arm of the sofa (God, my mother really would be ashamed of me). I felt so torn—part of me wanting to just fall into Alex's arms, and at the same time part of me wanting her to leave me alone so I didn't have to feel this uncomfortable, this scared. It was all too complicated, too difficult. Maybe I should just go off and join a nunnery or something. Maybe I should take a vow of celibacy and dedicate myself to feeding the poor and changing the world. I could become the new Mother Theresa—Sister Lou, role model for confused lesbians everywhere.

I noticed some shuffling about at the other end of the sofa. I looked up to see Alex pick herself up and move only inches away from me. "So, what do you want to do with the rest of the evening?" she asked, taking my hand and looking into my face. "Are you hungry?"

"Well, I…er…" Her skin felt warm, I liked the way she intertwined her fingers with mine. "I guess it would be nice to go out and get something to eat. I'm not much of a cook, I'm afraid, and I really don't have much in my kitchen…unless you like baked beans and instant mashed potato. Of course we could always order a pizza, there's a place just down the street that does a really good…"

Alex raised her other hand to my mouth and placed two fingers over my lips. "How about we get dinner later?" she said, and then wrapping one of her arms around my shoulder, she pulled me towards her and pressed her lips into mine.

Her kiss was hard, compelling, and for a few seconds I felt overawed. But then a spark seemed to ignite inside of me, like a match flaring in the dark. I felt desire rise, and I kissed her back eagerly. I was surprised, but it just felt so right, so easy. I ran my hands over her wide, strong back, pushed my fingers through the tangle of her curly hair, and relished the satin texture of the skin on her face, her arms. Each place we touched, every point of contact sent a blast of energy through me, left me gasping in achingly long breaths. I tugged her T-shirt from out of her jeans and moved my hands over her to feel the amazing pattern of bone, muscle and tissue beneath her hot flesh. She planted kisses on my neck, her tongue trailing wet over my skin, as she moved her hands slowly over my thighs, my stomach, my chest. Under my clothes my flesh felt like it would implode.

Suddenly Alex pulled away. "Lou," she said, looking so hard into my face that it seemed she was trying to see behind my eyes, "is this what you want?"

I hesitated for a moment, searching my mind for an answer. Then I nodded. "Don't worry, I'm not going to run away this time," I replied.

"Good," she whispered, smiling, "then why don't you show me the way to the bedroom?"

We finally ate pizza after midnight, sitting on the dishevelled sheets, the pizza box perched precariously on the edge of the bed. We dropped crumbs over the bed clothes and licked tomato sauce from each other's fingers and lips, or wherever else we might dribble it. When we finally fell asleep it was almost dawn. The last thing I remember hearing was the hopeful chirp of early morning birds. And then I fell asleep, Alex's arms around my shoulders, her soft breaths like a warm breeze across my face.

I woke on Sunday morning to an empty bed and the sound of loud, angry chanting coming from outside. On the bare and wrinkled sheet next to me was a note. "Didn't want to wake you, had to go to work. Thanks for a wonderful night, talk to you soon. Alex." I felt a pang of disappointment, I had been looking forward to a lazy morning spent in bed wrapped in Alex's embrace. I just hoped I would get a chance at that experience sometime soon.

The chanting outside became even louder, the words of some political slogans I couldn't quite recognize. God, those people were irritating. Didn't they have anything better to do with themselves at eleven on a Sunday morning? Talk about inconsiderate! I sat up in bed, shuffled over to the window and peered out through the blinds. Across the street the brilliant green oblong of Dolores Park was adorned with a large, milling crowd. More people meandered from the sidewalks across the grass. They carried painted banners and rainbow flags which surged and flapped in the morning breeze.

Immediately, I felt thoroughly ashamed of myself. I couldn't believe I could be so thoughtless, so forgetful, so self-absorbed. After all, those inconsiderate chanters were only readying for the march to protest Mario's arrest! And here was I, his so-called best friend, languishing in bed after a night of passion ready to forget his plight completely. Mumbling a litany of colorful curses and self-admonishments, I jumped out of bed and headed for the shower.

By the time I strode across the street to join the assembling crowd, it had grown to number what I estimated at around five thousand—not a bad turn out for a march called just a couple of days ago. Many of the various San Francisco lesbian and gay organizations were represented, including Queer Nation who were already lifting their voices in an enthusiastic chant, The Sisters of Perpetual Indulgence whose costumes, a flamboyant drag parody of the traditional nun's habit, seemed strangely appropriate for this Sunday morning gathering, and the Latino Gay and Lesbian Alliance. Now that I was closer I could make out the text on the fluttering banners; they read 'Mario Fuentes is innocent' and 'Fight hate crime, not queers'. The mood was mixed, some appeared in high-spirits, smiling as they greeted friends with wide, exuberant hugs, while those who shouted out slogans waved angry fists at the dark line of police already lining Eighteenth Street.

I wandered into the thick of the crowd and eased my way towards what

I guessed would form the front of the march. I made slow progress as I kept stopping to say hello to various friends and acquaintances who bombarded me with questions regarding the murder and Mario's case. It was when I was turning away from one of these conversations that a surge in the crowd caused me to lose my balance, stagger unevenly forward and step on someone's foot.

"What the hell do you think…?" An enraged male voice bellowed as he swung around, his face a picture of rage, hands shaped into hard fists.

"Hey, I'm sorry," I said, glaring to meet his malevolent scowl. For a moment he glared at me, a near-manic glint in his eyes. It was about as pleasant as turning around to face Jack Nicholson on the set of *The Shining*. Then recognition dawned upon each of us almost simultaneously.

"It's Lou, right?" He took a step back and his angry expression transformed into a broad smile.

"Hello, Daryl," I said, still frowning. It was Daryl Banks, the friend of Peter's that Mario had introduced me to at the memorial service.

"Sorry about that," he placed his hand on my shoulder as I pulled away. "Hey, you know how crowds can be, people pushing and bumping into you from all directions. Makes me pretty damn irritable."

I nodded. "Yeah, I suppose it can affect some people that way." By now, I was sure that my first impressions of Daryl had been correct. His gestures, his expression, even his voice held a false ring that made almost everything about him appear insincere. Neither did I like the fact that he had been so aggressive when I had bumped into him. It was almost as if he'd been looking to pick a fight with someone. But when he discovered it was me, he became almost fawning.

"So, Mario's been charged with Peter's murder." He creased his face into an imitation of sympathy. "That's too bad. He seemed like such a nice guy, I'm sure he can't be guilty."

"He's not," I said firmly.

"Well, no, of course not." He coughed out a sharp laugh. "Anyone can see it had to be a hate crime. Although sometimes Peter could be pretty annoying, you know. He used to drive me crazy. In fact there's been times when…well, what I mean is I could understand it if Mario lost his temper and, well, you know…" He shrugged and pulled what I can only describe as a conspiratorial grin.

"Mario did not kill Peter," I said slowly.

"No, no, of course he didn't. That's why I'm here today, to protest his arrest."

"Well, I'm glad about that," I said as I turned away, eager to put an end

109

to our conversation.

We finally departed the park, the march headed by a line of Community Coalition leaders who strode beneath a multi-colored banner. Amanda was among them, holding a megaphone to bellow slogans which were echoed in a chanting chorus from the crowd. I marched close behind, with several members of my soccer team. We walked under a banner that Terri had made; it read 'SF Dynamite Dykes are in your corner, Mario. It's our goal to set you free'. It was corny, but I knew Mario would appreciate the sentiments, and besides, I was just glad that the team was helping out.

"How you feeling, Lou?" Terri stood on tip toes to put her arms around my neck and give me a tight hug.

"Okay, I suppose," I said, hugging her back. "Things are crazy, everybody at work is completely stressed out and we're all so worried about Mario. And I'm absolutely knackered," I added, suddenly aware of how my night with Alex had allowed me very little sleep.

"Yeah, I bet you're knackered," she said, smiling fondly as she mimicked my British slang. "This must be a pretty hard time for you. But, hey, didn't you have a second date with that cop?" She nudged me as the march came to a temporary standstill and we waited for the cops to direct a MUNI train across Church Street. "How did it go?"

"Okay," I shrugged.

"Oh, come on, Lou, you have to do better than that. Look at that smile on your face. I want details." Terri bounced up and down, grabbed at my sleeve and gave me her most beseeching look. I said nothing and did my best to look inscrutable. "Stop teasing me like this, Lou," Terri protested.

"Okay," I laughed. "Well, suffice it to say I'm no longer a virgin."

"Congratulations," she shrieked, "just wait until I tell the rest of the girls."

"No," I said firmly, "just for now this is between you and me. I want to see how things go. Okay?"

"Okay," Terri nodded. "I guess no one could ever accuse you of throwing caution to the wind, Lou Spencer. Though one day it might be good for you."

As we turned the corner onto Castro Street, a group of young activists ran alongside the march and inserted themselves in front of us. Jasmine was among them. She wore a T-shirt bearing the slogan, 'Safe Sex is Hot Sex', and a picture of two women engaged in exactly that. Fist raised into the air, she yelled at the line of police that accompanied us. She seemed to be having a great time. When she glanced back and saw me she stopped mid-chant and scooted through the moving crowd. "Great demo, huh?" she said, breathlessly.

I nodded.

"Show them jerks what we think of them, that's for sure." She gestured towards the police. "Look, they're just dying to cause trouble, you can see it. Fucking fascists," she snorted. We were surrounded by lines of police, most of them white, male and almost inevitably straight. They eyed the drag queens and butch dykes distastefully, their gloved hands grasping and ungrasping their nightsticks. For a moment I found myself thinking of Alex and how people like this were her colleagues. It was an idea I did not care to dwell upon.

The march moved sluggishly and it was almost three o'clock when we reached Bryant Street and the crowd settled around the steps of the Hall of Justice to wait for the speeches to begin. As Amanda and several other Coalition leaders mounted the steps, sheaves of prepared notes in their hands, I noticed Jasmine and her activist friends gather into an excited, whispering huddle then break apart and make their way to the edge of the crowd.

I was relieved to see that the police seemed to have decided on a hands-off approach. Apparently happy to stand back and rake in the overtime pay, they didn't even react to the downright insults that came from some of the more radical speakers at the podium, insults that were greeted by the crowd with stamping feet and thunderous applause. I kept looking up at the ugly building, thinking of Mario imprisoned somewhere inside and hoping that he could hear us all outside, that he'd know that he wasn't alone.

There were several powerful and moving speeches, though Amanda's speech was by far the best. "Every day a gay man is beaten because he is gay," she began, her clear and steady voice reverberating over the hastily-assembled P.A. system, "every day a lesbian is attacked because she loves women. Both Mario Fuentes and Peter Williams worked at Stop The Violence Project to help fight this senseless hatred. Meanwhile the police and the mayor stood by and did nothing!" She stabbed the air with her index finger. "And now, now that Peter lies dead, the victim of yet another hate crime, the police arrest his friend and co-worker, Mario Fuentes. This is typical of the kind of treatment our community can expect from this administration. And we will not put up with it any longer." She shook her right hand, clenched into a fist, high into the air. "We will fight back!"

A roar of approval rose from the crowd, some lifted their hands in fervent applause, others waved banners and flags in a swirling, colorful dance above our heads. I, too, was straining my voice in a loud, throat-tearing cheer, but I stopped when a sudden rush of dark blue bodies on the fringe of the gathering caught my eye. I turned to see a group of uniformed cops run towards the building and disappear into a side entrance. A few moments later, while the crowd still roared and Amanda nodded encouragement at their rowdy support, the same group of police returned, followed by more cops in full riot gear. My whole body tensed in dread and anticipation; it looked like they were preparing to launch a full-scale charge against the crowd. Then I realized they were already busy with something else.

About twenty Queer Nation members were being dragged, pushed and pummeled as they were herded towards a couple of police vans parked across the street. The activists responded in turn by yelling, kicking and struggling to free themselves from the vicious grip of the angry-faced cops. It seemed like no one else had noticed what was going on as the cries of approval at Amanda's words continued and the protests of those being arrested were lost in the noise. I stood open-mouthed for a moment, not sure what to do until I suddenly saw Jasmine, kicking and flailing as two cops grabbed her, lifted her off the ground and lugged her away from her screaming companions. Immediately I pushed past the people around me, bumping shoulders and stumbling over feet before I broke free from the assembly to run across the street.

"What's going on?" I demanded of the two cops, their fresh-faced countenances contorted into an ugly, emotionless brutality. "Put her down, she hasn't done anything." Jasmine was yelling out expletives and writhing in their grip.

"If you don't get out of the fucking way, we'll arrest you, too," the taller of the two cops spat at me before digging a hard elbow into my side and pushing past me towards the van.

I staggered back for a moment before continuing after them. "What's she being charged with?" I shouted.

"Conspiracy to damage city property, now fuck off you fucking dyke," the shorter one yelled as they tossed the squirming Jasmine through the open doors of the van. She landed, next to several of her companions, with a thud on its metal floor. Her eyes took on a shocked glaze for a few seconds until she seemed to reorient herself and her face shaped into an expression of rage. "Goddamn fucking pigs, you wouldn't believe it, Lou…" I moved towards her, reaching out my hand, but was thrust out of the way by the taller cop who landed a powerful and violent blow to my chest. I was sent reeling, gasping desperately for breath as pain resounded through my body. The cops climbed in to the van, the doors were slammed shut and it lurched away leaving me only to cough and sputter a tirade of feeble curses.

By this time the rest of the marchers had realized what was going on and a tidal wave of bodies flooded across the street. Some yelled angrily, others tried to reason and argue with the cops as more of the Queer Nation contingent were tossed into the second van. The cops' response was cruel and instantaneous. In a sweeping, dark line they began to move forward, raining down indiscriminate blows onto arms, shoulders and heads of the screaming demonstrators. I joined the panicked retreat and watched in horror as people fell like skittles under the vicious whack of police nightsticks. From the steps I could hear Amanda bellowing into the microphone, making a desperate appeal for calm. Her words, however, were soon swallowed by the screams and yells of the terrified and injured marchers.

By the end of the afternoon there had been over fifty arrests. Many others had sustained cuts and bruises. Several people had been taken to hospital with suspected broken bones, a couple of women sought treatment for deep and heavily-bleeding gashes. The area outside the Hall of Justice looked like an abandoned battlefield, with hats, banners and broken placards littering the street. A few dazed marchers sat on the stone steps and surveyed the desolate scene. Amanda was among them.

"Are you okay?" I asked as I approached her.

"Yeah, I'm fine," she replied, pressing a hand up to her forehead. "But God, what a mess—we try to get one person out of jail and end up with a bunch of others arrested." She pulled a handkerchief from out of a pocket and dabbed lightly at her cheeks.

I sat down beside her, wincing slightly at the stab of pain in my side and chest that came with any sudden movement. "How come the cops started those arrests in the first place? I saw them dragging a group of people from the side of the building before the violence began."

"Oh, that?" Amanda stuffed the handkerchief back into her pocket as she shook her head regretfully. "Queer Nation had planned this great action, they were going to break into one of the side entrances and occupy the whole first floor. It would have been an excellent way to get public attention. Unfortunately, from what people say it looks like the cops knew about what was going to happen before it started. I've no idea how because it was kept a tight secret."

"You think there was an informer?" I asked.

"It's a definite possibility," she answered glumly. Groaning, she heaved herself up from the steps. "I guess I'd better get myself together. I need to coordinate some press releases, make sure our version of what happened here makes it to the media."

"Can't you leave that to someone else in the Coalition?" I asked. She didn't look too well, her face looked strained and pale, there were heavy shadows under her eyes.

Amanda swung around. "No," she said sharply. "It's important I oversee what gets out there." Then in a more measured tone she added, "I have a lot of experience in public relations, I want to make sure my expertise gets used to help our cause."

I watched as she made her way across Bryant Street to where some of the Coalition leaders formed a tight huddle. Immediately she began talking, making broad gestures as those around her nodded. I envied her apparently unflagging energy. While she seemed determined to rally her forces and push on, I was rapidly sinking into the depths of depression. The march had ended in disaster, Queer Nation's action had been aborted, the cops had ridden roughshod over us, and here I was nursing what were probably going to be some very spectacular bruises. And after all that Mario was still in jail. Pulling myself to my feet I breathed a defeated sigh.

I walked heavily down the steps. As I did so I noticed a couple of uniformed officers emerge from the main doors of the Hall of Justice. One of them was Alex Ramon, the other I recognized immediately: it was the young thug who had arrested Jasmine and who had hit me. They were both nodding and smiling, apparently engaged in some highly entertaining small talk. I couldn't believe it. Cartoon-fashion, I closed my eyes, shook my head and then did a double-take. And there they were, the woman who I had shared a bed with just last night and the cop who had viciously assaulted me, walking together like they were the very best of pals. I wanted to throw up. No, I wanted to march right over to the both of them and bang their heads together. I wanted to yell and scream and tell them and the world exactly what I thought of them. I wanted to do anything I could to make the little scene in front of me disappear. So I turned around and walked away.

I spent the next couple of hours working with several Coalition members to arrange legal representation for arrested marchers. Amanda took charge of dealing with the television reporters who descended upon us in search of a lurid story for the normally slow Sunday evening news. Most of them demanded interviews with the injured. Apparently it helped their ratings if they were able to show some real blood on the air. Unfortunately, none of the reporters had been around at the crucial moment when the police attacked the crowd and I heard several of them speculate that perhaps it had been the 'radical gay elements' who had instigated the violence. So much for media accuracy.

I was tired, aching, and in very low spirits when I finally made my way home that evening. The last thing I wanted to do was keep my appointment with Patrick Tanner. But I knew it was important to talk to him if I were to hope for any success in my investigation. Reluctantly, and cautiously, since I was feeling noticeably stiff where my bright new bruises were starting to show, I pulled on my jacket and ventured out.

Chapter Sixteen

"So, you think you can make them do something so that fucking driver gets fired?" Patrick Tanner sat on his living room sofa amid a shambles of magazines, newspapers, dirty cups and fast food take-out cartons. He wore a T-shirt patterned with what appeared to be dried-up pizza sauce and a pair of pants that looked like they hadn't seen the inside of a washing machine in a very long time. He balanced his bare feet on the coffee table in front of him. From my seat across the room I had a lovely view of his long, callused toes and dark-stained soles.

"I'll do my best, Patrick," I answered. "The information you've given me should be pretty helpful. Donna's your advocate so I'll have to clear anything I do with her. But I'm sure she won't have a problem if I write some letters, make some phone calls and try to get some publicity for your case. I know you deserve to get some justice after everything you've been through."

"No shit." He spat out the words, nodding furiously and pressing his gaunt features into an even deeper frown. "That's what no one seems to understand. No one." He punched the sofa cushion next to him sending a squall of dust flying into the apartment's musty air. Being here certainly made me feel better about my own housekeeping habits.

He sighed and sprang from his seat, making towards the window with stomping, furious steps. He looked out at the glimmering lights that sprinkled the vista from his third story Upper Castro apartment, but his glazed eyes seemed oblivious to the view. He took a breath and began banging his forehead against the glass in a slow, shuddering rhythm. I'd known that Patrick was pretty messed-up, but as I sat there witnessing this impromptu headbanging session, I began to wonder if, as we say back home, he might be completely off his trolley. I didn't know what to do, but I knew I couldn't just watch him while he bruised his face black and blue.

Cautiously, I lifted myself from my chair and walked over to him. "Patrick," I said softly, "why don't you go sit down? I'm sure you'd be more comfortable."

He stopped and turned to look at me, his expression as disconcerted as if I'd just woken him from a dream. "Oh, yeah, okay." Meekly, he shuffled back to the sofa where he sat down, arms folded about his body, legs tucked tight under him. His eyes moved jumpily around the room, like any moment someone could burst through the wall and attack him.

I cleared away a pile of magazines and a couple of crumpled MacDonalds wrappers and sat down at the other end of the sofa. "Can I get you anything?" I asked, leaning slightly towards him.

He shook his head swiftly. "No, I'm fine," he breathed. "Just a little jumpy these days, that's all." (Now that was an understatement, if ever I've heard one.)

"Er… have you thought about seeking professional help, Patrick? I know that—"

"No, I don't need that kind of help, I'm fine."

"But if you saw a professional…" I let my suggestion fade to nothing as Tanner shot me a fierce glare. I shrugged. "It's your choice, I suppose." He replied by nodding silently. For a few moments I sat quietly as Tanner heaved several audible breaths. I wondered if now was a good time to proceed with the questions I had for him, after all, I didn't want to upset him any further. But then, I asked myself, when would be a good time since Tanner's behavior seemed so unpredictable? I needed to find out this information if I was going to help Mario. "So, Patrick," I said gently, "if you don't mind I just have a couple of questions about that last night you saw Peter."

"Go ahead. But anything I tell you stays between us, otherwise I'll—" He pushed his body away from the back of the sofa and I thought for a moment that he was about to jump up to give a repeat performance of his head-banging routine. I was definitely relieved when he merely sighed, dropped back down onto the rumpled cushion and waved a loose hand in front of him. "Just don't tell anyone else, okay?"

"I only want to follow up on some of the things you said the other day. And this is strictly between you and me." I gave him what I hoped was a reassuring smile. "First I want to ask you about when you left The Project on Friday. Do you remember if Peter locked the door?"

Tanner creased his heavy brows and looked pensive. Then he nodded. "Yeah, Peter locked the door. He followed me down the stairs and locked up after me."

"And it was after that you saw Julia?"

"Julia?"

"Yes, the woman on the magazine cover."

"Oh, yeah, right. Yeah, she came up to me as I was walking away. I told you what she said already."

"Do you know if she went inside The Project? Did she knock on the door?"

Tanner shrugged. "I don't know. After I spoke to her I walked back home. Didn't look around, so I wouldn't know what she did next."

"And did you see anyone else hanging around, or anyone go into The Project?"

"Nope." He shook his head swiftly. "No one else."

"Thanks."

"Is that all?" he asked.

"Yes, that's all I wanted to know." I nodded as I pushed myself up from the sofa.

Tanner jumped up after me. "So, you gonna work on my case tomorrow?" he asked eagerly as I negotiated my way towards the door through the clutter covering the worn carpet.

"I'll do my best, and I'll let you know what I find out."

"Good, good," he nodded. "It's about time somebody helped me out. Peter never really did much, you know. Always making up excuses for why nothing was happening. You ask me, he didn't have a clue...you people should get someone better to replace him, someone who makes things happen." He pointed a surly index finger towards me.

"Yes, well I'm sure we'll get the best person for the job," I said as I reached for the door handle, eager to escape before Tanner began another one of his ranting diatribes.

He, however, seemed equally anxious to detain me as he deftly slipped between me and the door. "You know in all the times I met with him I don't think he ever—"

"By the way, why did you meet with Peter on Friday?" I inquired.

The stream of words suddenly dried in Tanner's mouth and he stepped away from the door. "It was just a regular appointment," he said tersely.

I frowned at him. "But wasn't it only ten minutes?"

"Yeah, we didn't have a lot to discuss." Suddenly, he seemed eager to have me leave as he scrambled to undo the two large bolts above the locks on his door.

"But what did you talk about?" I persisted as Tanner slid back the bolts.

"I don't remember, to tell you the truth," he replied as he pulled the door open and a cool draught gusted its way into the stuffy apartment. "Something about my case, of course. But I don't remember exactly what." His gaze flitted about in all directions, he seemed steadily determined to avoid meeting my eyes. He seemed also determined to ensure my swift departure. "Well, goodnight, then," he said, placing a hand against my back and almost shoving me out the door. "And don't forget to call me when you get news of my case."

"I won't," I answered, turning to catch a last glimpse of his anxious face before the door was firmly closed.

Back at my apartment I spent the rest of the evening zoning out on bad television. What can I say, I love seventies re-runs. When I first came to the States I thought I'd died and gone to heaven when I discovered cable television and found everything from *Charlie's Angels* to *Columbo* to *Hart to Hart* playing back to back from morning until night. I know, I should be extolling the virtues of the BBC and all that 'quality' drama they're so famous for. And it's true, I do miss decent British television every now and again, but give me a *Fantasy Island* re-run any day and you'll make me a very happy woman. Anyway, I spent a couple of very enjoyable hours in front of the box, before deciding it was time for bed. .

As I brushed and flossed, regarding my reflection in the bathroom mirror, I let my mind wander back to my meeting with Patrick Tanner. With the information he'd provided it seemed I could conclude that Peter had indeed locked the door. Did that mean the murderer was someone either known to Peter or someone who had their own keys? It was always possible that the killer could have been a stranger who gave Peter a beseeching look through the door's glass panel and Peter, surmising it was someone who needed services, let them in. It was unlikely that he would have done that—all of us were very cautious about who we let in the office after hours, but anything was possible. The fact that Tanner still insisted that he had seen Julia made me even more determined to speak to her. As well as being a suspect herself, she might be able to provide me with important information.

Then there was Tanner. Until that evening I hadn't even thought of him as a suspect, but his wacky behavior left me wondering. And why had he become so defensive when I had asked him about the content of his meeting with Peter? What was it that he had to hide? A motive for murder perhaps? And if that was so then how much could I trust any of what Patrick Tanner had told me?

I slid into bed, pushing my hand across the sheet to touch a crumpled piece of paper. It was the note left by Alex that morning. The day had seemed so long it was hard to imagine that less than twenty-four hours ago we had fallen asleep together on these very sheets. And so much had happened since then. I recalled the previous night and could almost sense the beautiful smoothness of Alex's skin against my palms and fingertips. I remembered the demonstration, the screaming marchers and the cruel, enraged faces of the police. And I remembered Alex walking casually down the steps of the Hall of Justice engaged in happy conversation with the very cop who had assaulted me. The anger I had felt then came back in full force. How could she even think of talking with someone like that? How could she be friendly with such a thug? And how could I have foolishly ignored my own rational instincts, choosing rather to get swept along by lust and a silly attraction? And now I had lain myself open to yet another betrayal. Okay, so Alex might not have hit me like Justine, but as far as I was concerned, the fact that she was chummy with the cop who had assaulted me came a very close second.

I picked up her note and read slowly over the looped, gently sloping handwriting. But this time her sweet message only made me scowl and shake my head. Then, breathing a weary sigh, I balled up the paper and tossed it across the room.

The next morning I called my office and left a message on the machine to say I wouldn't be in until after lunch. Then, after showering, gulping down a couple of cups of tea, and taking Hairy Boy for his morning constitutional, I set off for the BART Station at Sixteenth Street.

It was rush hour and the BART train was crowded. I found myself squashed between a middle-aged man scowling over the front page of the *Wall Street Journal* and a young woman apparently trained in the Tammy Faye Bakker school of cosmetology who stared into a compact mirror to put the finishing touches to her overpowering eye make-up. I was relieved to step off the train at Embarcadero and make my way towards California Street where the offices of City Models were based. I had decided that an in-person visit would probably be the most effective in helping me find Julia. Experience had taught me that people who were cooperative over the phone would bend over backwards for you in a face-to-face meeting. And I wanted to locate the mysterious Julia as quickly as possible.

City Models was located on the thirty-second floor of a concrete building that rose to dizzying heights above the busy downtown sidewalk. After struggling through the crowded lobby, I got on the elevator and stepped into a bright, airy office with high, domed ceilings and an incredible view across the San Francisco Bay (and quite a striking contrast to my own dismal work environment, but no, I wasn't envious, not even for one minute). The windows were enormous and the walls offered vast expanses of white, decorated intermittently with framed monochrome photographs of young and beautiful women. On a raised platform directly in front of me a receptionist sat at a curved glass-topped table. Carefully groomed, wearing lipstick that matched her blood-red suit, her dyed black hair shaped in a bob around her face, she raised one thin eyebrow as I approached. A chrome name-plate on her desk told me her name was Linda Morgenstein.

"Can I help you?" Her expression suggested she thought not, that a woman wearing faded Levis, Doc Martin shoes, and an over-washed sweat-shirt could only have wandered into this office by mistake.

"Yes, I'm here to see Julia." I pulled my most friendly of smiles.

The eyebrow was raised again. "Julia?" Her tone was icy cold. Beneath the glass desk she crossed her legs, smoothing hands over her skirt. Her nails were painted the same shade as the suit and lipstick. If Disney had seen Linda, I swear she'd have beaten Glen Close hands-down for the part of Cruela de Vil.

"Yes, she's a model with your agency. Tall, blond, thin…"

"Well, I'm afraid that describes a lot of the women who work with us," she said, rolling her contact-tinted blue eyes.

"She was on the most recent cover of *San Francisco Freedom."*

"And what is your interest in Julia?"

I had considered earlier what approach I should take and had fantasized creating some elaborate story: pretending I was Julia's long-lost sister, say-ing I was a reporter wanting to do a feature on her career. But I'd decided that my best chance of success probably lay in sticking as close to the truth as possible. "Julia knows, I mean knew, someone who was a friend of mine. He died recently and I wanted to let her know."

"I see." A flicker of interest showed in her face. "So you just want her to know her friend died?"

"Yes, he was murdered actually."

Her eyes became wide. "Really?" The Cruela persona suddenly disap-peared to be replaced by an expectant, puppy-eyed expression that would have fit well on any of the one hundred and one Dalmatians.

I gave a swift nod. "Yeah."

"Well, that's just awful. How did it happen? Did they catch the person who did it?" From her enthralled expression I got the impression that Linda's work days didn't contain an awful lot of variety. It was nice to know my visit brought her some excitement.

"The police are still investigating," I said solemnly.

"Oh," she said, nodding. "That's terrible." She chewed slightly at her lower lip and a stripe of lipstick appeared across two of her front teeth.

"Anyway, I was wondering if you could let me know how I can get in touch with Julia. I'd hate for her to find out from a stranger."

Linda seemed to consider this for a few moments, stretching out her fingers to stare at her crimson nails as she did so. "Well, I wouldn't normally give out this kind of information, but since it does seem important..." She gave a quick glance behind her, at the door that seemed to lead to the rest of the offices. "She's on location." She lowered her voice to a whisper. "In the East Bay...let me see..." She turned to a computer behind her, tapped the keyboard a few times and then turned back to me. "She's in Oakland, of all places, in Jack London Square. They started there at seven and will probably stay all day. Mind you, from the way she's been behaving recently there's no telling if she'll be there or not." Her eyes signaled a look of disapproval.

"Why? Is she unreliable?"

"No, not normally, but just recently, well, we've had several complaints." Linda Morgenstein lowered her voice again. "Like last week, Monday and Tuesday she didn't even turn up for this major, and I mean MAJOR assignment. She just called in and said she didn't want to do it, said she was feeling upset."

"Is that unusual?"

"Oh, yes, very unlike Julia. I mean, that woman is ambitious, very ambitious. And she needs to be—this is a cut-throat business. And that's not the sort of thing that does your career any good, let me tell you." Linda tossed back her head, amazingly not a hair on her head moved. Apparently when it came to hair spray, moderation was not a word she was familiar with. "Hey, when did your friend die? Maybe she found out and that's what upset her."

"Maybe," I said, thoughtfully.

Chapter Seventeen

Even at ten-thirty the traffic on the Bay Bridge was heavy, a slow moving river of cars and trucks that edged its way towards the East Bay. I fiddled with the dial on the aging radio in my Datsun, wondering for the umpteenth time why it was that the only stations it seemed capable of picking up without static either played country music or were run by Christian evangelists. Was this what Pat Robertson meant by God's punishment, I wondered. Finally I settled on a station whose version of 'all day news' ranged from reports on the National Spelling Bee contest to interviews with Michael Jackson's ex-bodyguard. No wonder people make such informed decisions come election time, I thought bitterly, as I braked behind a noisy and exhaust-spewing truck.

After more than forty frustrating minutes in stop and go traffic, I took the exit to downtown Oakland and headed down Broadway. It was considerably warmer on this side of the bay, in San Francisco the entire city had been shaded in gray cloud, but here in Oakland, the fog had already burned off completely. I was sweating by the time I pulled up to a meter by Jack London Square.

A collection of tacky tourist stores, overpriced seafood restaurants and bars, the square overlooks the Oakland estuary. Named for the author who grew up in Oakland, it boasts an incongruous-looking log cabin that is said to have been occupied by London during his Gold Rush days in the Yukon. (If you ask me, it bears a very striking resemblance to my granddad's garden shed, but I'm sure that's just coincidence).

I fished a couple of quarters out of my pocket, pushed them into the meter and headed towards the waterfront where Linda Morgenstein had told me I would find Julia. She and a couple of other models were working on a promotion for a chain of restaurants, one of which was based on the square.

I spotted the photographer first, a middle-aged guy with a sagging belly and round shoulders, he moved about crooning and calling as his camera clicked and whirred. I moved closer and the focus of his attention came into view; it was Julia. Wearing spiked high heels and a silk dress that had it been any shorter the hem would have caught in her armpits, she smiled, leaned forward, pushed her arms back and thrust her breasts towards the camera. I found myself wondering if fashion models have to sign up for compulsory yoga, after all, every other pose you see them in looks either highly unnatural or very painful. Astonishingly, even in such a ridiculous position Julia was still able to communicate a very magnetic quality.

I stood several yards away, watching Julia primp, pout and twist her willowy body until a frown suddenly settled across her features, she pulled herself up straight and muttered, "I need a break." Then, kicking off the treacherous shoes, she shook her blond mane back from her face and strode over to one of the other models who handed her a pack of cigarettes. Julia pulled one out, lit it and sucked in hard, closing her eyes and throwing back her head as she breathed out the smoke in a long, loud gasp. After receiving the attentions of the make-up artist, the second model stepped in front of the camera and took up another contorted pose. Cigarette in hand, Julia walked away from the group. I decided now was the time to talk to her. "Julia," I called as I approached.

In a slow, somewhat exaggerated gesture, she took another drag on her cigarette and gave me an appraising glance. "Do I know you?" She asked in her throaty, resonant voice.

"You may remember me, I work at Stop The Violence Project."

"Stop The Violence Project?" She feigned confusion but I could tell from the recognition that flashed in her eyes that she remembered The Project well.

"Yes, you were there just over a week ago. You came to see Peter Williams."

She sucked on her cigarette, looked out over the water and narrowed her eyes. "Oh, yes, you're right. Peter and I had lunch. But I'm not sure I remember you. You're name is…?"

"Lou, Lou Spencer. I'm the Office Manager, we met very briefly."

She pushed a strand of windblown hair away from her face and gave me a hard stare. "No, I don't remember meeting you. But anyway, what do you want?"

"Well, I'm here to talk to you about Peter."

Momentarily, the muscles on her face tightened, she swayed back slightly on her heels. If I had blinked I would have missed her sudden show of anxiety, for the next second she appeared perfectly at ease. Her hand made a languorous movement up to her mouth as she dragged on her cigarette again. "Peter?"

"Yes. About his murder."

"Murder? You mean Peter's dead?" She widened her eyes, put her hand up to her mouth and staggered back. I couldn't help thinking that if Julia was considering expanding her career into television or movies she was going to have to do a lot of hard work, either that or try out for one of the daytime soaps where her brand of overacting would blend in well.

"Yes, murdered. Surely you must have seen mention of it in the news-papers, or on the television?"

"No." She shook her head emphatically. "I don't really keep up with the news. I'm just so shocked. Poor, dear Peter. How did it happen?" She had managed to squeeze out a couple of tears; they rolled gracefully down her cheeks.

"The police think it was a co-worker, but I have other ideas. I thought you might be able to help me."

"Me?" She said as she tossed away her cigarette and dabbed the tears with the back of her hand. "How could I help?"

"I thought you might know something about what happened to Peter the night he was murdered."

Just then a harassed-looking young woman holding a clipboard ran over to us. "Julia, they're waiting for you. We need you for these next shots." She tugged at Julia's arm.

"I'll be over in a second, okay?" Julia answered and pushed the young woman away. Then she turned to me. "I'm sorry, I wish I could help you but I only saw Peter for lunch and he seemed fine then. Now if you don't mind I have to get back to work."

"I have a witness who says he saw you outside the office that Friday evening," I said as Julia turned to walk away.

She turned back abruptly. There was anger, or perhaps it was fear, in her fiery expression. "Look, I really can't talk to you…I'm way too busy." She cast an anxious glance towards the photographer who was standing with his hands on his hips staring in our direction.

"I need to talk to you," I insisted. "If you have something that may help me, I need to know."

She breathed an exasperated sigh. "Why don't you come to my apart-ment this evening? I can talk more then."

"Great," I nodded. I handed her a pen and paper and she quickly scrib-bled down her address and phone number for me. "It's pretty easy to find," she said. "Come anytime after seven-thirty." Then, in a slow, hip-swaying stride she made her way back to the waterfront.

"I'm glad to see you're out of jail," I commented when I arrived at The Project that afternoon to see Jasmine bustling around the office.

She shrugged. "If it was up to me I'd still be inside. There's a whole bunch of people not released. We'd planned to stay together in solidarity but my damn parents got wind of what was going on and came down and bailed me out." She wrinkled her nose and gave a slow shake of her head.

"That's great that they support you," I commented.

"Oh, it's not that," Jasmine said dismissively. "They're just worried about dishonor coming on the family. And besides that, they're always interfering. I want to be represented by Legal Advocates like everyone else but my mother's talking about getting me some damn expensive lawyer. Can you believe it?"

"What are you charged with?" I asked.

"Oh, I don't know, same as everyone else. Disturbing the peace, assault on a police officer, resisting arrest, and a couple of other things I can't remember now. It's kind of exciting really." She grinned wide. "Makes me feel like I'm really standing up and striking a blow for freedom. You know what I mean?"

I gave a brief nod. However naive I might think Jasmine was, I couldn't help but admire her enthusiasm. In ten years time, when she reached my age, she'd probably be a little more jaded. But I sort of hoped that she stayed the same.

"We're doing our best to get everyone released." Amanda had wandered down the hall to stand by the door. "And some of the people injured at the demo are talking about starting legal proceedings against the city. Though it seems like the mayor is bending over backwards to be vague and evasive. Though he did make some pretty messed-up comments."

"Yeah, you should have heard him, Lou," Jasmine interrupted. "He was rambling on about San Francisco's image, how it needs a solid law abiding citizenry, how all this political activism makes the wrong impression. All he's worried about is the business sector and tourism."

"If we're not careful Mario's going to end up one of his scapegoats," Amanda sighed. "Just one more way Finch can prove we're all violent trouble-makers. I'm going to make sure the Coalition continues our campaign. We need to get Mario and everyone else out of jail as soon as possible."

I nodded an agreement. "How's it going raising bail for him?"

"Okay, I guess," Amanda replied. "It's a lot and we may have some trouble raising the full amount, but we're doing our best."

"I'll certainly put in as much as I can," I said. "Unfortunately, that's not very much."

Jasmine looked wistful. "God, if only I could persuade my parents to bail out Mario. Now that would be neat, wouldn't it?"

Donna had been holed up in her office almost the entire afternoon, it wasn't until five o'clock when she made a fleeting trip to the bathroom that I was able to accost her in the hallway and ask for a quick word.

"I'm kind of busy, actually, Lou. Can it wait?" She snapped, backing towards her office as she spoke.

"It won't take a minute," I persisted. "It's about Patrick Tanner."

"Oh, well...then okay. What can I do?"

I didn't tell her about my meeting with Tanner but I did tell her that I wanted to help out on his case. "It seems pretty complicated and since you must be so overworked right now with Peter no longer here, I thought I'd be able to do something."

"Sure." She smiled.

I told her of my intention to write letters on Tanner's behalf lobbying for disciplinary action against the bus driver.

"Well, I'm glad that you share the same approach as me to his case. Patrick just needs a lot of intensive attention. He's suffering from pretty serious Post Traumatic Stress, you know. Unfortunately, Peter didn't seemed to understand that." Donna shook her head in a gesture of exasperation.

"What do you mean?" I asked.

"Peter was planning to terminate Patrick. When I looked through his notes to familiarize myself with the case his last entry said he'd set up a meeting to do just that."

"Why?"

Donna shrugged. "Peter seemed to think that Patrick needs psychiatric help. He'd told him that if he didn't agree to see a psychiatrist then he couldn't continue to get help through The Project."

"And Tanner wouldn't agree to that?"

Donna shook her head. "No way. He's too suspicious of any so-called professionals. But Peter didn't leave him with any choices, he pretty much offered him an ultimatum."

I was thoughtful for a moment. "That must have left Tanner pretty pissed off."

"Yeah, I guess so," she said lightly. "But that's not important now because with you and me helping him he's getting the services he needs. Right?"

"Right," I said, nodding slowly.

"So, thanks for your help, Lou." Donna patted me lightly on the shoulder. "Just give me copies of any correspondence so I can keep it in Patrick's file. Now, I'd better get back to work." She glanced at her watch and sighed. "I've a ton of things to get done before I leave tonight." She turned towards her office. As she swung around I was suddenly reminded of seeing her on Saturday at the beach and the way she had turned and hurried away from me then.

"Hey, Donna, were you at beach on Saturday? I thought I saw you...you and this other woman..."

Donna turned around slowly. "Beach, what beach?"

"Muir Beach, I could have sworn..."

"I don't think so, Lou. Maybe you got me confused with someone else," she said decisively.

"Yeah, maybe," I nodded. But as Donna strode back to her office I knew that I had not been mistaken.

Chapter Eighteen

At seven-thirty that evening, I climbed into my Datsun and set off for the Inner Sunset address that Julia had given me. Twenty minutes later I pulled up outside an apartment building located on one of the tranquil residential streets. It was a modest building with a painted stucco exterior, neat strip of lawn, and carefully-tended succulents edging the sidewalk leading to the main entrance; not what I'd pictured as suitable accommodations for an up-and-coming model—I'd imagined something much more ostentatious. But then, maybe I've been influenced by watching too many episodes of *Lifestyles of the Rich and Famous*.

I parked my car across the street and climbed the single flight of stairs to the second floor apartments. I rang Julia's doorbell and waited. From behind the door I could hear a shuffle of footsteps and the sound of a bolt being pulled back. The door opened and Julia greeted me with the merest suggestion of a smile. "Come in," she said flatly, signaling me inside with a languid motion of her long, thin arm.

Wearing a pair of faded jeans belted at the waist and a plain black T-shirt, she looked quite different from when I had seen her earlier. The elaborate mask of make-up was gone, revealing a fair, unblemished complexion. Her hands and neck were free of jewelry, and her hair was tied in a thick braid down her back. It was as if the glamorous persona she wore for the outside world, like armor, had been stripped away. Here she seemed fresh-faced, young, almost delicate.

If the unassuming exterior of Julia's apartment had made me think that she herself was modest, the decoration on the walls of her living room soon set me right. They bore perhaps fifteen or twenty large photographs, some in black and white, some in color. Each one featured Julia, her lithe body arranged in a variety of alluring poses. One, above all dominated the room, it hung, almost life-size, over the sofa. In shimmery soft focus, it showed Julia standing, legs apart, in a field dotted with bright red poppies. With lips painted the same crimson shade, she pouted towards the camera. Her hair hung loose around her shoulders and the only clothing she wore was a tiny black leather skirt and a pair of knee-height lace-up leather boots.

"Pretty tacky, huh?" She said, following my gaze to the picture.

"It is a bit…seventies," I agreed.

She laughed. "Yeah, those were exactly my thoughts when it was taken. I often think about taking it down but it has sentimental value, one of my first sessions. Back in the days when I wasn't sure I could even make a living modeling." She picked up a pack of cigarettes, pulled one out and lit it with the gold lighter she kept in the pocket of her pants.

"Seems like you're doing pretty well now," I commented, sweeping my hand over all the other photographs.

"Yes," she said, puffing eagerly on her cigarette. "But it's still difficult to trust my success. The way I see it, one day you have it and the next it can be taken away." Momentarily, her face was clouded with a troubled frown. "But I guess that's just the way life goes for someone like me." She exhaled in a loud gasp.

She sounded so insecure, and I wondered why. After all, she seemed to have everything going for her. Was there a reason for her to be fearful? Did she have some kind of degenerative disease? Or a hidden mental illness? Or perhaps she was just the victim, like so many others, of a profession that allotted status, fame and fortune to women on the basis of their looks alone. In those circumstances even the mere passage of time became an enemy. But I got the feeling it was more than that for Julia.

"Why don't you take a seat." She motioned me towards a massive blue velvet couch. "Would you like something to drink?"

"No, thanks, I'm fine." I answered.

"Well, I need a drink. I'll just go fix myself something." She spun around and, trailing a ribbon of smoke behind her, disappeared down the hall. While she was gone I looked around the room. Apart from the extravagant display of photographs, the decorations were spartan. A hardwood floor offered a broad, polished expanse mitigated only by a small, Indian motif rug at the center of the room. Other than the sofa upon which I sat, the only furnishings were a matching armchair and a square coffee table which held a vase of carefully-arranged long-stemmed white roses.

Julia returned holding a glass of red wine. She eased herself into the armchair across from me, balancing her glass on one arm of the chair. On the other there sat a large glass ashtray. She took out another cigarette. "You smoke?" she asked, offering me the pack.

I shook my head. "No, and I was pretty surprised to see you do. I thought you models were all clean-living and health conscious."

She barked a derisive laugh. "Oh, you'd be surprised. This little habit helps keep down my weight, though I know several other girls who use somewhat more drastic measures—you know, drugs, liposuction, and good old vomiting when all else fails. Personally I've had to go through more than enough. Using a pack and a half a day is my limit."

"I've never understood the habit myself," I said, wafting away the cloud of smoke that drifted towards me. "I guess it helps with stress, too, right? A friend of mine just started again after giving up for years. He's under a lot of stress."

"Is that the guy they hauled in for murdering Peter?" She asked.

"I thought you said you didn't know anything about that," I retorted.

She shifted her gaze away from mine and took a sip of her wine. "Well, I guess I do know a little. Peter was a good friend of mine, you know. We met when we were both at Berkeley. He never turned his back on me, not like some people...well, not until..." She shook her head as if trying to push an unhappy memory away. "I'm really sorry that he's dead. He was a good guy at heart." Tears welled up in her eyes and spilled slowly down her cheeks. This time, however, they seemed quite genuine. "I heard about him getting killed, but when you came asking questions I just didn't want to get involved."

"Why?"

She made a dismissive gesture and picked up her wine. "Oh, it just wouldn't look good for my career, that's all."

From the look on her face, I guessed there was more to Julia's fear than that, but I decided not to push it. Instead I asked her about the Friday night Peter was killed. "So what were you doing outside the Project?"

"I wasn't there!" She threw out her arm in an angry gesture and her fingers caught the glass perched on the arm of her chair, sending it flying. It hit the wooden floor with a crack, splintering apart as the red liquid spilled out into a dark, expanding pool. I looked at the broken glass lying in the red wine and I was suddenly reminded of Peter as I had found him, dead in a congealed pool of his own blood. I shivered and glanced up to meet Julia's eyes. From the fear and dreadful recognition in her face, I guessed that she too was thinking of Peter. It made me wonder if she had also been a witness to that scene. I looked at her more intently, trying to read her troubled countenance. Quickly, she looked away.

"Did you kill Peter?" I demanded.

"Don't be ridiculous, Peter was my friend," she said, shaking her head and then muttering something about having to clean up the mess. She stood up and strode from the room.

She returned carrying a sponge and a dustpan and brush. After refusing my offer of help, she spent the next few minutes sweeping up the pieces of broken glass and wiping away the wine. Her gaze remained fixed in avid concentration on the floor. When she finished she disposed of the garbage then sat down and tugged out another cigarette, lighting it with an unsteady hand.

"What do you know that you're not telling me?" I said, leaning towards her.

"Nothing, absolutely nothing." She did her best to sound measured, calm, but there was a nervous edge to her voice.

"Look, Julia," I reasoned, "I have a friend in jail charged with this murder. I know he didn't do it. Do you want an innocent man to go to jail for something he didn't do?"

"Believe me, I just can't help you."

I wasn't sure if I imagined it, but she sounded almost regretful. I said nothing, letting my gaze wander once again over the glamorous photographs. None of them showed the real Julia, they were all as posed and as false as the photographs they had been taking at Jack London Square that morning. I found myself wondering what kind of fragile ego needed such constant reminders of her own obvious beauty and success. Finally I turned back to her. "You know, if you were at The Project on Friday night and you saw something…" Julia shot me an alarmed glance. "…you could be protecting a murderer, you know."

"I can't help you," she repeated.

I let out a frustrated sigh. "Okay, so you won't admit you were at The Project on Friday night. Maybe you can help me, though. You had lunch with Peter, right?" She gave a quick nod. "Can you tell me what he talked about? Did he by any chance mention someone called Malcolm?"

"Is that the guy he was dating?"

I nodded.

"Yeah, he told me he was about to ditch him. He seemed pretty pissed."

"Did he say why?"

"Not really." She folded her arching brows into a deep frown as if trying to recollect the exact content of their conversation. "He kept saying how spineless this guy was, how he couldn't believe that he could date someone like that. And then Peter said something about him deserving everything that was coming to him."

"Did he say anything else?"

She shrugged. "Not about the boyfriend or, rather, ex-boyfriend. But he was pretty pissed at his boss, too. Spent quite a long time ranting about that."

"Really?" I pushed myself to the edge of the sofa. "What did he say?"

"You know, I don't really remember. To tell you the truth I was a little distracted. He kept saying how disappointed he was, how he thought she was different and now he felt really let down. Something like that."

I was thoughtful for a moment. So Peter was angry with Amanda. I wondered why. Was it connected to the 'confidential personnel meeting' they had later that day? I felt ever more curious to find out what had actually been discussed there.

"Anything else you can remember?" I asked Julia. She shook her head. I was certain that she wasn't telling all she knew, though for now, at least, I knew of no way to bully it out of her. There was nothing I could really threaten her with and even if I went to the cops it seemed like Cochran was determined not to listen to me.

"Well, if that's all…" Julia stubbed out her cigarette and made to get up.

"Actually, there is one more thing. I met someone else who knows Peter from his time at Berkeley, a guy named Daryl Banks."

Her features suddenly stiffened, as if I'd just delivered some very, very bad news. "I see," she said dully.

"He says he doesn't know you, though it seems you know him."

"Unfortunately, yes."

"He said he was a good friend of Peter's."

She let out a short, bitter laugh. "I'm not sure Peter would've described their relationship that way."

"Oh, so they weren't close?" I asked.

She shrugged. "They used to be, but not any more."

"Any particular reason?"

"Peter didn't say much but I think Daryl had threatened him, maybe even more. And from the little interaction I've had with him, that wouldn't surprise me at all."

I nodded as I recalled my own reaction to Daryl Banks. "Do you know why he threatened Peter?" I asked.

Julia shook her head. "Not really. Like I said, Peter didn't tell me much."

"Were they serious threats?"

"I don't know. I just read between the lines of what Peter told me. And Daryl…well, he's weird, creepy."

"Did you ever think that…did it ever cross you mind that he could have murdered Peter?" I asked.

"I guess anything's possible," Julia answered vaguely.

Back at my apartment I was firmly ensconced on my living room sofa, zoning out in front of a vintage episode of *Mission Impossible* and occasionally letting my thoughts run over what I had learned during my visit with Julia, when my doorbell rang. I groaned, muted the TV, swung my legs to the floor and followed Hairy Boy as he raced in a barking frenzy along the hall.

"Oh, hi…this is er…a surprise," I said as I pulled open the door.

"Just thought I'd drop by on the off chance you'd be home. Looks like I got lucky." Alex Ramon stood, thumbs looped over the pockets of her jeans, a sheepish smile on her face. Hairy Boy sniffed insistently at her legs and she leaned down to pet him. "I have some information for you, about that stuff you wanted me to follow up on. And besides, I wanted an excuse to come see you." The smile became wide and her dimples began to show.

I replied with a slow nod and a glazed look. Behind my eyes my thoughts were scrambling and my emotions swirled like a river in flood. The last thing I felt equipped to deal with was a visit from Alex.

"Is this not a good time, Lou? You busy?" She shifted uneasily from one leg to the other. "I can always call you tomorrow if that would be better."

"No, come in, it's fine," I answered, moving away from the doorway to let her in. "I was just watching the telly."

She followed me to the living room where both our eyes wandered to the silent television screen. *The Mission Impossible* team had almost completed their mission and were just peeling off their stunningly realistic rubber masks (as a kid, I used to nag and nag my mother to tell me how they did that). I picked up the remote and turned it off.

"God, don't you love how TV is always so true to life," Alex commented as she sank to the sofa.

"Yeah, they might do better to air shows about cops beating up queers on demonstrations." I quipped, seating myself in the armchair across the room.

Alex gave me a wary glance. "Yeah, I heard about the demo…"

"What do you mean heard about it?" I interrupted, angrily. "I saw you there, afterwards. Talking merrily to the same bloody wanker who assaulted me."

"But Lou…"

"And maybe you're friends with the guy who elbowed me in the stomach. He's tall, dark hair, probably no more than twenty. If you see him tell him I said hello. All right?"

"I'm sorry, Lou, I really am. I had no idea that—"

I waved away her comments. "It doesn't matter. I suppose I should have known better."

"What do you mean?" She leaned forward.

"Well, it's obvious, isn't it? You and I are on different sides of the fence."

She sighed and sank back into the sofa. "I just don't get it. You talk like we're a couple of political candidates, not two human beings who happen to like each other."

"That's not the point…"

"Well, what is the point then, Lou?" she challenged me, folding her arms across her chest. "I didn't know that guy had hit you. He's not a friend, I don't even remember his goddamn name. And now after what you told me, I've no interest in talking to him again."

"Look," I said steadily, "I just don't think this is going to work out."

"Why do I get the feeling that you're just looking for an excuse not to get involved with me?"

"I don't know what you're talking about," I replied, turning slightly away. "This is how I feel—it's not about making excuses."

"Isn't it? Then why so hot and cold? Why are you so quick to jump to conclusions about me? Why do you keep running away?"

"I don't," I protested.

"Lou," she said calmly, "you know you do."

"Look, this is about you being a cop, about you hanging out with bloody thugs who beat up demonstrators. It's not about me."

"Whatever you say," she said, rising from the sofa, a grim frown set across her face. "But for your information, Lou Spencer, I do not hang out with thugs. I do happen to care about you, though, for all the difference that seems to make." She shook her head slowly. "By the way, here's the information." She pulled a couple of sheets of folded paper from the back pocket of her jeans, walked over and handed them to me at arm's length. Without saying anything I took them from her. "It's all written down. I hope it helps point the finger at someone other than Mario. I passed on the information to the Hate Crimes Unit and, of course, to Cochran."

"Thanks," I breathed as she walked past me and into the hall. A few seconds later the door closed behind her and I was left alone.

I sat up late that night, thinking about my conversation with Alex. Was there any truth in what she said? Was I really just looking for an excuse not to get involved? It was true that past experience had left me more than a little wary, could it be that I was overreacting because of my relationship with Justine? I told myself no. I mean, I had seen Alex with that cop, laughing and talking. I had every reason to feel angry and outraged by her behavior. And she and I really were on opposite sides of the fence, weren't we? So, okay, she had helped me out with trying to prove Mario's innocence, but that didn't really mean anything. I had every reason not to trust her.

Chapter Nineteen

The next morning I decided not to let myself get distracted by my conflict with Alex. I needed to focus on helping Mario if I was ever going to get results. So, after making myself some tea, I sat down at my kitchen table with the two sheets of paper Alex had left me the previous night. What they contained could indeed have an impact on Mario's case. They detailed the activities of Frank Frederickson since his acquittal of the assault charges he had faced.

Apparently, Frederickson had become something of a celebrity after the trial. He was a charismatic speaker and within only a couple of months had been recruited to the ranks of the far-right group, American People for Freedom. In no time at all, he had become their San Francisco spokesman and under his leadership much of their literature and materials had become less anti-immigrant and more anti-gay. Frederickson himself had made several virulent anti-gay speeches and in an interview given just a few days ago on one of the many right-leaning talk radio shows he had mentioned Peter's murder. He was reported to have said, "It's about time someone shut that interfering little fag up. Those people should know that not everyone will put up with their perversion and their anti-family political agenda."

I wondered how I could follow-up on this information. After all, I didn't exactly have the resources to put a tail on Frederickson or conduct an investigation of his organization. And then I thought of Jeff Easton. He was always after a hot story. I didn't see any reason for him to turn this one down.

After calling Jeff, I picked up the telephone to make another call. I had another suspect I had to follow up on. What Julia had told me about Daryl Banks and his threats to Peter surely gave him a motive for murder. I needed someone to help me find out if there were any records of such threats. Despite our previous night's conversation, I was sure Alex would have helped me, but I thought it better if I got assistance elsewhere.

I decided to call Reggie Johnson, a cop who worked out of Taraval

Station. A couple of years ago, before joining the force, Reggie had been beaten unconscious by a group of drunk sailors on shore leave from a navy destroyer. After the attack, The Project had provided him with services and since one of the advocates had been out on disability leave, it had come down to me to work with him. As well as offering emotional support, I had referred him to a lawyer who had recently managed to get an out-of-court settlement for him in the region of three-hundred-thousand. I figured Reggie might be willing to help me out a little. When I called him he seemed more than happy to hear from me. "Hey, Lou, how's it going?"

"Okay," I answered. "Congratulations on your settlement."

"Yeah, that's pretty good news, huh? Though to tell you the truth, no one could pay me enough money to go through that experience again."

"Yes, I know," I agreed, remembering the terrible state in which Reggie had first visited our office.

"Hey, you wanna join me for dinner sometime and celebrate. I feel like I owe you a lot for all you did for me."

"Sorry, I can't—The Project has pretty strict policies about not socializing with ex-clients. But if you'd like to make a donation the money is always welcome."

"Sure," he answered brightly "I think I can manage that."

"Actually Reggie, I was calling to ask a favor." I explained to him that I was interested in finding out anything the SFPD might have on a certain Daryl Banks.

"Sure, I can probably get back to you in a day or so. That okay?"

"Yes, thanks, Reggie."

"No problem—I owe you big time."

After walking Hairy Boy I left my apartment and set off for the county jail to visit Mario. Although I had talked to him a couple of times on the phone and he had assured me that he had plenty of friends visiting and offering support, I really felt guilty that I hadn't been to visit him earlier. Of course, he had been on my mind constantly, but in the whirlwind of the last few days I had had little time to get to see him. But that was no excuse, and on my journey over there I swore to be a better friend in the future. There was no doubt in my mind that he was going to need one.

It took forty-five minutes from my arrival at the jail until I finally got to sit and talk with him. And after those forty-five minutes I was feeling angry and frustrated with the institution and its officials who gazed at me with sneering condescension, triple-checked my ID, and seemed to take delight in keeping me waiting. The whole experience left me wondering what effect being in this place twenty-four hours a day was having on Mario.

I didn't have to wonder long. Mario looked awful. His face was drawn, there were lines over his skin that I had never noticed before, and his eyes were dull, shadowed by dark gray circles. A deep frown had set in his forehead. He smiled when he saw me, but it was a half-hearted smile shaped for my benefit.

"How are you?" I asked, stretching across the table between us to touch his hand.

He shrugged. "Okay, I guess." I noticed that this time he didn't seem to have any cigarettes on him, but I could smell their stale scent on his clothes.

"I should have thought to bring you something," I said, suddenly feeling bad that I had arrived empty-handed.

"Hey, seeing you is wonderful by itself, Lou." He smiled again, this time with a little more conviction. "And anyway, people have brought me all kinds of stuff, I really don't need anything—just to get out of here, it's the worst hotel I've ever visited." It was a brave attempt at humor, but it did little to hide his depression.

"There's lots of people working on it," I said. "I expect you heard about the demonstration."

He nodded. "Yeah, and I heard about the arrests and the violence. I hate to think of people getting hurt 'cause they were protesting to support me."

"It's not your fault, Mario. People really want to see you get out of here. Everyone's doing whatever they can. The Coalition's working to raise bail for you as well."

"Yeah, I know. Gay Legal Advocates have been great, I don't know what I'd do without them. Even my family have been real supportive. Of course, they're not too thrilled to have my relationship with Peter all over the newspapers and television, but they're doing their best. They may not approve of my being gay, but they certainly don't think I'm a murderer."

"Good," I nodded, "I'm glad they're standing by you. That must mean a lot."

"Yeah, I guess…I'm just not sure that's going to do any good in the long run. I mean, if they have all that evidence…and if they can convince a jury that I'm guilty…" His voice trailed off.

I hadn't been sure whether to tell Mario about my investigation of the murder, mostly because I didn't want to raise his hopes too high. But he seemed so despondent that I thought letting him know what I'd discovered might just cheer him up.

"I can't see how anyone is possibly going to convict you," I began. "Not only is it ridiculous to think of you as a murderer, but there are plenty of others who could well have had a motive to kill Peter. And I don't just mean the bonehead responsible for those hate calls."

"What do you mean?" he asked, looking decidedly unconvinced.

"Well, since the cops seem to think they have this thing all sewn up, I thought I should make a few inquiries of my own." I winked at him. "And what I've found out so far is very interesting…"

"Go on," he said eagerly.

"Well, there's one guy who seems to be a prime suspect if this was a hate crime." I told him about Frank Frederickson, his connection to The Project, and his activities with American People for Freedom. "I've passed on the information to Jeff Easton, he's going to write a piece in *The City Reporter*. That way maybe we can at least put pressure on the cops to investigate the hate crime angle. And you never know, maybe someone will come forward with some information after reading the article."

"That's great," Mario nodded.

"Yes, well that's not all," I continued. "After you told me about Cochran's theories it started me thinking. And I guess there is a possibility that this might not be a hate crime after all. As much as I resent saying it, what Cochran said about the murder weapon makes sense—any basher in their right mind would take something with them. And why would Peter let in a stranger?"

Mario nodded in agreement. "But who else would want to kill Peter?"

"I'm not sure," I answered truthfully, "but I've discovered more than one candidate."

"Who?"

I told him everything I had found out so far. I told him about Patrick Tanner's appointment with Peter on Friday evening, about Tanner's claim that he had seen Julia outside the office, about the phone conversation I had overheard between Peter and Malcolm. Then I gave him summaries of my meetings with Julia and Malcolm, and Julia's comments about Daryl.

"So you think one of them is the murderer?" he asked.

"Possibly," I answered cautiously, "I'm just not sure. There's a chance the murder is somehow connected to the meeting that Peter arranged with Jeff Easton that night, the meeting he never made. He told Jeff he wanted to expose someone…"

"And you think whoever it was killed Peter to stop him telling?"

"Well, that would explain why Peter's keys were taken and his apartment was searched—that way the murderer could make sure nothing incriminating would be found."

"So that probably leaves Malcolm as your prime suspect," Mario concluded, "sounds like he had a lot to lose if he was outed." He rolled his eyes. "God, I can't believe what Peter would see in someone like that. He was always so, you know, concerned about being politically correct."

"That's exactly why he might have wanted to out Malcolm. I mean, they weren't exactly long-term relationship material. Once the passion died down the differences between them would've become irreconcilable. Peter might even have felt it was his duty to expose him."

"Yeah," Mario nodded, "that sounds like Peter all right." Sadness settled fleetingly in his eyes. He let out a sigh. "And what about Julia?"

"Well, she's definitely hiding something. According to Patrick Tanner she seemed pretty anxious to see Peter that night. But to tell you the truth she just doesn't strike me as being capable of murder. She was genuinely upset about Peter's death."

"Yeah, but she never showed up for his memorial service and she even pretended she didn't know anything about him being murdered when you first saw her, right?"

"Right," I conceded. "And she's definitely afraid of something. She's so bloody insecure. It's a bit odd really."

"Sounds like she could be the murderer to me," Mario stated.

"Maybe," I answered, frowning. "I just got the feeling she wanted to help me out, but something was stopping her."

"Like guilt," Mario suggested.

"Or fear," I answered thoughtfully.

"So what about this Daryl guy? I remember you didn't like him when we met him at the memorial service."

"Yeah," I answered, "he gives me the creeps. Peter never mentioned him to you?"

Mario shook his head. "The only friend from school that Peter told me about was a guy named Joshua Bryson, said they were really close. In fact Peter talked about him often. But this guy Daryl, no, he never mentioned him to me."

"Well, like I said, Julia said he'd threatened Peter. I'm checking into that to get more specifics."

Mario nodded. "And what about Patrick Tanner?"

"Tanner's definitely a suspect. He complains about Peter constantly and I found out from Donna that Peter had decided not to let him come back to The Project for services."

"Why?"

"According to Donna, Peter thought Tanner needed psychiatric help. But Tanner refused to see anyone. And to tell you the truth, Mario, I think Peter was probably right." I told him about Tanner's weird behavior when I had visited his apartment. "When Peter met with Tanner on Friday evening I think it was to tell him he couldn't come back to The Project."

"So that could've sent him over the edge and he could've ended up killing Peter, right?"

I nodded. "He could even be lying about Julia being outside The Project that evening just to take suspicion away from himself."

"You think so?" Mario asked.

"Maybe. But when I talked to Julia, I did get the feeling that she had been there, even if she's not admitting it."

Both of us sat silent for a few seconds, thoughtfully staring at the stained wooden table between us. "Hmmm, it all sounds pretty interesting," Mario said. "You have any other theories or suspects?"

"There is one other thing that's bothering me," I said.

"What's that?"

"Do you remember just before Amanda left the office for her interview that Peter requested an urgent meeting with her?"

Mario frowned. "Yeah, kind of. Why?"

"Well, I don't know if it means anything but Julia told me that when she met him for lunch Peter was furious with Amanda. He was saying how disappointed he was with her, how he felt let down or something like that."

"So?" He looked at me quizzically.

"When I asked Amanda about the meeting she had with Peter that day she got pretty defensive and the only thing she would tell me was it was a confidential personnel matter."

"Sounds pretty mysterious. But how's it linked with Peter's murder?"

I shrugged. "Oh, I don't know. But it seems weird. I mean, I've never heard of anything being a confidential personnel matter at The Project before. It makes me very curious."

"Yeah, me too," he said. "Hey, maybe they were discussing pay raises."

141

His voice was full of irony.

"Yeah, right, and I'm French."

"But I hardly think Amanda could be involved in the murder, do you, Lou?"

I shrugged. If Mario had asked me that question just last week I would have answered with a definite no, but right now I was just trying to keep an open mind. As far as I was concerned, Amanda was as much of a suspect as any of us. And until I found out what that 'confidential personnel' meeting was about, that wasn't going to change.

"So, anything else about this murder investigation of yours you have to tell me?"

"Well, there is…something…"

"What?"

"Oh, it's nothing…"

"Come on, Lou, don't get all coy with me. This is my future we're talking about here." He gestured at the bare walls and the flickering fluorescent lights.

"You'll probably think it's silly and it's not even something I can put into words. It's just that ever since I found Peter's body I feel like there's a clue at the murder scene that I'm just not seeing. I can't put my finger on it, but I just know that if I could work it out then I might even know who the murderer is. It's pretty stupid really."

Mario shook his head. "No, I believe real strongly in gut feelings like that. All I can hope is you keep racking your brains until you come up with the answer."

"Yeah, I suppose so," I answered, thinking that gut feelings were pretty damn useless if you couldn't work out what on earth they were about. For a second, I considered visiting a psychic, maybe one of those New Age gurus could help me figure out just what those feelings were about. But almost immediately, I brushed that thought away—I might have done a pretty good job of assimilating into Bay Area culture, but not that good. Like almost every other Briton, I still prided myself on having both feet planted firmly on the ground.

"I suppose you're going to have to go soon." Mario sighed as he pointed at my watch. It was almost eleven-thirty.

"Yeah, things are pretty overwhelming in the office without you and Peter."

"Speaking of the office, any news or gossip I should be made aware of?" For a moment he flashed me his mischievous smile and I had a glimpse of the happy, upbeat Mario I knew so well.

"Actually, there is one thing that might interest you."

"What?" He asked, making his eyes wide.

"Well, Donna has a girlfriend."

"No way!"

"Uh-huh, I saw her at the beach with some woman."

"That's it!" Mario exclaimed. "You've got to break me out of here immediately. I'm the one who's supposed to know all the dirt on everyone. This is not fair." He huffed and folded his arms across his chest. "So who is she?"

"When I saw her she looked a little familiar, but I don't know."

"You don't know? Well, you had better find out immediately—why don't you ask Donna who she's seeing."

I shook my head. "I saw them together at Muir beach when I went for a hike the other day. But when I called over to them they virtually ran in the opposite direction. And then, when I mentioned to Donna that I'd seen her there, she pretended like she didn't know what the hell I was talking about."

"You know why?"

"No. I suppose Donna could be annoyed with me and that's why she's being so secretive. I went out for coffee with her last week and it didn't end exactly amicably."

"How come?"

"Oh, I just asked her why she and Peter weren't getting on well. I noticed the day that Peter died that things were a bit strained between them."

"Oh, that," Mario said, making a dismissive gesture. "They had a fight a while ago, must have been at least a week before Peter died. I never did find out what it was about, though. Both of them were very tight-lipped about the whole thing. Anyway, if you can't find out who Donna's dating, I'll have to find out myself."

"From jail?" I asked incredulously.

"I have my contacts," he said, winking as he tapped a finger to his nose.

I merely shook my head and smiled.

"Hey, before you leave you better update me on what's happening with you. Aside from running around trying to solve a murder, of course."

I shrugged. "Not a lot."

"What about Alex, you been seeing much of her?" He nudged me from across the table.

"No, that didn't work out," I said, looking away.

"What do you mean, didn't work out? I thought you were real well-suited, I even told Alex so much myself."

"Yeah, she told me about your little conversation with her about me," I said, mock disapproval in my voice.

"But seriously, what happened, Lou?"

"Oh, we're just too different, that's all. I mean, she's a cop, for God's sake."

"So?"

"So, we just wouldn't get on." I shrugged.

Mario let out a sigh. "How could you possibly know that unless you give it a chance?"

"Look, I just don't want to talk about it, okay?" I said flatly.

"Lou," Mario regarded me seriously, "she really likes you, she's a nice person, she's cute. I hate to say this to you, but I think you're making a big mistake."

"What do you mean?"

"This isn't about Alex, and you know it. You've got to move on. You can't protect yourself by just not letting anyone get near you."

"Why not?"

"Because you'll end up miserable and lonely, that's why. And someone as nice as you deserves better than that." Mario said, glaring at me.

I rolled my eyes and breathed a deep sigh.

"Lou, I really think it's time to deal with stuff, don't you?" He sighed and reached over to touch my arm. "I mean you have all these issues and they're just getting in the way of—"

"Don't start that California therapy speak with me, Mario—save it for the clients. I'm fine. And anyway, it's got nothing to do with any of that. This is just about the two of us having nothing in common. All right?"

"Whatever you say, Lou." Mario shook his head, eyebrows raised, and not looking particularly convinced.

When I arrived at the office things were crazier than ever. Several people I recognized, and many others I didn't, rushed around the office, sending out faxes, making phone calls, caucusing in corners, and brewing a never-ending supply of coffee (these people seemed to treat caffeine like it was one of the major food groups).

"Amanda said she wants to see you when you get in," Jasmine called to me, muffling the mouthpiece of the phone. "She's in her office." She nodded towards the end of the hallway.

"I was just wondering how Mario's bearing up?" Amanda sat at her desk chair. The computer screen in front of her showed a page of dense text. She was surrounded by a frightening chaos of manila folders, paper, open accordion files, and what looked like the discarded wrapping for several sandwiches. Though she always insisted she knew exactly where everything was, Amanda had never kept her office particularly tidy, and in the wake of recent events things had deteriorated badly.

"He's holding up, I suppose, considering the circumstances."

She nodded her head solemnly. "Yes, it must be very hard for him. I hope he still knows he has our support. I'm just working on a press release to counter the comments Finch made yesterday. And the people out there," she gestured down the hall to the marauding hordes who had taken over the office, "are doing everything they can to bring community and press attention to our campaign. We're doing some great coalition building with some of the other communities in the city. So far we've had some great responses from homeless activists and a number of women's groups. I think we can see some really productive long-term relationships come out of this."

"That's great, Amanda, but I just hope Mario doesn't get lost in all this politicking."

"Good God, no, Lou. I am doing everything I can to highlight his case and we really are struggling to raise bail for him. I'm as concerned about Mario as you are. He is, after all, a casualty in this larger battle. Don't worry, he is very much on all our minds."

"Amanda." A voice called from down the hall. "Amanda, can you come and give us some input on this?"

Amanda stood up. "I guess I'm needed for advice again," she commented as she brushed past me.

I watched her stride down the hall and was about to follow her when I noticed something out of the corner of my eye. In the disarray and clutter of her office Amanda had left two of her file cabinets unlocked, their drawers pulled halfway open. One of them was the cabinet that housed the personnel files. If I wanted to discover the contents of the mysterious meeting between Amanda and Peter, now was my chance. A confidential personnel matter was bound to be noted in his file.

I glanced down the hall. Amanda stood in a huddle with two or three others, they pored intently over a sheet of paper. I decided to take advantage of the moment and, negotiating the jumble of papers on the floor, I strode over to the file cabinet.

The personnel files were arranged alphabetically, Peter's was at the very back. With one ear on the conversation in the hallway, I pulled out the manila folder and began leafing through the sheets of paper it contained. There was Peter's résumé, notes from two hiring interviews with him, his references, an evaluation of his work after his three month probationary period was over, and a few notes regarding changes in vacation and sick benefits. I looked through everything carefully, but there was nothing at all regarding the meeting he and Amanda had had the day he had been killed.

As I replaced the file and made my way back to my office I wondered what the absence of notes on this 'confidential personnel matter' meant. Did it mean that Amanda hadn't had the time to write anything up at the time and afterwards, since Peter had been subsequently killed, had not bothered to do so? I thought that scenario unlikely. It was my experience that she was scrupulous in keeping employee records, and since even now, after Peter's death, Amanda refused to discuss what they had talked about, it must have been serious. So why was there nothing in his file about it? It was a question for which I didn't yet have an answer.

I was beginning to feel I had far too many unanswered questions in this investigation. That evening, I sat at home watching a seventies episode of *Columbo* and hoping for a little inspiration from the bumbling, yet brilliant detective. Unfortunately, none came and a little after ten I found myself pulling out both Malcolm Devreaux's and Daryl Banks' business cards, and Julia's number which she had given me when she'd handed me her address. I just felt like I should be doing something. So I picked up the phone.

The first number I called was Daryl's. It rang several times and then a machine picked up. The message was brief and to the point, "Leave a message after the tone," it said. Even over the phone Daryl's voice gave me the creeps. Without thinking I put down the phone.

Next I called Julia. She too had a machine. "Hi, you have reached Julia Bryson at six-six-eight two-four-three-one. I'm so sorry not to be able to take your call. Please leave a message after the beep and I promise to call you back. Bye." In her message Julia sounded buoyant and confident, there was no trace of the fear I had witnessed when we spoke. What was it she was so scared of? I left no message, instead I dialed Malcolm's number. I was surprised when he picked up.

"Hi, this is Lou Spencer," I began.

"What do you want?" He didn't seemed very pleased to hear from me.

"Oh, I…er…I was just wondering if you thought over what we talked about the other night. Maybe you came up with something else that might help me find out who killed Peter." I knew it was a stupid question but I couldn't think of anything else to say.

"No, I haven't. And anyway, the police have the person responsible locked up in jail, so why don't you stop pestering me?"

"Well, I happen to believe someone else killed Peter. In fact, that someone could even be you. Peter had lunch with his friend Julia on Friday and she tells me that he talked about you a lot. He was very angry at you, it seems he might even have been prepared to tell the world about your little secret."

"Oh, don't be ridiculous."

"Well, if you did murder Peter you should be careful," I warned. "There were other people who could well have seen you leave the office—both Julia and a client of Peter's were around—"

"Look, Miss Spencer," he interrupted, "I am sure that if you had a shred of evidence to suggest that I killed Peter you would have taken it to the police already. But since I am completely innocent, I have nothing to worry about." There was a tremor in his voice that suggested that he might not be quite as unflustered as he would like to make out. "Now, if you don't mind, I have things to do." With that he put down the phone. I was left wondering if I had in fact managed to hit a nerve or if it was just my over-eager imagination.

Chapter Twenty

The next morning I was sitting at my desk sipping a cup of tea and checking through a stack of invoices when I heard a familiar voice over the intercom. Jasmine hit the buzzer and a few moments later Natalie Featherstone, the woman who had almost been strangled to death and come to The Project for services, stood in front of my desk. I was glad to see she looked a lot better than the last time I'd seen her. The string of bruises around her neck had faded to a pattern of dull blue marks, her eyes were clearer, the irises mottled only slightly red. Under her smile, however, she appeared troubled.

"I just came by to say hello," she said, shuffling her feet awkwardly. "I hope you don't mind." She eyed with uncertainty the cadre of Coalition members and volunteers who breezed through the office. "Seems like you're pretty busy right now."

"No, it's good to see you," I smiled. "It's a bit nutty here, but why don't you take a seat?" She dropped into one of the chairs across from my desk. "So how are you?"

She thrust her hands into the pockets of her jeans. "Oh, not too bad, I guess."

"You look a lot better," I said.

"Yeah, almost completely human again, huh?" She let out a short laugh before her features folded once again in distinct tension.

"Not feeling very well though?"

Her gaze dropped to the floor. "No, I'm not doing so good."

"I'm not surprised after what you went through."

"Yeah, I guess I expected to start feeling better right away, but I'm beginning to realize that I kinda need some help. Peter said if I needed anything else I should come back and see him but I heard about him getting murdered. That was awful…" She shook her head. "I guess hearing about that really upset me, too. Made me think how easily it could've happened to me." Her voice was thick, despondent.

"Yeah, that must be really hard," I said, nodding and wishing that instead of hollow platitudes I could say something to really make her feel better. Nothing came to mind.

She pursed together her cherub lips. "Peter said something about maybe seeing a therapist, said it might help in the long run." She looked away, embarrassed.

"I could give you some referrals if you'd like."

"Yeah, that…that would be great." She pulled a hesitant smile. "I mean I'd feel a lot better if you could give me some people to call. I'd rather do that than just pick names out of the yellow pages."

"No problem. Just wait a minute and I'll look some up for you." I pulled out the agency's list of referrals and resources. On a piece of paper I wrote down the names and phone numbers of two lesbian therapists. I was relieved she was interested in getting some longer-term counseling, at least that way she could really start to recover from the assault. "Here," I said handing the paper to her, "these are women we've referred to before and several clients have said they worked out well. But let me know if they're not what you need and I'll find you some others."

"Thanks, I'll probably call today." She seemed visibly relieved.

"So how's your case going? Have you spoken to the police recently?" I asked.

She breathed an exasperated sigh. "Yeah, but they don't have anything to tell me. The woman who called them didn't get a good look at the guy and without any witnesses they say it's unlikely that they'll ever find him. It makes me so furious to think he might go doing this to someone else. And maybe next time he won't get interrupted."

I nodded.

"You know what else annoys me?"

"What?"

"This happening to me has made me realize how much shit I get from people because I'm a dyke. I mean, I've always been the butch type, even when I was a kid. Always got teased and made fun of y'know. Got called tomboy as a kid, then dyke and bulldagger when I got older. And where I grew up in Minnesota there weren't exactly a lot of great lesbian role models. That's why I came to San Francisco. And now I find out I'm not even safe here. Makes me wish sometimes that I could pass as straight, y'know." She looked down the length of her short, broad body. "Not that I'd ever be very successful at that," she snorted. "It's not that I'm ashamed of what I am, I'd just like to get less hassle for it."

I nodded, considering Natalie's remarks. It would be hard to mistake her for anything other than a lesbian. And it wasn't just the short hair, flannel shirt and jeans that gave it away. It was in her body language, her gestures, the way she spoke. "But you shouldn't be hard on yourself, Natalie. It's not your fault that people are so homophobic."

"Yeah," she said, wrinkling up her button nose. "But I can't help but think that being taken for a straight girl sometimes might make life a lot easier. Yeah, there's a lot to be said for passing when you need it."

Natalie's words struck a chord and suddenly an enormous realization dawned on me. It was like I could finally see something that, now I saw it, had been staring me in the face. I nodded as Natalie continued to talk but my thoughts were racing. Perhaps now I could finally get some answers about Peter's murder.

"...so, thanks for these phone numbers," Natalie said, folding the piece of paper I had given her into her back pocket. "I really appreciate your help." She pushed herself up from the chair. "Better go now, though. I'm sure you got a lot of work to do."

"Oh, er, yeah, but I'm glad you came by. And if those referrals don't work out, just let me know. Okay?"

"Okay," she nodded as she rose to leave.

As soon as Natalie was gone I picked up the phone. "City Models," Linda Morgenstein answered. "How can I help you?"

"Hi, Linda, I don't know if you remember me. My name's Lou Spencer, I came to see Julia..."

"Oh, yes, of course, you're the one with the dead friend, right?" She said cheerfully.

"Yes, that's me," I answered, shaking my head. It never ceased to amaze me how much entertainment some people could get out of others' misfortunes. Linda was probably one of those rubberneckers who held up traffic to gape at gory road accidents, or tuned in to every natural disaster shown on CNN. She really needed to get a life.

"How can I help you?" she asked eagerly.

"I need to get in touch with Julia, can you tell me where she is today?"

"Your guess is as good as mine," she said acidly. "She's supposed to be on a shoot this morning but she never showed up. The photographer's going crazy and the head of the agency is about to fire her— I mean we're talking big money on this project. If you want to get a hold of her you might try calling her at home, but you probably won't have much luck there, she's not picking up her phone."

"Oh, well, thanks."

"Sure. And by the way, if you do manage to get a hold of her, tell her she better come into work prepared for big trouble. She's really put her career on the line this time."

I did try Julia at home but like Linda said, she wasn't picking up her phone. I thought of leaving a message but decided against it. What I wanted to talk about needed to be discussed in person.

It wasn't until after six that I was finally able to get away from the office. After going home to pick up my car, I drove to the Inner Sunset with the conviction that I was finally going to get what Lieutenant Columbo would call 'a break in the case'.

I listened to *BBC World Service* on the way over. The news readers might have annoyingly pompous accents, but you do get the best international news from them. And it helps me stay in touch with events in Britain, which at times, can be quite a laugh. For instance, the day I found out that they were undergoing a heatwave in which traffic nationwide was brought to a standstill because several motorways had *melted*! Apparently, vehicles had been literally sticking to the asphalt—brings a whole new meaning to the term gridlock.

I was giggling all the way over to Julia's, but when I turned the corner onto her street, I abruptly turned the radio off. Outside her pink stucco apartment building there was a swarm of cops, police cars, and a couple of ambulances. Distorted voices rung out over the static of radios, flashing lights blinked on the top of the chaotically parked vehicles. I drove by neighbors gaping from their driveways, and pulled up by a group of excited children who ran along the sidewalk, laughing, screaming and pointing gun-shaped fingers at one another.

I walked towards Julia's building, a feeling of nausea rising in my stomach as I caught some of the whispered conversations around me. "…lovely girl, she was, very sweet…" "They say she was murdered, shot, I never heard a thing…" "…worked as a model, I guess, at least that's what her neighbor says…"

As I approached two men emerged from the building, they were carrying a black body bag. I stood still. The ground started to move and swell under me, at the edges of my eyes I could see bright, silvery lights. I felt lightheaded, extremely lightheaded…

I reached out to lean against the front gate of one of the neighboring houses and took some long, deep breaths. I felt sad and sick and angry all at the same time. The murder of two people I knew in two weeks was overwhelming. And no one needed to confirm for me that the latest murder victim was Julia, it made complete sense.

"Why Miss Spencer, funny we should bump into one another here." It was Inspector Cochran. His hands thrust into the pockets of a dark, wrinkled raincoat, he strode towards me. "You live round here?" he asked.

"No, I'm visiting someone," I answered warily, pushing my hair back from my face and trying to compose my expression.

"Someone who lives here?" He asked, pointing to the apartment building.

"Julia Bryson." I tried to sound casual.

He frowned and pushed his hands deeper into his pockets. "She a friend of yours?" He asked gruffly.

"An acquaintance."

He coughed and looked away before turning back to me. "Well, I'm sorry to tell you this, Miss Spencer, but she's been shot, murdered."

I didn't have to pretend shock, I was still reeling from the knowledge of Julia's death. My throat was dry and my heart beat furiously. Tears welled into my eyes, with the back of my sleeve I rubbed them quickly away. "I think her death is connected to Peter's murder," I told him shakily.

He let out a sharp laugh. "I hardly think so, Miss Spencer. This was a robbery. The place was turned upside down, valuables were taken. It looks like the victim walked in, disturbed the intruder and ended up with a bullet in her brain. Of course, if you have another theory..." His tone was mocking. "I mean, maybe you think it was another hate crime."

"It's a possibility."

"Why, this acquaintance of yours, she a lesbian or something?"

"Or something." I answered.

He narrowed his eyes. "What do you mean?"

"Julia Bryson was a transsexual."

"That's ridiculous."

I shook my head. "No, it's true."

"But I just saw her, saw the pictures of her on her walls, she couldn't be...I mean can't you tell that she, I mean he...well, I know they do surgery but..." I must admit I got a certain satisfaction seeing Cochran stumbling so clumsily over his words.

"Maybe you should look a little more thoroughly around her apartment, there's probably something there that will tell you that Julia was born Joshua Bryson."

This time Cochran said nothing, just looked at me open-mouthed and said, "Wait here."

Chapter Twenty-One

"How did you know?" Cochran demanded as he emerged from Julia's apartment and marched across the neat little lawn to where I waited on the sidewalk. The street was quieter now, the ambulances and most of the police cars had departed and only a few curious neighbors remained, the rest having retired inside where, in the comfort of their own living rooms, they could continue to watch cops, murder and violent crime on prime time television.

"I put several things together," I answered. "And through meeting her a couple of times. Julia was the woman Patrick Tanner saw outside The Project the night Peter was murdered. The one I tried to tell you about."

"Yeah, right," he said, raising his dull eyes skyward, "and Tanner denies being anywhere near your offices. Now what you trying to say, that this Julia or Joshua person murdered Peter Williams?"

I shrugged. "I'm just trying to tell you what I know."

"Still trying to get that little friend of yours off the hook?" he snarled. "Well, you might as well give it up, Miss Spencer, because we have enough evidence to lock him up and throw away the damn key."

"But I'm trying to help," I protested. "I know Mario didn't do it."

"Look," he said, reaching out a fat hand to grab hold of my wrist, "I don't need help like yours. And if you don't stop interfering in this case I'm gonna start investigating you as an accessory." He pushed his face up to mine. "Now goodnight, Miss Spencer." He said, dropping my wrist and turning away.

I was awakened the next morning by the telephone shrilling at my bedside. Eyes still closed, I reached over and searched blindly for the hand set. "Hello." My voice came out slow and slurring.

"What the hell is going on, Lou?" It was Mario, he sounded close to hysterical. "I just got hauled over the coals by that goddamn Cochran again. He kept asking me questions about that model that came to the office to have lunch with Peter. You know, the one I saw on the front of that magazine."

I immediately sat up and tried to shake myself awake. So Cochran had been asking Mario questions about Julia's murder. Maybe he'd taken me seriously after all. Maybe I'd convinced him to search for links between the two murders. Maybe he would see the light and release Mario, maybe I wouldn't have to continue trying to look into things myself...

"Lou, are you there?"

"Yes, sorry, I was just thinking—"

"Well, what's the deal with this Julia?"

"She was murdered," I answered.

"What?"

"They found her body yesterday at her apartment, she was shot." I rubbed sleep from my eyes and let out a loud yawn.

Mario said nothing.

"I think her murder is linked to Peter's," I explained. "And that might be why Cochran was talking to you. It could be that he's having his doubts that you killed Peter."

"I don't think so," Mario said bitterly. "At least not from what he was saying to me. Seems more likely at this point that he thinks I somehow spirited myself out of jail and killed Julia myself. That guy really has it in for me. Anyway, what makes you think the two murders are connected?"

"Remember how I said I thought Julia was afraid, how I thought she was hiding something?"

"Uh-huh."

"Well, I figured out what she was afraid of."

"What?"

"She was a transsexual, afraid of being outed."

"Are you serious?" Mario sounded almost as shocked as Cochran had. "Wow...Cochran never mentioned anything about that."

"Well, it's true. I figured it out yesterday. It made me realize why she was so uptight. She knew something about Peter's murder, maybe even knew who it was that killed him. But she was probably afraid that if she came forward then the police or the press would go sniffing around into her personal life. Pretty soon they would've found out that Julia Bryson was really Joshua Bryson, and that'd be the end of her big modeling career."

"Joshua Bryson...but that's the name of the friend that Peter had at Berkeley. He talked about him to me several times..."

"Yeah, I know. That's how I worked out who Julia was. I always knew there was something about her that was...different. There was just this feeling I got from her that there was more than showed on the surface. And when we talked to Daryl and he said he had no idea who she was even though they were both supposed to be friends of Peter's at Berkeley, well, that really intrigued me."

"Yeah, Daryl was pretty insistent that he would have known her," Mario commented.

"Well, he didn't know her because when they were at school together Julia was still Joshua."

"But I still don't get how you figured this out."

"It was when I went to Julia's apartment that I really began to wonder. I remember looking at the photographs of her on the walls—she has them everywhere—and she made some comment about being really insecure about her success and then she said something like, "I suppose that's just the way life goes for someone like me" and I just kept wondering what she meant by that. But it wasn't 'til I called her answering machine the night before last that I got the most important clue. In her message she gives her full name—Julia Bryson. It didn't ring a bell with me until yesterday morning when I was talking to a client who came by. She was saying about how hard it was that she couldn't pass as straight and for some reason everything just clicked. I suddenly realized that Julia and Joshua had the same name, I thought about what Daryl had said and put that together with my own intuition. I figured out what Julia was hiding. She didn't want anyone to know about her sex change—she was so invested in passing that she was too afraid to come forward with any information she might have. It just made sense."

Mario was quiet for a few moments, as if digesting this new information. "But didn't it ever cross your mind that she might have been the murderer? I mean, if Peter knew that she was a transsexual then he could have threatened to out her. That could be a perfect motive. It could even have been Julia he was planning to expose in *The City Reporter*. Julia could be the murderer after all and maybe the fact that she was shot yesterday is some sort of weird coincidence." He sounded distressed. "And if that's true it means Peter's killer is dead and there's not much chance of me getting out of this damn jail."

"But I'm sure Julia didn't kill Peter. Don't ask me why, I just know it in my bones." It was another gut feeling, intuition, call it what you will. But I knew I had to go with it.

"But you think she was at the office when Peter was murdered?" asked Mario.

"Yes. Of course I'm just speculating, but I think after she saw Tanner outside the office, she probably waited a while longer, hoping that Peter would come outside."

"Why do you think she wanted to see him?"

"I'm not sure but something she said to me makes me think that Peter actually was thinking about outing her."

"What did she say?"

I tried to remember Julia's exact words when I had been at her apartment. "Something about Peter being a good friend of hers who'd never turned his back on her until now."

"But then it would make perfect sense if Julia killed him."

"You're right," I agreed, "it's always a possibility. But I just can't believe that the fact that she's been murdered now is a coincidence. I think Julia was waiting to talk to Peter that Friday night, but before she was able to someone else went up into The Project office and killed him. And of course at some point, maybe not until she saw the news of Peter's death in the papers on Monday, she put two and two together and figured out that the person she saw go into the office had to be Peter's murderer."

"So if what you say is true, then how did the killer know that Julia was there? How did they know that they had to get rid of her?"

"At this point I'm not really sure," I answered. But the question made me feel decidedly uneasy, it was something that I intended to find out.

Mario let out a loud sigh. "God, this whole thing is such a nightmare. Two people dead, me in jail. You need to be careful, Lou, whoever is responsible for this is pretty damn scary. Don't go taking any unnecessary risks, okay?"

"Don't worry, I won't. But I'm still determined to do my best to get to the bottom of this. I want to get you out of there as soon as possible."

"Now that I like to hear." He paused. "Hey, while I have you on the phone, I might as well let you know that I found out who it is that Donna's dating."

"Really?"

"Yeah, and you're not going to like this, Lou."

"What do you mean?" I asked, puzzled.

"She's seeing one of her clients."

Now it was my turn to be shocked. My mouth literally dropped open. It was a several seconds before I spoke. "You're kidding me."

"No, it's for real. From a very reliable source. Apparently they've been seeing one another for over a month now."

"Well, no wonder I thought I recognized that woman at the beach, I must have seen her in the office. But surely Donna would know better than that…"

"Well, you'd think so, but I can assure you that she doesn't."

"Great. Well at least we can be thankful that Peter isn't around to find out, you know what a stickler he always was for procedure. He'd go nuts if he found out Donna was violating personnel policy like that."

"I'm not so sure that he didn't know," Mario said.

"You think so?"

"Well, it would certainly explain their argument and the icy atmosphere between them, wouldn't it?"

"I suppose you're right," I answered.

Later that morning as I walked down Castro Street towards work, the events of the last twenty-four hours spun through my mind. Mario had posed a troubling question. If, as I speculated, Julia had been killed because she knew something, how had the murderer known that she had been outside the office that night? It was hardly something she would have been likely to broadcast. Of course, she could have been trying to extort money from the killer, but that didn't seem very likely. She was on the way up in a career that paid very well so I was pretty sure that she didn't need money. And besides, there was my instinct that she wasn't a criminal. There were two other alternatives—one was that the killer had actually bumped into her at the office that night. Patrick Tanner had already mentioned the fact that he had seen her, it was possible that someone else could have too. The second alternative was one I did not like to think about. The night before Julia's murder I had called Malcolm and mentioned that Julia had been outside The Project when Peter was killed. Only now did I realize what a stupid idea that had been. If Malcolm was the killer I'd virtually told him he needed to get rid of Julia to ensure his own safety. I shuddered when I thought I might be responsible for Julia's death.

And without Julia around to share what she knew, finding the murderer was going to be very difficult—she had really been my only hope of getting somewhere with this case. Now that she was gone I didn't know where to turn. And suddenly it seemed that the killer had upped the stakes, first by using a letter-opener, perhaps in a moment of passion or anger, but had now graduated to deliberate, cold-blooded murder. Julia had been shot in the head and the killer had taken care to make it look like a robbery. He or she was obviously willing to go to great lengths when they felt threatened. I felt the hairs over my skin rise as I contemplated dealing with someone who was so ruthless. The fact that they had killed the first time could quite possibly have been shocking to them, but the second was probably easier, and the third…I decided that Mario was right to caution me. If I was seen to be a threat, I could quite easily become the next murder victim.

Chapter Twenty-Two

"Lou, we got another one of those goddamn calls," Jasmine announced as I walked into my office.

"What did they say this time?" I asked, sighing.

"Oh, the usual, something about how all us fucking perverts should die."

"Great. Well, can you make a police report, and give Inspector Cochran a call, too?" It wasn't like I held out much hope that another threat was going to persuade Cochran that Peter's murder was a hate crime (in fact, I was sure the entire staff could be gunned down by the Ku Klux Klan, white robes and all, and Cochran would still be looking for other 'likely suspects'), but I wanted to make sure he knew we were still getting the calls.

As I sorted through my messages I was surprised to find one from Malcolm Devreaux. He wanted me to call him. The number he'd left connected me to a receptionist at City Hall. It took her a good five minutes to locate Malcolm and put me through.

"Hey, Malcolm, it's Lou Spencer returning your call. How's it going? Come out of the closet yet?" Maybe I was being mean, but I just couldn't resist the temptation to bait him.

"Very funny, Miss Spencer, very funny indeed." He didn't sound in the least bit amused. "I called because I need to talk to you…there's something I'd like to discuss."

"Well, good because I want to talk to you, too. How about tonight?"

"Tonight's fine. What about eight o'clock at that same bar we met in before?"

"I can't wait. That was such a lovely little place, and we did have such a fabulous time."

"I'll see you at eight," he said stonily.

"Hey, Lou. Oh hi, Jasmine." Donna strolled into the front office at close to half past ten, hands stuffed deep into the pockets of her jeans. She had

158

called in late again, mentioning something about a rescheduled doctor's appointment. "You guys seen *The City Reporter* yet? The front page has a big spread about the protest outside the Hall of Injustice and something about who the mayor might appoint to that vacant supervisorial seat. 'Course I'm more interested in browsing through the personals myself, but I know what political animals you are in here." She tossed the paper onto my desk with a mischievous grin.

"Yeah, I'd like to see it," said Jasmine. She looked up eagerly from the computer. "You never know, maybe they'll have a picture of me being hauled away by the cops." She was close to rubbing her hands in excitement.

As Jasmine unfolded the paper, I thought about what Mario had told me earlier. The idea of Donna having a relationship with a client did not make me happy. We had pretty strict policies around conduct with clients, and intimate relationships were definitely on the list of grounds for dismissal. But where did that leave me now? What was the right thing to do? Mario seemed to think that Peter had known what was going on. I wondered what course of action he had considered. The fact that he'd had a row with her just a few weeks ago made me think he'd decided to confront her. Is that what I should do? Or should I take it straight to Amanda? If I did, Donna would be furious, she'd probably want to kill me—

The phrase stopped my thoughts short. Did Donna find out that Peter was planning to tell Amanda about her affair with a client? And if so did she make up her mind to try to stop him? I couldn't help thinking that one very effective way of doing that would be to kill him.

"If anybody wants me I'll be in my office." As Donna left us, flipping her long locks over her shoulder, she flashed us both her sweetest, warmest smile and instantly I felt ridiculously paranoid for even thinking that she could have killed Peter. This murder investigation stuff was getting to be too much and I was beginning to see killers everywhere. It was just plain silly to imagine Donna as a murderer. She might be capable of breaking person-nel policy by dating a client but I was almost positive she couldn't really do any harm to someone. Then again, if she had fought with Peter and lost her temper...

"Hey, Lou, you seen this piece by Jeff Easton?" Jasmine waved *The City Reporter* towards me, pointing to an article heading the inside page. "It's about this guy, someone who bashed one of Peter's clients. Apparently he's an agitator on the far right and he's even said threatening things about The Project. It says here how the cops should consider him as a suspect in the murder. That should help Mario's case, huh?"

I hope so, I thought to myself.

"Can I see that?" Amanda strode into the office and gestured towards the copy of *The City Reporter*. Jasmine handed it over with noticeable reluctance.

"This information about Frederickson, it's very interesting," Amanda said as she scrutinized the article. "I wouldn't be surprised if a hate monger like him was behind Peter's murder. I always thought there might be a possibility that one of the perpetrators involved in Peter's cases could be responsible for his death. It would certainly make sense. I should make some calls, see if the cops plan to follow up on this." She finished reading the piece and turned to the front page. Her eyes moved back and forth through the two main articles. After a few moments she gave a slow, satisfied nod. "This is more like it," she commented.

"What?" asked Jasmine.

"I think we've really started to turn the tide of Finch's hate. All this pressure we've put on this week, it's really starting to pay off. This piece…" She held up the paper so we could both see the heading over one of the articles. It read, *Mayor thinks twice about new supervisor*. "…it says that Mayor Finch is re-thinking who he might appoint to replace Patricia Jones. Apparently there's some rumors going round City Hall that he's trying to find someone acceptable to the gay and lesbian community. He's finally coming to his senses and realizing he can't keep on alienating our community."

"That's good news," I said, "and it's good to know that all the work you've been doing is finally paying off, Amanda."

"Yes, it certainly is. I just hope people appreciate what a difference I've been able to make. Finch's backtracking doesn't come out of a vacuum, you know." She quickly leafed through the rest of the paper, pausing once or twice to scan its pages before returning it to Jasmine. "Well, better get back to work, there's still plenty to be done. By the way, Lou, we're working hard on raising bail for Mario but right now it looks like we're going to come up short. So get the word out there, we need all the help we can get."

When Jasmine had finished looking through *The Reporter* she passed it on to me. I read the main articles and then leafed casually through the rest of the paper until I turned to page ten. There I was shocked to see a photograph of Julia under the headline, "Secret life of model fatally exposed." It was only to be expected that the story of Julia's murder be picked up by the press, and considering the standards of *The City Reporter*, I was surprised they hadn't tried to give it a more sordid slant and plant it on page one. The article they had run was journalism á la *National Enquirer*, all gossipy phrases and lurid insinuations. There were few facts beyond what the police were saying, and that wasn't much. Cochran was quoted, still sticking to his idea that the murder had happened in the course of a robbery. And no one else connected with the case, it seemed, realized that Julia had been a close friend of Peter's, or if they had, they'd deemed this to be a fact of no significance to either case.

At one-thirty I decided I needed to escape the tumult of the office and get lunch. I bought a sandwich and hurried on to my apartment. I wanted to get home in time to give Hairy Boy a decent run through the park. Walking with my head to the ground, focused on my swiftly-moving feet, it wasn't until I heard my name spoken in soft, smooth tones and I looked up to see the midnight blue of an SFPD uniform that I realized I was almost face to face with Alex Ramon.

"How are you, Lou?" She smiled awkwardly as her arms swung at her sides. She looked about as uncomfortable as I felt.

"Okay. How are you?" I tried my best to sound casual.

"I'm doing okay, I guess."

"Well, good, that's good." I found myself nodding and scrambling for something else to say. The embarrassment of just standing there in silence was too much to bear. "Things are really busy at the office, I've been swamped. You know, the usual clients as well as all this stuff related to Mario and the er...demo on Sunday. There were a lot of arrests and so there's a lot of work to be done on that."

She nodded slowly. "I guess you guys are pretty crazed. It must be real stressful."

"Yes," I said absently, "it is. Anyway, look, I have to go." I glanced at my watch. "I've got to get back and feed my dog." I gestured up Eighteenth Street towards my apartment and began backing away.

"Actually I've got to go this way myself." Alex began to walk with me, matching my quickening pace. "Got to take a report of petty vandalism from the owner of the laundromat down the street. Poor woman, I must talk to her at least every other day. Those high school kids really do give her the run around."

It was so painful, the way both of us were trying to act normal—and both of us doing a rather pathetic job of it, I have to say. As we walked for several seconds in silence, I even entertained the fantasy of leaping out in front of an oncoming MUNI bus—a bit of an overdramatic gesture to get me out of the situation, but I'll admit it, I was feeling desperate.

"By the way," Alex finally spoke, "I wanted to let you know what I'd found out about Frederickson."

"You've been making inquiries?"

"Not me, actually, but the friend of mine in Hate Crimes. They're just interested in keeping an eye on his activities. Apparently, the night Peter was murdered Frederickson has a solid alibi—he was at some Survivalist conference in Idaho, stayed there from Friday afternoon all through the weekend."

"Damn," I exclaimed. "I was really hoping that might be a lead that would help out Mario."

"I'm sorry, Lou. I was hoping it might help him too. Say, how is Mario?"

"Oh, holding up under the circumstances. He has a lot of support but I think he feels pretty scared. It's not easy being locked up in the county jail."

"He's still in the jail?" Alex looked shocked. "How come he's not out on bail?"

I shrugged. "His family hasn't any money and the Coalition's been trying to raise it for him but so far we've come up short. I'm not sure how much they need but it's quite a substantial sum."

"That's too bad. It must be really hard on him."

"Yes, it is."

"Well, this is where I have to take my report from," she said, stopping outside the door of The Golden Gate Wash'n Dry. Through the window I could see an elderly woman in a floral nylon overall, an anxious expression on her heavily made-up face. She paced the floor, apparently awaiting Alex's arrival. "It was good to see you, Lou," Alex said before pushing open the door.

"Yes, you too," I replied without thinking, but realizing, to my surprise, that was really how I felt.

I returned from lunch to find Patrick Tanner occupying one of the chairs in front of my desk and looking his usual happy-go-lucky self. He was frowning over a magazine, gripping the pages tight with both hands. When he saw me he tossed it aside and leapt to his feet. "You done anything on my case yet?" he demanded, pushing his face so close I got a great look at the nose hairs sprouting out his flaring nostrils.

I took a step back. "I've written some letters, but so far I haven't heard anything." Following up on my promise to Tanner, I'd sent letters to several managers at MUNI. I'd also written to the mayor and several of the city supervisors about Tanner's case. I didn't expect to get replies for a while, I doubted Tanner's dilemma was at the top of anyone's priority list—except, of course, his own.

"Well, let me know soon as you hear. I want to know what those assholes have to say for themselves."

"I'll let you know, Patrick," I nodded. "Now is there something else I can help you with?"

"I need to see an advocate." He stamped his foot on the floor, like a small child about to throw a tantrum. "She," he pointed an accusing finger at Jasmine, "said that Donna's out to lunch. I need to see someone now." He set his hands on his skinny hips and glared at me.

At that moment Donna's footfalls on the stairs announced her return. She bounced into the office. "Any messages?" she asked.

"No, but Patrick's here to see you," I said, gesturing towards Tanner who stood hunched by my desk.

"I need to see you right away," he barked.

Donna pulled a conciliatory smile. "I'm sorry, Patrick, but I can't see you right now. I have a meeting scheduled in just a few minutes. But I'm sure we can make an appointment for tomorrow."

Patrick Tanner's face turned crimson, his eyes bulging out so far they looked like they might pop right out of their sockets. "What do you mean, you can't see me?"

Donna kept her voice calm. "I already have a meeting scheduled, I'm sorry, Patrick, but I do have other things..."

Donna's words died in her throat as Tanner lunged forward, and with a flat, skinny hand made a swipe at the side of her face. Fortunately, she anticipated the blow, ducked, and Tanner was sent stumbling forward as his arm swept through the air above Donna's head. At the same time, Jasmine and I sprang toward Tanner, grabbed and attempted to restrain him. He wasn't strong, but his energy was immense, and we just had to hang on until his stamina gave out. He flailed and thrashed about like a wild bull, shaking Jasmine and me round the room like a couple of bare-back rodeo riders. All the time he kept yelling. "You people don't give a goddamn shit about me. First that fucking Peter, now you. I'll show you I can stand up for myself. I'll show you."

Finally, he seemed to run out of steam and we were able to push him back into one of the chairs where he collapsed like a rag doll. All three of us stood over him, breathless and watching for his next move. We needn't have worried, however, since it was apparent that he was completely sapped. In a few moments he began to let out loud, gasping sobs.

I turned to Donna. "Are you all right?"

She nodded, pushing her hair back from her face and straightening her disheveled clothes.

"What should we do?" Jasmine whispered, giving the weeping Tanner a wary glance. "You think he's really flipped? Maybe we should get him, you know, committed or something. Isn't that what you do with people like that?"

"I think he's just in a lot of pain," Donna said. "I'll cancel my meeting and talk to him."

"Have you completely lost your marbles?" I breathed, moving away from Tanner in the hope that he wouldn't hear me. "The man just attacked you. He could be dangerous. And I don't know if it's escaped your memory, but Peter was killed in this office only days ago. For all we know, it could be Patrick here who was responsible."

Donna laughed. "Oh don't be silly, Lou, we know that was a hate crime. I know Patrick wouldn't really hurt me."

"Donna, he just tried. I don't like the idea of you seeing him alone."

"Okay, then, I'll leave my door open and then you can be sure everything is okay. I just can't leave him in this state, can I?"

I shrugged. As far as I was concerned Jasmine wasn't too far from the mark, maybe he did need to be committed, or at least sent to bed with a nice cup of cocoa and a couple of very strong sedatives.

"Look, I know he didn't mean to hurt me. I'll see him in my office, okay?"

"It's your decision but I really don't feel good about this, Donna. I don't see how you can overlook the fact that he just attacked you. I mean, look at me, I'm still shaking." I held up my hand, it was indeed trembling. "I don't want to have to intervene like that again."

"You won't," she said curtly. "Believe me, it'll be fine." She moved towards Tanner who was still bent over and crying. She placed a hand on his shuddering shoulder. "Now, Patrick, why don't you come with me and we can talk about what's going on."

As I watched Tanner get up and shuffle after Donna, I couldn't help thinking that it was going to take more than just talking to solve all his problems.

That evening, when I got home, there was a message from Reggie Johnson on my answering machine. He said he had come up with some information about Daryl Banks. I called him right back. "I don't know why you want to know about this guy, Lou," he began, "but he sounds like a nasty piece of work. If you want my advice you should steer well clear." He then proceeded to go over the extensive information he had gathered. Over a period of two years Daryl had been arrested on four separate occasions in Berkeley and Oakland on charges ranging from vandalism to assault with a deadly weapon. In all four cases the complainant had been Peter Williams and each time after a few days the charges had been dropped. "Seems like Peter was reluctant to turn his friend over to the law. If it wasn't two guys involved, I'd swear this was one of them classic domestic violence situations" Reggie commented.

"And it still could be," I said. "Don't think that it doesn't happen among same-sex couples as well."

"But I thought it was just straights…"

"No, Reggie," I said firmly, "believe me, it happens among gays and lesbians, too." If it hadn't been for Justine, I, too, might have been skeptical of the existence of gay domestic violence. But there's nothing like first hand experience to open your mind.

"Oh, well, anyway, I guess Peter Williams finally got sick of being the victim. He took out a restraining order against this guy, sometime in May."

"Were there any incidents after that?" I asked.

"None that were reported," Reggie answered. "Seems like it did the trick."

Maybe it did. Or maybe it had provoked Daryl to a more serious crime—murder. As much as I balked at the prospect, I decided I needed to talk to Daryl Banks again. But before I could do that I had to head over to the Hotsy Totsy to make my meeting with Malcolm.

Chapter Twenty-Three

Thursday was not a busy night for The Hotsy Totsy. Malcolm was the sole occupant of the tattered, vinyl-covered stools that flanked the bar. Two guys sat in a corner, leaning back in their chairs, feet propped on the table as they swigged beer from bottles and stared at a television bracketed to the wall. It was tuned to MTV with the volume turned down. Neither of the men seemed to notice me as I entered; they were too busy staring at the TV screen and the heavy metal band who were frantically throwing their instruments into a swimming pool filled with bikini-clad women.

"We have to stop meeting like this," I commented as I slid onto the stool next to Malcolm.

The bartender strode over and scowled in my direction. "Mineral water?" he snarled. I nodded, making a mental note to myself that if Malcolm and I were to meet again, then I would pick the venue. As far as I was concerned, the fact that the bartender remembered what I drank was not a good sign—one more visit and he'd be thinking of me as a regular. And maybe I'd get my forearms tattooed and start appreciating heavy metal music just to fit in. The thought was scary.

"So, what's up?" I asked after my drink had been slammed in front of me. Malcolm shrugged and downed what was remaining in his glass. Once again whiskey seemed to be his beverage of choice. He signaled to the bartender and another was duly delivered. As he wrapped his fingers around the glass, I squinted through the half-light to study his face. He looked tired, in fact haggard was a more appropriate description. His carefully nurtured tan had faded to a drab yellow, his hair was dull and uncombed. Despite the expensive suit, the poise and authority were gone. Instead he looked sad and defeated. The transformation was disconcerting.

"Are you okay?" I asked.

Malcolm turned slowly to regard me through glazed, reddened eyes. An inane grin stretched slowly across his lips as he slurred, "hello Misssspencer." He was drunk. And not just tipsy or a little bit high, but, as we put it back in England, completely bloody plastered.

"How long have you been here?"

"Since six, maybe a little earlier."

"And how many of those have you drunk?" I pointed to his glass.

He rested his elbow on the bar and leaned on his hand. "Don't know, maybe ten, twelve, twenty. It's hard to say," he said, the silly grin becoming wider.

"Don't you think you've had enough."

His hand slipped from under his chin and his face almost hit the bar. "Probably." He tried to straighten himself up but it seemed beyond his capabilities, as if his broad shoulders and back were too heavy for him to support. He hunched over the bar and leaned once again on his hand. "I need to talk to you." He gave me a watery, unfocused look. "It's very important."

"Well, good, because I need to talk to you, too. It's about Julia."

"Yes…Julia." He looked wistful as he reached over to take another swig of his drink. He drained his glass and the bartender moved expectantly towards us. "I think he's had enough," I said flatly. The bartender lifted his upper lip in an Elvis-style snarl, stuffed his hands into his pockets, and swaggered to the other end of the bar where he joined the two guys staring at a noiseless MTV video. Now they were watching a rap star and another group of half-naked women. This time the women were confined in cages, gripping the bars and writhing in time to the thudding bass. It warmed the cockles of my heart to see misogyny was alive, kicking and being beamed into millions of televisions all over the world. I turned my attention back to Malcolm. "What do you know about Julia?"

Malcolm pursed his lips and looked down at the bar to study the pattern of scratches and stains over its surface. "It's just such a…waste of young life, and for what? It can't be worth it, don't you think?"

"Worth what?"

"I tried to warn him…I tried to tell him. But then… it's all my fault. I just couldn't help it…I really couldn't, you know." He started to cry, tears flowing silently down his cheeks and dripping from his chin to the bar.

I stared at Malcolm. What was he trying to say in these drunken ramblings? Was he confessing to a murder or was he just trying to impart some information? It was impossible to tell. But what was obvious was that he knew something important. He knew that Peter's and Julia's murders were connected. What he knew could well be the key to finding their killer. Maybe he was their killer. I should try to push him now while he was drunk, after all, he might tell me something that he might not reveal sober.

"And now I don't know what I should do…" He gave me a desperate look then suddenly collapsed to slump over the bar where he continued to cry in loud, heaving sobs. While I watched him I reflected that this was the second time in less than twenty-four hours that I had seen a grown man cry. Who knew, maybe all this men's movement stuff really was helping them get in touch with their feelings. I glanced down to the end of the bar where the two customers and the bartender were eyeing Malcolm with a mixture of puzzlement and derision. Unlike me, they didn't seem particularly impressed by his ability to spontaneously express emotions.

I sat on the bar stool, swinging my legs and waiting for Malcolm to calm down. I was about to ask if he had a handkerchief when I realized that the sobbing had stopped only to be replaced by loud, throat-gurgling snores. He had fallen asleep.

"Malcolm," I said, taking hold of his shoulder and shaking him. "Malcolm, wake up." He responded by shaking my hand away and snoring even louder. "Great," I sighed, "this is all I need." I signaled over to the bartender. "Can you call me a cab?" I asked.

"You're a cab," he answered, letting out a loud guffaw and throwing his head back so I could see the impressive array of gold-fillings in his back teeth.

"Very funny," I said. "Now can you call a cab? My friend here seems to need some transportation."

"Some people got no sense of humor," he muttered as he pulled a telephone from under the bar. Yeah, and some people are complete idiots, I wanted to say. But recognizing I wasn't in entirely friendly territory, I thought it wise to keep my comments to myself.

When the cab arrived I managed to rouse Malcolm enough so that he was able to stagger inside and inform the driver of his address. If he fell asleep during the journey, which I judged to be more likely than not, then as far as I was concerned that was the cab driver's problem.

As I drove home I thought over what Malcolm had revealed in his incoherent ramblings. None of it made very much sense, but what was clear was that Malcolm Devreaux had something on his conscience. And it was also clear that I had to find a way to make him tell me what that was.

I managed to fit in a much too brief visit with Mario before I went into work on Friday morning. He was anxious and exhausted and chain-smoked through almost the entire visit. After I informed him of the progress of my investigation, however, he seemed a little more cheerful. Both Daryl and Malcolm were beginning to look like very strong suspects, and as Mario pointed out, if worse came to worse and his case went to trial then at least his defense could use what I had found out to help cast that all-important 'reasonable doubt' on Mario's guilt. I left him in good spirits and with the promise that I would visit him again as soon as I could.

Donna accosted me in the hallway as I made my way towards my office. "Lou, I need to talk to you. Do you have some time now?" Her tone was clipped.

"Well, I just got in…"

"This won't take long."

"Okay," I said reluctantly.

She turned around, and in her heavy leather boots stomped down the hall to her office. I followed close behind. Leaving the door ajar, she turned to face me, anger was painted all over her face. "I cannot believe what happened yesterday! I cannot believe you questioned my judgment about how to deal with a client! How dare you do that, and in front of the client and a volunteer? As far as I'm concerned, your job here is Office Manager. I'm the advocate, I deal with clients." Her hands rested, in tight fists, on her slender hips.

"But, Donna," I tried to reason, "the bloke attacked you. If me and Jasmine hadn't intervened he could've seriously hurt you…"

"Look, I know my clients better than you do, Lou. It is my job after all. Now you need to butt out, okay? And let me get on with what I have to do."

I could feel my temper rising. As far as I was concerned we should have thrown Patrick Tanner out on his ear. He might have been victimized but that wasn't any excuse to do the same thing to a staff member. "I can't believe you're saying this…"

"Well, believe it. I'm tired of people here telling me what to do, how I should or should not relate to my clients. It's none of their damn business."

"Is that what you told Peter when he confronted you about dating a client?" It slipped out before I had time to censor myself. And I was so furious with Donna that I didn't even care.

For a moment she looked stunned, the outrage in her eyes replaced by astonishment. "I don't know what you're talking about."

"I think you do."

She laughed. "You're being ridiculous, Lou. Like I said, I have no idea what you're talking about." She attempted a look of confusion. It wasn't very convincing.

"I know you're having a relationship with a client, Donna," I said steadily. "There's no point in denying it. I even saw you with her at the beach."

She sighed, walked over to her desk and dropped into her chair. For several seconds she was silent, chewing her lip and contemplating the floor. "So, what are you going to do, Lou? Are you going to tell Amanda? Are you going to make me lose my job? What exactly are you going to do?" Her voice was panicked.

"To be honest with you, Donna, I don't really know. I don't want to see you fired but what you're doing is wrong."

"Well at least that's one way you're different from Peter," she said quietly. "He wanted me out, I know he did. All he cared about were his fucking precious personnel procedures."

"I'm sure he was in as much of a quandary as I am."

She let out a harsh, sputtering laugh. "I don't think so. He wanted me out of here. He was such a stickler for procedure. God, did he have a bug up his butt about the whole thing." She pulled a slight, caustic smile.

"Well, he was right. You can't go on dating a client."

"So what do you want me to do?"

"I'm not sure. Maybe you should give it some thought over the weekend and we can talk early sometime next week."

"Whatever," Donna said sulkily. "I guess I'm at your mercy just like I was at Peter's."

"Knock, knock." Amanda gently kicked open the door with her black patent pump. "Not interrupting anything am I?" Her face puckered into a frown as she looked from Donna to me and then at Donna again. "You two look a bit...serious. Anything wrong?"

"No, no," Donna responded breezily. "We were just...er...discussing a client matter. Right, Lou?" She shot me an imploring glance.

"Yes," I nodded, "we were going over Patrick Tanner's case."

"Oh, well are you done?" Amanda asked. "Because I wanted to talk with you, Lou."

"Yes, we're done," I said, glancing over at Donna before stepping out into the hall.

"Lou, I've been thinking, we haven't really had much chance to talk in a while." Amanda patted a hand over her bobbed hair. "I know there are several things we really need to talk about and since it's so crazy here in the office I was wondering if we could have lunch today. You know, get away from the chaos so we can really check in. I want to make sure you're getting the support you need to do your job." She pulled her glossy lips into a reassuring smile.

"Yeah, that would be good. We do need to talk about some stuff. How about one?"

"That works for me."

"Good, so I'll talk to you then."

"This is on me," Amanda said as we sat down to lunch at the second floor Chinese restaurant overlooking Castro Street. I began to protest but she reached over to touch my hand. "No, Lou, I insist, I feel like I've been so caught up in all this furor and you've had to do a lot of extra work to cover for me in the office. This is just something to make it up to you."

"Thanks." I smiled as the young waitress handed me the menu and placed two glasses of ice water on the table.

"And before we start talking business I just wanted to show you this." She rifled through her attaché case and pulled out a copy of *The National Gay Times*. "They printed that interview they did with me the other week. I'm quite pleased with it. I'd like to get your feedback." She thumbed through the pages. "Here it is."

"That's the interview you did the evening Peter was killed?"

She nodded.

I took the magazine from her to glance quickly over the article. Headed 'Lesbian Leadership', it was a double-page spread that featured a couple of photographs of Amanda at a podium gesturing to a crowd.

"They had a photographer come later to the conference I went to in the evening—the one I was the keynote speaker at. What do you think of that one?" She pointed to the picture in the right hand corner. In a deep red jacket and light gray shirt, Amanda was caught in mid-gesture, pounding the podium.

"I suppose that's what they call an action shot," I commented.

"Yes, I was pretty fired up that night." She smiled as she bent to study the photograph again. "Anyway, why don't you take it with you and read over the piece? It gives some great national coverage to The Project, and I think I did a good job of covering the issues. You might find it informative."

"I'll take it home," I said, setting the magazine next to me on the table.

The waitress arrived to take our order. I decided on Braised Tofu with Chinese Greens and Amanda ordered Chicken Chow Mein. We handed back our menus and Amanda brought up the issue of searching for Peter's replacement. His job had been advertised a little over a week ago and we had already received some résumés. Amanda wanted to outline the procedure for selecting interviewees. "It seems strange, almost disrespectful, to be replacing him like this," she sighed, "but I suppose we have to fill the position as soon as possible."

The food arrived and as we spooned rice and noodles onto our plates we began to talk about several other administrative issues including grant applications that were pending, reports to be written, bills to be paid.

I was just chewing my last piece of braised tofu when Amanda said, "Lou, I've been thinking." There was something ominous in her tone that made me stop mid-bite and look over at her. "This is a little awkward…but it's about Donna. I found out recently something that is very disturbing to me…" She paused, picked up her glass and took a sip of water. "…I have information that suggests she might be having a relationship, an intimate relationship, with a client. Do you know anything about this?" Dabbing her mouth with her napkin, she stared at me intensely.

I hesitated, not sure of what to say. I didn't want to go back on what I had told Donna; after all, I had said I wouldn't do anything until after the weekend, nor could I lie to Amanda. "I just found out." I said.

"I see." Her tone was solemn. "Well, that would seem to confirm my information. It was brought to my attention a little while ago. You remember that meeting I had with Peter, the one you asked me about?"

"Yes."

"I told you before that it was a confidential personnel matter that we discussed. Well, the matter was Donna. Peter found out that she was having a relationship with a client and wanted me to do something about it."

So that was why Peter had been so adamant in demanding a meeting with Amanda. It also explained why I had found no note in Peter's personnel file about the meeting—any notes about it would be in Donna's file.

"Peter was furious," Amanda continued. "He wanted me to fire Donna immediately, which of course, I refused to do. I couldn't act without looking into the matter further. And I had fully intended to deal with it the next week, but what with Peter's death and everything, I just haven't had a chance to give it my attention. Now I realize I can't put it off any longer. I was wondering if you had any advice on what I should do."

"Me?"

"Yes, I thought you might have some insight."

I shook my head. "Not really, and besides, as Donna's co-worker I don't really think it's appropriate for me…"

"I'm asking you, Lou, because I trust you and I know you have a good head on your shoulders. I feel in a quandary myself. We're already one advocate down—without Donna things would be a nightmare. And besides, she's given so much to The Project…I know this is a very serious violation of our policies, but maybe there's a way things can be worked out."

I shrugged. "I'd love to help you, Amanda, but this really is something that you need to talk to Donna about."

"Yes, I suppose you're right. It's just…very difficult, you know."

"Yes, I know," I nodded. But I had to admit to feeling a little relieved. After all, I no longer had to worry about what to do about Donna's violation of personnel policies; it was in Amanda's hands now. I was also happy to realize that I could erase Amanda's name from my list of suspects now that her meeting with Peter had been explained. It was always good to narrow the field.

The waitress brought the bill along with two fortune cookies. I picked one up and cracked it open. 'Life is full of surprises,' it read. There was certainly a lot of truth in that. A couple of weeks ago I had hardly expected to have to deal with two murders and my best friend in jail. I wasn't sure I could take many more surprises on that scale.

Amanda ignored her cookie and placed a twenty dollar bill over the check. "By the way, did you find any information that could help out Mario?"

"I think so." I said nodding as I crunched away at my cookie. "You know, I really get this feeling that if I could just put together all the pieces I have already then I'll work out who the killer is. I feel like I'm really close."

"That's great news, Lou. I'm sure that with all the work I'm doing and these inquiries you're making, we'll be able to get this murder charge dropped very soon."

"Hey, Lou, Amanda, did you hear what happened?" When we returned to the office Jasmine was virtually bouncing on her seat, her eyes blazing wide. "There's been a whole bunch of arrests, four Coalition leaders and some others. Stevie just called, said they've been charged with some sort of conspiracy."

"What do you mean, conspiracy?" Amanda frowned.

"I dunno. Something about subverting something or other. Don't ask me the exact charges. Stevie thinks it's pretty serious, though. He thinks someone on the inside passed the cops some information. When they searched they seemed to know where to look and what to look for. They hauled off several boxes of stuff with them."

"This is ridiculous, it's like we're under siege." Amanda slammed her attaché case onto Jasmine's desk and breathed an indignant sigh. "It's clear that because we've made progress against Finch the cops have been ordered to crack down. Those charges will never stick. I'll make sure they don't. Where is Stevie, did he leave a number?" Amanda snatched the message slip that Jasmine handed her. "I'll be in my office if anyone needs me. Someone's got to do something about this god-almighty mess." She picked up her case and strode angrily down the hall.

Within half an hour the office once again became a chaotic hive of activity. Outraged activists arrived to help plan strategy, make phone calls and statements to the press, negotiate legal issues, and once again, consume our entire supply of coffee within a few short hours—all these crises were playing havoc with my petty cash budget.

By the time six o'clock came around no real progress seemed to have been made. The mayor and police chief were unavailable to take calls, those arrested were still in jail, and Stevie from Legal Advocates was saying that the charges, at least in the short-term, were going to stick. I would have stayed late to help out, but the office was so full of enthusiastic helpers that I thought it could well develop into a case of too many cooks. So I decided to leave, make a quick stop over at my apartment and then head over with Hairy Boy for my Friday night soccer practice in Golden Gate Park.

"Lou, I cannot believe you." Terri peered over the mound of whipped cream on the top of her mocha to give me an exasperated look. After practice we had headed over to the coffee shop on Haight Street with the rest of the team. We sat at a table slightly apart from everyone else. "One minute you're starting a love affair, the next you're ending it. I got the impression you really liked this…what's her name?"

"Alex."

"Yeah, I thought you liked this Alex. What's the problem?"

"Well, I do like her, but she's a cop and…and I just don't feel like I can trust her."

"Why?" She popped a spoonful of whipped cream into her mouth and looked at me expectantly.

I explained what had happened outside the Hall of Justice and how I'd seen Alex with the cop who'd assaulted me.

"And did you give her a chance to explain?"

I nodded.

"What did she say?"

"She said she was sorry, and had no idea that he'd hit me. She also said she thought I was making excuses for not wanting to get involved with her."

"Forgive me for saying it, but she might not be too far from the mark. And if you know what's good for you, Lou Spencer, you might just give her a chance to prove she's not the same as that damn ex-girlfriend of yours."

By the time I parked on a side street and walked to my apartment building with Hairy Boy, it was eleven o'clock. As so often happened in the evenings in the city, the wind had picked up and the leaves of the palm trees lining Dolores Street flapped like oversized fans. Under the yellow halos of the street lamps I could see figures moving at the edges of the park. Cars hummed by and a bus pulled up to the bus stop on the corner. Its doors opened, and a drunken, laughing straight couple stumbled onto the sidewalk. Arm in arm, they began weaving their way across the street. Hairy Boy dodged around them and bounded in front of me to the main door of my building.

"Bloody hell," I muttered as I reached the third floor and realized that the light at the top of the stairs wasn't working. I was forced to fumble around in the dark trying to find my key. As I was clumsily trying to place it in the lock Hairy Boy began to growl, at first a low moan that developed quickly into a threatening snarl.

"What's up, Boy?" I asked.

He growled again. I looked around, unable to make out anything other than shadows in the grainy dark. "It's okay." I tried to sound reassuring, but I wasn't feeling particularly reassured myself, all these threats and murders were definitely getting to me.

When I went back to trying to fit my key in the lock I noticed that my hand was shaking, and I had to fumble around for several seconds before I finally managed to slide the key in the door. As I did I heard the distinct shuffle of footsteps behind me. Hairy Boy growled again and I had time to tense, shape my hands into fists and turn half way around in anticipation of defending myself against a potential attacker when I was struck by a hard, heavy blow to the back of my head.

I saw stars, yellow and orange and purple ones, and big red bursts of light. It would have been a lot of fun if it wasn't for the burning pain that blasted its way over my skull and left me staggering against the wall. Fear pumped through me, adrenaline took over and I thought quite clearly that if I didn't do something to stave off another blow then it was almost certain I was going to die. My mind scrambled through the self-defense moves I had learned in class. I bent my knees (which right at that moment felt about as steady as a bowl of Jello in an earthquake) to lower my center of gravity and tried to steel myself against the possibility of another blow. At the same time, Hairy Boy stood at my feet, barking and growling and gnashing his teeth as he lunged at my attacker who was somewhere out of reach in the dark. I heard scuffling, and then the dull sound of some kind of blunt and heavy weapon hitting flesh. Hairy Boy let out an ear-splitting yelp.

Almost immediately a door opened and an oblong of light illuminated the end of the hall. "Man, will you shut that damn dog up or do I have to do it myself? It's almost midnight, for god's sake. Shit, and this goddamn light's not working again." It was Bill Smart, one of my neighbors. He was in his forties, an ex-hippie with dubious personal hygiene. I usually did my best to avoid him, but at that moment I could have kissed him on his grubby little cheek.

As Bill shuffled his way towards us, I heard my attacker hesitate, back off, then run towards the stairs. Hairy Boy ran in pursuit, but weakly I called him back. "Stay, boy," I said as I sank down to the floor. He came to sit at my side. With a trembling hand I stroked his head and heaped praise on him like I never had before. After all, I was convinced that he had just saved my life.

Chapter Twenty-Four

The nurses in the emergency room told me I would probably be fine. They prodded my head, X-rayed my skull and at two-thirty in the morning sent me home. I was told to come back if I felt any dizziness or nausea.

"You'll probably have a colossal headache for the next couple of days," one of them commented, "but thankfully nothing more than that."

Hairy Boy was doing okay, too. Bill Smart had called Terri to come over and she had taken Hairy Boy to the Emergency Vet. No bones were broken, no internal damage was done. He had escaped with some severe bruising over his back. I was left with instructions to have him avoid any vigorous exercise for the next few days and to take him back in if he appeared in any serious pain.

The police took a report from me at the emergency room, but I wasn't able to tell them very much. I hadn't been able to see anything other than looming shadows.

"Probably some wacko preying on women. You need to talk to your apartment manager about better security there," one of the cops suggested. "You were pretty damn lucky this time, we wouldn't want to see this happen again."

Me neither. But I had a feeling that I was no random victim. Whoever had attacked me had gone to a lot of trouble. It's not easy to get into my building—all the tenants were pretty vigilant about who they let through the locked main door at night. But this person had somehow gotten in, broken the light on the third floor and then lain in wait for me to return. I just knew that I had been very specifically targeted. Someone was trying to stop me investigating Peter and Julia's murders, there was no doubt in my mind about that.

I didn't get to sleep until four in the morning so I was not at all happy to be woken by the insistent buzzing of my doorbell a little after eight. "Go away," I muttered, pulling the pillow over my head as Hairy Boy barked his little head off at the visitor on the other side of the door. But they didn't go away, in fact they buzzed more insistently, Hairy Boy barked louder and eventually I dragged myself out of bed and headed grumpily to the hall. I was pretty cautious when I pulled open the door, after all, I didn't want a repeat of the previous night's experience. Hairy Boy had no hesitation, however, he pushed past me, wagging his tail and jumping wildly at the person who stood in front of me.

"Mario?" I rubbed the sleep from my eyes, squinted and studied his face to make sure that this wasn't some hallucination brought on by the recent blow to my head. But it was indeed Mario standing in front of me so I wrapped my arms around his shoulders and gave him a huge hug. "God, is it good to see you." I stepped back. He looked tired, gray around the eyes and perhaps a little skinny in the cheeks, but his smile was radiant. "Hey, you're not a fugitive from the law are you?"

"No, I got out on bail late last night. Apparently Gay Legal Advocates raised some more money. I left you a message on your answering machine, didn't you get it?"

I shook my head. When I had returned from the hospital the last thing that had been on my mind was checking my messages. "Come in," I said, gesturing him into the apartment. "Let me make you a cup of tea."

We went into the kitchen and as I made the tea I kept glancing over at him, meeting his smile with a big fat grin. It was wonderful to finally see him outside the confines of that damn jail.

Tea mugs in hand, we moved into the living room and sat close on the sofa. I leaned into him and held his hand, still needing to reassure myself that he really was there in flesh and blood. I flooded him with questions about his experience in jail, how his lawyer thought his case was shaping up, and what he had to expect in his future dealings with the criminal justice system. He sounded hopeful, but under his optimism I could tell he was afraid. "And what about you?" he asked, draining his cup and placing it on the table in front of him.

I told him of all the recent happenings at The Project, Patrick Tanner's violent behavior, my run-in with Donna, Amanda's knowledge of Donna's inappropriate behavior, and the arrests of some of the Coalition leaders. "And you know what?—I really think I'm close to finding the real killer. I'm sure of it."

"What makes you think that?"

"Well, last night when I came home to my apartment someone jumped me in the corridor..."

"What?" Mario pulled away from me to glare into my face. "What do you mean? Are you okay? Did you get hurt?"

"Well, I'm a little shaken up, of course. I have this big bruise on the back of my head and a bit of a headache, but I'm okay…"

"Lou, you have to stop this investigation thing right away. You hear me?" He gave me a long, stern stare. "It's too dangerous. You could have been killed. How come you got off so lightly?"

I told him about Hairy Boy's heroic actions and the prompt intervention of my neighbor. Mario leaned down to pat Hairy Boy on the head. "Best thing I did was get you this dog. He might look cute and fluffy, but I always knew he had killer instincts." Hairy Boy nuzzled against Mario's hand and licked his fingers. "See, he's what they call a stealth guard dog—lulls people into a false sense of security and then, bam, bites off their arm. Right Hairy Boy?" Hairy Boy responded by licking him again. "But I'm serious, Lou," Mario continued, "you have to stop right now. Can you imagine how I'd feel if you got killed in the course of trying to keep me out of jail?"

I shrugged. "But I'm really close. I'm convinced if I put everything I know together I'll work out who did it. I just know it."

"I don't care, I don't want you putting yourself at risk for me. Just tell my lawyer everything you've found out so far and we can use it in the trial, okay?"

"But Mario…"

He lifted his palm towards me. "I don't want to hear it, Lou. You have to promise me that you won't carry on with this investigation." His tone was insistent.

I sat thoughtful for a few moments. "I don't think I…"

"Promise me."

"Okay, I promise." It was the only time that I'd ever lied to him.

I spent the rest of the day with Mario. We lounged around my apartment and in the afternoon, when the sun finally found the strength to burn off the fog, we went over to the park. We lay on the grass and talked about everything except the murders of Peter and Julia. It seemed easier for him to pretend that life was back to normal and that he didn't have a murder charge hanging over his head. He was doing his best to appear relaxed, but when he pulled a packet of Camels from his pocket and lit up a cigarette, it was obvious that the stress of his predicament was not far from his mind. Around four my head started to really pound and I decided that I could benefit from a nap. Mario said he'd stay over at the park. "It's so nice to finally be able to be outside, I don't want to miss a minute of this sunshine. Besides," he said, winking, "I've been exchanging glances with that very cute guy over there in the cut-off jeans. I'll see if anything comes of it."

My afternoon nap developed into something a lot more substantial and when I finally woke it was dusk outside. Since Mario hadn't returned I guessed that something had indeed come of his flirtation in the park, and I probably wouldn't hear from him at least until Sunday.

After making myself something to eat, I picked up the telephone and punched in Daryl Banks' number. I felt guilty for reneging so soon on my promise to Mario, but I wasn't about to give up when I felt I was so close to discovering the murderer. When the charges against him were finally dropped, I knew he would thank me for it.

"Hello," Daryl answered in his slippery voice.

"Daryl, this is Lou from Stop The Violence Project."

"Hi, how are you?"

"I'm doing okay, considering my little run-in last night. You wouldn't happen to know something about that now would you?"

"I have no idea what you're talking about," he replied firmly.

"And you probably don't know anything about that restraining order Peter took out against you, do you?"

He laughed. "Well, Peter and I did have our little disagreements. He never did have much of a sense of humor, always took things far too seriously."

"Really, so you think that a charge of assault with a weapon isn't serious?"

"Hey, look, the charges were dropped, it was no big deal. And anyway, what are you calling me about this for?"

"Were you and Peter lovers?"

"Sure, at one time. But Peter didn't think I was good enough for him. Thought he'd just get rid of me."

"And that made you angry?"

"Of course it did."

"So you decided to teach him a lesson once and for all, right?"

"What are you getting at?"

"Where were you on the Friday night that Peter was killed, Daryl? You have an alibi?"

"Look, the police have already talked to me about this. They checked out my story and I've got nothing to hide. I was with my boyfriend all night. I got over Peter months ago. Ask that Inspector Cochran, he checked my story out." With that he slammed down the phone.

So Cochran had considered Daryl as a suspect and ruled him out. I wondered how thorough his inquiries about Daryl's alibi had been. And for that matter his inquiries about anyone's alibi. I knew he hadn't followed up on mine by questioning the members of my soccer team. Maybe he hadn't followed up on Daryl's. As far as I was concerned Daryl was not yet out of the running.

I pulled a chair up to my kitchen table and thought about the rest of my suspects. There was Donna. Was it a coincidence that the night after I challenged her about her relationship with a client I had been attacked? Getting rid of me would certainly be one way to keep my silence. It seemed a bit of an extreme measure, but this was the United States, and if fired postal workers could turn on co-workers with automatic rifles then perhaps Donna was willing to murder just to keep her job.

Patrick Tanner had certainly proved himself capable of violence. It was possible that when Peter had met with him to tell him he was terminating him as a client, Patrick lost his temper and ended up terminating Peter. Then he murdered Julia when he realized she had been a witness.

And of course there was Malcolm Devreaux. Had he been on the verge of a drunken confession in The Hotsy Totsy that night? Or was it that he had information that would lead me to the murderer? It was clear that I needed to talk to him again. But sober he would probably be far more cautious and capable of hiding his guilty conscience and the secrets it contained. I needed to figure out a way to catch him off-guard.

As I leaned on the table, staring out of my window to watch the street lights flicker in the dark, I couldn't help but feel that there was something important I was missing. And like a lost jigsaw piece, until I found it I would never complete the puzzle.

First thing Monday morning, Stevie from Gay Legal Advocates stopped at the office to give us an update on the progress of the conspiracy charges against the arrested Coalition members. He didn't have much to tell, they were still in jail, and the police were continuing their investigation.

"Well, at least I can thank you for raising that extra money needed for Mario's bail," I said, giving him a warm pat on the back as he readied to leave. "I'm so glad you guys over at Legal Advocates got him out."

Stevie shrugged. "Wasn't us. We were just the people handling the money."

"Oh, then who was it?"

"Some woman friend of Mario's. I don't think she really wanted the credit. But she must be a pretty good friend because she put up her apartment as security. I think her name's Alex, yeah, Alex Ramon."

As Stevie made his way down the stairs I stood in shocked silence. I had been so ready to condemn Alex because she was a cop. And yet here she was risking her property and security in support of Mario. That was more than anyone else had been prepared to do.

Mario arrived soon after Stevie left. "God, is it good to see you here," I said, patting his shoulder as he came into the office. "I'm so glad you're back."

"Yeah, me, too. Although if anyone had told me before this mess that I'd be ecstatic to come back to The Project after a few days' break, I would've said they were crazy. But here I am, thrilled to be here." He opened his arms wide.

"Are you sure you're up to working, though, Mario? Don't you think maybe you need to relax for a while?"

"Lou, believe me, relaxation is the last thing I need right now. If I sit at home I'll just be stressing out and going through everything in my head, if I'm here at least I can do something useful. Right?"

"Well, we certainly need you."

"Good, I was afraid while I was gone you'd've found a replacement."

"Never," I said firmly.

"God, you noticed how cold it is in here, Lou?" Mario said, shivering and wrapping his arms around himself. "I think I must've got used to it and now I've been away, I realize it's goddamn freezing in here."

I nodded. "Yes, I suppose it is."

"Don't you wish we had a decent heating system? I hate that it gets so damn cold. The only person who never seemed bothered by it was Peter—I don't know how he stood it, but even in the winter he never put the heat on." He laughed. "You remember how his clients used to complain?"

I looked over at Mario and nodded, slowly. What he said made me think back to that morning I had found Peter's body…something about the heater…about the heater in Peter's office. And in a startling moment of clarity everything fell into place.

"Are you okay, Lou?" Mario frowned.

I nodded absently as I pondered my realization. I had always felt uneasy about the murder scene, there had always been something that didn't quite fit. Now I knew what it was. And with that piece of information I saw what had actually been in front of me all the time. Suddenly, I knew the identity of the murderer.

Chapter Twenty-Five

That evening, I left my apartment to stride resolutely along Eighteenth Street, passing a huddle of teenagers on the steps of Mission High School, their cigarettes luminous orange dots in the gathering dark. At Church Street I waited for the MUNI train to trundle by, then continued towards Castro Street, which was as thronged with people as ever. When I reached the office I let myself in. I gazed up the stairway, the whole second floor was still and dark. My footsteps echoed over the steep wooden stairs. At the top of the stairs I turned on a light. I entered my office, sat down at my desk and made a quick phone call. When I was done, I checked my watch—it was five to ten. I sat back to wait and at ten o'clock precisely, someone buzzed the intercom. A few seconds later Malcolm Devreaux stood in front of me. Immaculately dressed, and looking considerably more sober than the last time I had seen him, he swept the office with an appraising glance.

"I'm glad you could make it," I smiled.

"Well, you didn't exactly give me any choice," he said bitterly.

"That's not true. You could quite easily have refused."

"And have my sexual orientation revealed to the press and the whole of San Francisco. That's hardly a choice. Now why don't you get whatever you have planned over with? And I don't know why we had to meet here, it's highly compromising for me to even be in this neighborhood, you know." Apparently, given some time to think things over, and without the assistance of alcohol, Malcolm Devreaux was a lot less eager to talk.

"I want to show you something," I said, standing up and walking towards the hall. He followed me cautiously. I stopped at Peter's door. "This was Peter's office," I said, taking a key from my pocket and placing it in the lock.

Malcolm took a step back. "I don't want to go in there," he said, his voice a desperate whisper as I turned the key.

"But why not?" I asked. "After all, I'm not sure you got a chance to see where he worked, where he put in so many hours providing support to victims of hate crimes. Or am I wrong, have you been here before?"

Malcolm slid his hands into his jacket pockets and said nothing.

I walked into the room and turned on the light. "Come on in," I said, motioning him forwards. For a few moments he stood, swaying slightly as if his feet were glued to the floor, then he inched a few steps into the room.

"Look, just what is this...?" He stopped suddenly, I followed the line of his eyes, they took in the faded blood spatters on the wall.

"Yes, it's Peter's blood," I nodded. "And all these stains on the floor," I said, indicating the dull brown patches, "that's his blood as well. Not a pretty sight, is it? Yes, his body's gone, but the stains will probably never come out. You see, he was lying here for over two days before I found him and once blood seeps in like that it's impossible to get rid of it." I folded my arms across my chest and stared at Malcolm. He blinked and looked away. "I remember you telling me one time that you really cared about Peter. I'm beginning to wonder if there was any truth to that. He was only twenty-four, you know, Malcolm. How old are you? Forty? Forty-five? It doesn't seem fair really, does it? I mean, he had so much of his life to look forward to. He was young, idealistic and politically committed. But that was his downfall, wasn't it?"

"I have no idea what you're talking about."

"Oh, but I think you do. Peter had more integrity than you have in your little finger. He was brave enough to live his life honestly, and he was honorable enough to want to expose corruption when he saw it. And it was that honor and honesty that meant he ended up dead." I walked over to the exact spot where Peter had lain, glanced down at it and then back at Malcolm. "If it's true that you cared about Peter then the least you could do for him now is tell what you know. Don't you think it's time you stopped living a lie?"

I noticed the muscles around his mouth twitch, his eyes were red and watery. "Look, I'm sorry that Peter died, he..."

"He didn't just die, Malcolm. He was murdered, and you know why. You have to speak up."

He turned away. "I can't...you're asking me to give up everything...my career, friends, everything I've worked for over the last twenty years."

"But at least you'd finally have some integrity."

Slowly, he shook his head. "I don't think I can."

"Look, Malcolm, I know why Peter was killed and I know who did it. What I need is concrete evidence and you're the one who can provide that. If you don't talk you're finished anyway because even if I can't prove anything I'll go to the press and tell them what I know."

"But you said if I came here you wouldn't do that."

"I'll also tell them how you were the only person who knew Julia was a possible witness to the murder. I told you that night I called you and strangely enough she was murdered the very next day."

"I didn't have anything to do with that," he protested, "I just told—"

"Who did you tell?"

"Well, after I talked to you I called and mentioned to—"

"I wouldn't say any more if I were you, Malcolm." The voice came from out in the hall. It was steady and cold. A moment later Amanda appeared in the doorway. My eyes moved from her frowning face down her body, they stopped when I noticed the black metal object she held in her right hand. It took me several seconds to realize it was a gun. She pointed it first at Malcolm then at me. "Sorry to stop you, I guess you were just getting to the good part. But since that's where I come in, I figured I should probably be present for that. Don't you think?"

I said nothing as I glanced about looking for some way to escape. There was none. Amanda blocked the doorway and the only other exit was the second floor window.

"How did you get in?" Malcolm asked, then looked over at me accusingly. "You told me there'd be no one else here."

"And I'm sure that's what she thought," Amanda nodded. "But I had so much to do. After I got back from a long and tedious meeting I decided to take a nap on the sofa in my office for a little while. I needed a break before starting work on an important press release. I didn't hear you come in but I was surprised to hear voices when I awoke. I've been listening to your conversation for the last few minutes or so and it's been very interesting indeed."

"I hope you don't think I was going to say anything, Amanda." Malcolm pulled a nervous smile. "I mean she really did have me over a barrel here. But she wouldn't have been able to prove anything afterwards."

Amanda chuckled. "You really are so pathetic, Malcolm. You should get yourself into counseling and get used to who you are. That way, next time a lover of yours gets murdered and you know who did it, you can speak out instead of sniveling about it in some corner."

Malcolm pursed his lips and looked at the floor.

I stared at the gun that Amanda now pointed steadily in my direction, at her finger as it wavered ever so slightly on the trigger. I had never seen a gun before, and especially not from this angle. It was definitely disconcerting. I found myself musing how small the hole was from which the bullets would emerge. It seemed strange that my life could be put to an end so quickly by such a silly looking contraption. But all Amanda had to do was pull the trigger and then, like Peter and Julia, I'd end up just another murder statistic. I really didn't want to die, but there didn't seem to be much I could do about it. So I found myself wondering what people would say about me after I was gone and who would come to my funeral, what kind of music would they play, and what kind of food would be served afterwards...

Fortunately, before I started to ponder the benefits of cremation over burial or asked Amanda for a couple of minutes to write out a will, something in my brain snapped into action. I managed to pull myself together, tell myself that death was not yet inevitable and I might still be able to do something to avoid it. Lacking any other alternatives, I decided to play for time.

"You know, Amanda," I began, "I really don't understand why you had to do this. I mean, it doesn't make sense to me."

"Oh, come on, Lou, you're the one who figured it all out. I mean, you told me yourself last Friday that you were very close. That's why I had to try to stop you. Sorry about that nasty bump on your head. And sorry about that little dog of yours. You know, you really should learn to keep him under control." Her lips moved to form a thin smile.

I wanted to leap right over and slap her across the face, but I decided under the circumstances that wasn't very practical. I suppressed my anger and stayed calm. "I should have guessed earlier," I said, "but I suppose I wasn't looking at things right. It was hard to imagine that you, Amanda Jensen, gay and lesbian community leader could be responsible. And you really were very clever."

She grinned and nodded her head slightly. Apparently my flattery was working.

"But, you know," I continued, "I still don't get everything. And the very least you could do is tell me before you shoot us."

"You're going to shoot us?" A look of sheer panic flashed across Malcolm's face. Then he became unnaturally pale. I thought he was going to faint but after swaying a little, he managed to stay upright.

"Of course I'm going to shoot you, Malcolm. What else did you think I had in mind? A picnic? No, shooting you here will be perfect. Then I'll do exactly what I did with Peter. I'll leave a little hate note and not long after your bodies are found the community will be up in arms. Why, they'll even ask me to lead them in demanding that this time the police do a thorough investigation. Then, if our hate caller doesn't make a few threats, I'll call and make a few myself—just to keep everyone going, of course."

"But you didn't plan to kill Peter, did you?" I said.

She nodded. "You're right, it's just that Malcolm here revealed our little plan. Didn't you Malcolm?"

Malcolm said nothing.

"What plan was that?" I asked.

"Why, the plan the mayor and I cooked up to appoint me supervisor. It's brilliant, really. A wonderful alliance of left and right. For my efforts I'll be rewarded with a supervisorial seat and become the de facto leader of the lesbian and gay community in San Francisco. All I had to do was inform him of the planned actions of the Community Coalition, leak some names and information. That way he could look like the committed enforcer of so-called traditional values and law and order that those conservative voters love, and still court the gay vote by appointing me supervisor. I guess you'd say we used each other." She lifted the hand that did not hold the gun and pushed her hair away from her forehead. It was a gesture of pride and self-satisfaction.

"Yes," I said, "I figured you were the one responsible for all those leaks. After all, no one was so well-informed about Coalition actions as you. I'm surprised no one else suspected you."

"Me?" Amanda laughed. "Why they all think I'm so wonderful, they would never dream that it could be me. They're all so naive—it's quite sad really."

"So you were responsible for all the times the police were able to antic-ipate political actions? And it was because of you that Coalition leaders are charged with conspiracy?" I asked the question in the tone of an interested observer, trying to hide the outrage I felt.

"It was for the greater good of the community, Lou. Don't you see?"

"No, I don't," I said flatly.

"Yes, that's how Peter saw it too. He came to me that Friday, demand-ed to meet with me. Told me that Malcolm here had revealed my and the mayor's little plan."

"I was never quite convinced by your story of it being a confidential personnel matter. It did make me very curious. But when you told me Peter had met with you about Donna and her relationship with a client, well, that put me off the scent for a little while."

"Yes, I thought that was rather clever," she said. "And it was just on the spur of the moment really. I didn't even know about Donna and her client until I happened to be standing outside her door when you confronted her. I knew you were suspicious about the meeting I had with Peter and telling you it was a confidential personnel matter only made you more curious. Using that story about Donna seemed like a good way to put you off."

"Well, it did work for a while. But then when I thought more about it later I remembered that Julia had said Peter was angry with you at lunch time, before his meeting with you. So your story about Donna didn't really fit. I guess you weren't that confident about it yourself since you attacked me later that night."

Amanda shrugged. "Like I said, I'm sorry about that little incident, Lou."

"Only sorry that you didn't succeed, I suppose."

"You could say that."

"And what about that meeting with Peter…?"

"Yes," she sighed. "It was rather inconvenient. You see, I hadn't even known that Peter was sleeping with old Malcolm here. If I had, believe me I would have been a lot more cautious. But he's the mayor's chief aide, so of course he knows everything. You'd think he'd know how to separate his professional and personal life a little better." She glanced at Malcolm contemptuously.

"I do." Malcolm spoke up in his own defense. "But he was goading me. Said that I had no convictions, no political integrity. And then he compared me to you, and I had to laugh. You know, he really admired you, thought you were a wonderful leader. Well, I had to burst that little bubble, didn't I?"

"So you jeopardized all my plans. And I had to deal with Peter threatening to go to the press to expose me. Can you imagine? I couldn't let that happen. So I told him I would come back to the office after my interview and we could talk things over. You see, the interview didn't end quite as late as I said it did. I made it to the office at a little after six-thirty, almost bumped into that client of Peter's—Patrick Tanner, but fortunately for me he didn't see me. Of course the office was locked and I let myself in."

"And when you got up to Peter's office it was cold and you asked him to close the window and put the heater on," I added.

"Yes, that's right, I did."

I nodded. It was the fact that the heater had been on and the window closed that hadn't made sense. Peter would never have worked in such a stuffy atmosphere. Amanda was always cold and she was the only person who could ever bully him into turning up the heat. When this realization dawned on me all the other little clues that pointed to her as the murderer suddenly fell into place.

"I thought I could persuade him to keep quiet," Amanda continued, "you know, for the greater good of the community. But he wouldn't come round. He was naive and young, way too idealistic. So one thing led to another and, I guess, I sort of lost my temper. Next thing I knew I was stabbing him with that damn letter-opener. Of course, then we got into a bit of a struggle and it all got rather messy." She puckered up her face in a look of disgust. "But I suppose at some point I managed to slash his jugular and he wasn't able to put up much of a fight after that. Luckily I was wearing gloves, that way I didn't leave any prints. But unfortunately for Mario, it also meant I didn't have to wipe it clean, and his prints were left on the top end of the hilt where he'd held it when he'd been playing with it. And of course, my clothes all got covered in blood—"

"And you had to change into another outfit," I interrupted.

"Yes, how did you know?"

"You showed me yourself."

"I did?" She looked perplexed.

"Yes. There was always a question of how the killer had got away so inconspicuously when they almost certainly would have had blood on them. But someone who comes and goes from this building frequently and who always keeps a change of clothes in her office could most certainly escape without much notice."

Amanda nodded.

"I didn't even think about it until you showed me that interview in *The Gay Times*. Those photographs of you at the conference were taken the same day. Yet, when you arrived at the office you were wearing a blue pant suit. In the photograph at the conference you had on a red jacket and gray shirt. It's a pity that the cops didn't check your alibi a little more thoroughly. I'm sure they would have discovered some troubling time inconsistencies."

"Yes, I suppose that's true. You're a very smart woman, Lou. I'm sorry you decided to investigate this little mess. You and I always had a good working relationship; I was hoping that would continue. You would have made a great supervisor's aide." She sounded genuinely regretful. "It's a pity that's not going to happen."

"But why did you take Peter's keys?" I asked, hoping to keep her from the idea of killing me for a little while longer.

"Why, I had to make sure he hadn't left any evidence of my connection to the mayor at his apartment, didn't I? Of course, once I left the office I had to rush over to my conference. But afterwards I had plenty of time to go over to his place and check through his things."

"And what about Julia?"

"Well, you have Malcolm to thank for that, too. You see, Malcolm wasn't entirely happy with the idea that I killed Peter. Of course, he didn't know for sure that it was me. But he had known why Peter was meeting with Jeff Easton, so he had a pretty good idea, right Malcolm?"

"I knew," Malcolm said solemnly.

"After you met with him, Lou, it really shook him up. Didn't it Malcolm?" She flashed him a taunting smile. "And then when you called and told him Julia had seen the murderer, he called me. I'm not sure why, perhaps to warn me, perhaps to convince me to turn myself in. But I don't think he quite wanted that, because if I confessed, that meant that everyone would find out about Malcolm being gay." She whispered 'gay' in exactly the way Malcolm had whenever he used the word. If he realized that she was mimicking him, he didn't respond. "So, he was in a bit of a quandary really. But I solved that. It wasn't hard to find out where she lived, so I just went over there and killed her. It was a little easier than Peter, I mean, not nearly so messy. After that nasty struggle with him, I thought it best that I go out and buy a gun. I mean, you never know when you might have to protect yourself…" She pulled her lips into a momentary smile.

I was beginning to realize just how crazy Amanda really was. And it didn't reassure me at all to know I was in the company of a one hundred per cent certifiable lunatic. I decided to keep talking. "But still, wasn't it hard to kill Julia in cold blood?"

She shrugged. "It gets easier, believe me. I guess the third and fourth times," she said, gesturing to Malcolm and me, "will be a piece of cake."

"But what about Mario? Didn't you feel bad that he was charged with murder?"

"Of course I did, Lou, of course I did. But when you're in my position, and you have to focus on the great things you'll do to benefit people once you have power, well, that's what's most important."

"I always felt like you weren't quite working as hard as you could to support him," I said. "It always left me feeling a little uneasy. But now of course it makes sense."

"As long as they had charged Mario they weren't going to look very hard for someone else, were they? I'd be cutting my own throat, if you'll excuse the expression," she paused and pulled an amused smile, "if our protests succeeded and we got the charges dropped. But they certainly gave me a chance to get my face in the papers and in front of all those television cameras. I'm sorry for what Mario has had to go through, but I suppose you can look at it as being for the larger cause."

I found myself wondering how I could possibly have overlooked Amanda's absolute focus on achieving power. As far as she was concerned, the community's fate was welded to her own and what was good for Amanda Jensen was good for everyone else—whether they wanted it or not. Talk about megalomania, the woman had it spilling out of her ears.

"I'm sorry that you won't be here to see me take the supervisorial seat in a few days," she continued, "but I guarantee, it will indeed be a wonderful moment…"

"That's not going to happen." Malcolm's voice was dull and even.

Amanda let out a high laugh. "What do you mean, it's not going to happen? You think you can do anything to stop it in your present situation?"

"I'm telling you it's not going to happen, Amanda," he repeated.

The smile fell from Amanda's face, replaced by an expression of simmering anger. "Just what do you mean?"

Malcolm raised his head to stare steadily into her eyes. "Mayor Finch has no intention of appointing you supervisor, he never did. Even before Patricia Jones resigned he had a candidate ready, someone who shares his political agenda. The only way you could become supervisor is to get yourself voted in, and with the electoral reforms he's proposing to bring in next year, I think that's highly unlikely. You think a man like him would ever really see you as an ally? It's ridiculous. You've been used, Amanda."

Amanda looked like a three-year-old who has just had her shiny new toy snatched away. Unadulterated rage burned in her eyes. "You're lying, you've got to be lying. Even the press have been saying he's going to appoint someone good for the community."

Malcolm shook his head slowly. "Yes, I believe I heard about those leaked pieces of information. But it's not true, just part of Mayor Finch's political game."

"I don't believe you."

"Oh, but you should. After all, I know what I'm talking about."

"But he can't do this to me... I'll—"

"You'll do what?" he asked. "Tell the press? Or the voters? Or perhaps the police? I think you're as eager to make your life open to public scrutiny as I am. And when the mayor leaks the story about the exact circumstances in which you left your previous job, then I think you may find yourself even more shy of media attention."

"What are you talking about?" I asked, frowning.

"Yes, I'm not surprised Amanda's never shared that particular story with you. She prefers to paint herself as a wronged refugee from the discrimination and hollowness of corporate life. Isn't that right, Amanda? Well, I can tell you, nothing is further from the truth." Malcolm seemed to be gaining in confidence, glaring at Amanda in self-righteous defiance. Amanda, in turn, glared back. I was impressed by Malcolm's willingness to take her on, in fact, I was shocked by his sudden show of courage. I wasn't sure it was all that advisable, however, since she was still the one holding the gun and her finger was looking more and more itchy on the trigger. Nevertheless, I was curious to know what he was talking about, after all, it might be my last chance to find out.

"You see," he continued, "Amanda was fired when it was discovered that she had been harassing, threatening, and coercing other company executives into giving her the best and most prestigious accounts. She used anything she could against them, right Amanda? Threatening to reveal adulterous affairs to spouses, telling people she'd make their lives hell if they didn't do what she said, why, she even threatened to out closeted colleagues just so she could get what she wanted. She built her career on terrorizing her coworkers. Of course, the whole thing was hushed up. The company didn't think it would be at all good for their image if such details came out."

I looked over at Amanda.

"So what? I was far better than any of them. It was in the best interests of the company to let me have those accounts. And those people who complained about me, well, they were a bunch of spineless fools anyway. Just like you." She turned the gun suddenly from me to Malcolm. Her hand shook as she raised it to point first at his chest then his head. With her eyes squeezed narrow, the corners of her mouth twitching, she spoke in a slow, enraged voice. "You useless piece of garbage." Her words burned like hot acid. "You think Mayor Finch would trust a little faggot like you?"

Her finger quivered on the trigger and it looked as if Malcolm Devreaux was about to be blown into kingdom come. With Amanda's attention directed elsewhere I knew it was time to act. Without thinking I dived toward the heater that stood a few feet away and flipped the switch to turn it on. As I had hoped, the old wiring in the office was unable to cope with the sudden demand on its resources and the power went out. We were plunged into darkness and a shot blasted across the room. I heard a groan and then the thud of a body sinking to the floor. Malcolm had been shot. I dropped down, and groping my way forward found the desk. I scooted behind it. At least now I had some cover.

"That was pretty smart, Lou," Amanda said, "but it's only going to prolong the agony. After all, I have a gun and you have nothing. It's just a matter of time." As if to emphasize her point she fired in my direction. She was close, the bullet lodged itself in the desk a few inches away from me.

My pulse thundered in my temples and my chest. My mouth was impossibly dry and my breaths came out in tiny, fast gasps. I felt icy cold and my palms were sweating. My whole body felt as stiff and hard as steel. So this is what people mean by an adrenaline rush, I thought to myself.

As my eyes got used to the darkness I could pick out the dark outline of Amanda's body close to the door. I contemplated trying to rush at her, taking her by surprise before she had a chance to fire, but there seemed little chance it would work. I also thought of reaching for the phone on the desk and dialing nine-one-one. But by the time I'd punched two of the buttons I'd probably be lying on the floor with a bullet through my brain. The odds were not looking good. For lack of any alternatives, I started to pray. Believe me, I am far from religiously inclined, but at that moment it seemed like my best (and only) option. I visualized the God I remembered from my childhood, the old white man with a silver beard and flowing robes, and I promised him I'd never do anything the slightest, tiniest bit dishonest for the rest of my life, that I would always remember family birthdays and never cut someone off on the freeway again—that is if he would just show up for me this one time and get me out of this horrible mess.

Another bullet whizzed over my head. I prayed even harder. And then I heard a noise downstairs. It sounded like the scraping of a key in a lock. Amanda seemed to hear it too because her shadowy shape backed away from me a little as if she were straining to determine the source of the sound. Then I heard voices.

"Hey, the power's out." It was Mario. For a moment I felt almost a giddy sense of relief. Maybe there was a God after all. "I'll just flip the switches," Mario announced.

My panic accelerated to new levels. "Don't turn the lights on," I found myself yelling. "Amanda's got a gun!"

As if to prove my point Amanda fired once again in my direction. I ducked low and the bullet flew over my head. There was a mumbling of conversation from downstairs, Mario and whoever he was with appeared to be strategizing. I hoped they weren't stupid enough to come up the stairs. Malcolm's prostrate body was proof enough that Amanda was serious in her intentions.

I heard some muffled footsteps on the stairs, then for a few moments there was nothing. All I could hear was my own breathing. Then in one dazzling moment the lights came on and I found myself blinking and dazed in the sudden brightness. I heard the sound of running along the hall. Two shots rang out. Someone gasped and then fell to the floor.

Chapter Twenty-Six

I raised my head from behind the desk and the first thing I saw was Alex Ramon. She stood in the doorway, her gun held steadily in two hands. Amanda lay on the floor next to her, a slow trickle of blood oozing through her white silk blouse.

"God, am I glad to see you," I said breathlessly as I pulled myself to my feet. "I thought I was a goner for sure."

"Yeah, and so did I," Mario said sternly as he appeared next to Alex.

"Well, how was I to know…" I began.

"Lou, you promised me," he interrupted, wagging a finger at me. "You said you weren't going to investigate…"

"But I had to…" I began to protest.

"Don't tell me…"

"Look, you two," Alex interjected, "maybe you can save the argument until later. We need to call an ambulance. Amanda here needs some attention and I'm not sure what kind of state the other guy is in." She nodded over towards Malcolm who lay in a silent and motionless heap.

"Of course," I said, embarrassed, and picked up the phone to dial nine-one-one.

It wasn't until the early hours of the morning that Mario and I were able to resume our discussion. Within minutes of my call two ambulances and several police cars arrived outside the building. Amanda had a relatively minor injury just below her shoulder. Malcolm, however, was less fortunate, he had been wounded in the stomach and was thought to have sustained some serious internal wounds. But one of the paramedics assured me that he would probably pull through.

After an initial barrage of questions from the officers who arrived first on the scene, we were subjected to another grilling by Cochran who staggered up the stairs about an hour later looking like he'd just been pulled out of bed. Naturally, he was skeptical of our story.

"So, let me get this straight," he said as he took a loud sip of coffee from a Styrofoam cup, "you're telling me that the mayor and this Jensen woman were involved in some political deal?"

I nodded.

Cochran sipped his coffee again. "And Peter Williams found out about the deal through this Malcolm Devreaux guy and threatened to go to the press?"

I nodded again.

"But this Jensen woman arranged to meet Peter Williams after work and killed him before he could spill the story?"

"Yes."

He shook his head slowly. "And how does this Julia person fit in?"

I managed to stop myself saying that I'd already tried to tell him all this when Julia was killed. Instead, I went over everything I knew.

"I'm going to have to look into this further," he said, looking at me with dubious scrutiny, "it sounds pretty far-fetched to me. I just hope for your sake, Miss Spencer, that this doesn't turn out to be another effort to get your friend Mr. Fuentes off the hook. Because if it is, well, this time I think you've gone a bit too far."

Finally, a little after three am, we were able to convince Cochran. And if it had not been that Alex, a fellow member of the SFPD, was able to back up our story, I suspect Mario and I would have been detained a lot longer. Cochran seemed far from thrilled to admit the possibility that he had been wrong.

We emerged onto an eerily quiet Castro Street. "Let me give you guys a ride," Alex suggested. We readily agreed. When she pulled up outside my apartment building I invited them in.

"Come up and have some tea," I offered, "I don't know about you two but I'm far too wired to be able to sleep now." They both nodded and within minutes we were in my kitchen sipping mugs of deep brown tea. "I think I owe you two a rather large debt of gratitude," I began.

"Yeah, I guess you could say that," Mario said, his tone still somewhat indignant. It seemed it was going to take him a little while to forgive me for almost getting myself killed.

"But why did you end up at The Project?" I asked.

"It was the message you left," he said.

"Really?" Just before Malcolm had arrived at The Project I had called

Mario. He wasn't home so I'd left a message on his machine. But I hadn't said anything about meeting Malcolm, or anything about my investigation of the murder. "All I mentioned was something about getting together with you later, right?"

Mario nodded. "Yeah, but don't you think I can tell when something's up with you, Lou Spencer? I haven't known you all this time for nothing. And I also know you well enough that when you told me you weren't going to carry on with murder investigation that you were telling me one big lie. When I heard that message I knew something was up, you just sounded so excited. I guess you could call it intuition or something. Anyway, I knew something was going down. And being the big old baby that I am, I decided to call Alex to help out."

"Yeah, he called me with this garbled nonsense about you being in some kind of danger," Alex said. "I wasn't sure how seriously to take it. But he had me worried enough to want to check things out."

"We went over to your apartment first," Mario said, "but you weren't there, so we thought the next logical place to try would be the office. That's how we ended up there."

"When you shouted downstairs that Amanda had a gun, I wasn't sure what to do," Alex said. "I did think of calling for back-up, but realized that in the time that it could take them to get there you could already be dead."

"Yeah, so we figured out that Alex should creep up the stairs and then I'd turn on the lights," Mario added. "In the time that it took Amanda to get used to the light, Alex had a chance to disarm her."

"It didn't quite work out like that," Alex frowned, "I hadn't planned on having to shoot her. But when she fired at me she didn't give me much choice. I hate having to deal with guns." She shuddered. "But I'm glad it looks like she's going to be all right."

"I'm more glad that Lou's all right," Mario said.

"Thanks," I said, reaching out to squeeze his hand. "I guess I was pretty stupid for thinking I could handle it all on my own. I'm sorry if I worried you."

He shrugged. "I guess it's okay. I mean, it looks like you've gone and got me off a damn murder charge, I think I can forgive you for that." His whole face lit up in a beaming smile and for the first time in a while he looked truly happy. "But you know, I just can't get over that it was Amanda. Of all the people, I would never have guessed…" He shook his head incredulously.

"Yeah, she always seemed so…committed, so in touch with the community. And such a really cool leader," Alex sighed.

"I know, I was certainly fooled," I concurred. "I sometimes thought she needed to be the center of attention a little too much, and she always did want to be in control when it came to any media coverage or political campaigns. But I put it down to her corporate background. You know, I thought she'd just learned to boss people around. Who knew she was so into power? It just goes to show that you can't judge people from appearances alone." I looked across the table and caught Alex's eye. She was nodding slowly in agreement.

"Well, I don't know about you guys, but I'm exhausted," Mario yawned loud, stretching as he stood up. "I'm ready for bed."

"You want me to drive you home?" Alex asked.

He shook his head. "Hell, no, I want to walk and enjoy my new found freedom. The way things have been going lately, you never know just how long it's going to last."

I saw Mario to the door. When I returned to the kitchen, Alex was readying to leave. "Thanks for the tea, Lou," she said. "And I'm really glad you're okay." Her voice was measured, sincere. A slight flush bloomed in her cheeks. She looked down.

For a few seconds we stood in silence. I looked at her face as she bent it to the floor. I took in her proud profile, the long, dark lashes, her loose curls as they tumbled over her forehead, the way she bit nervously at her lower lip. I remembered the night we had slept together, how we had fallen asleep in each other's arms, my skin soaking up her warmth, her smell. And I remembered how, in that moment I had felt calm and completely happy.

"Well, I guess I'd better get going." Alex lifted her eyes but avoided my gaze. "I'm sure you need some sleep." She moved towards the door.

"No." I reached out to tug at her wrist. "I want you to stay." She turned to look at me. Her eyes were full of questions. "I know, I wouldn't blame you if you were suspicious, or even if you told me to just piss off."

She smiled. "Well, I don't know about telling you to piss off, as you put it, but I guess I am a little wary. You do tend to run a little hot and cold, you know."

"I know," I said, nodding. "And I'm sorry. And maybe sometime soon I can tell you the whole story behind that. But I've thought about it a lot and I really would like to give things between us a chance."

"I'm glad to hear you say that, Lou. But how do I know that you won't change your mind tomorrow or the day after?" She narrowed her eyes and gave me an appraising stare. "How do I know our differences won't get in the way again?"

"I suppose that's the chance we both have to take," I said. "And I suppose I'll just have to learn there are ways to work out differences that don't mean I have to push you away." I took her hand, relishing the touch of her strong, slender fingers. "I really want to give this a shot, Alex. It's about time I started taking some chances again." I put one arm around her shoulder and pulled her to me, and closing my eyes I pressed my lips against hers.

Epilogue

It was Monday morning. A steel-colored fog hung over the city, the choke of morning traffic sputtered out foul-smelling exhaust. I hurried along Eighteenth Street, dodging pedestrians and a couple of hurtling roller-bladers, and scurried across Church Street against the light. I was running late and it was my turn to open up the office. During the last couple of weeks my punctuality had suffered noticeably. I tried to make the excuse that it was the stress of dealing with the aftermath of Amanda's arrest on two counts of murder—the constant calls from the media, the ongoing conversations with the police, the barrage of inquiries from the community. But if I was honest with myself I had to admit it was the nights of rather limited sleep spent in the company of Alex Ramon that was messing with my ability to get up in the morning. She, on the other hand, seemed to have no trouble surviving on a couple of hours rest, bounding happily out of bed with plenty of time to make her shift. The way things were going I might seriously have to think about sleeping alone for a while. But I brushed that thought away almost as soon as it entered my head. I loved spending time with her, and though our discussions about politics, the police, and the lesbian and gay community were lively to say the least, I felt like the ways in which we were compatible outweighed our considerable differences. Alex was good for me, there was no doubt in my mind about that.

As I approached the corner of Eighteenth and Castro, a group of Queer Nation activists were setting up a table. "Hey, Lou, sign the petition?" It was Jasmine. She bounded over to me sporting a head of bright blue hair and a fresh batch of facial piercings. She wore a T-shirt that proclaimed in big black letters, *No one knows I'm a lesbian.*

"What petition is that?" I asked, taking the clipboard that she thrust over at me.

"Oh, you know, about recalling Mayor Finch. I cannot believe that he's still in office, it's outrageous."

"Yeah," I nodded, "it certainly is. He's clinging onto office for dear life but to be honest I don't think he can last much longer. At least once Amanda's trial starts and all the evidence comes out, I definitely think he's out of there." I signed my name anyway, happy to do something to support any efforts to get rid of him. I handed back the clipboard to Jasmine.

"So you think he knew about the murders?"

I shrugged. "I don't think so, but it's hard to tell. But he certainly was up to his neck in it with Amanda. Hopefully when he's fully discredited we'll see someone decent come into office."

Jasmine looked dubious. "I'll believe it when I see it. And what about that Malcolm guy? Don't tell me he'll be back at work soon."

I shook my head. "It's going to be a while before he's well enough to work anywhere. And from what I heard from our friend Inspector Cochran, there's still the possibility that there'll be charges filed against him, too."

"Good, it's about time these people were held accountable," she declared.

I shrugged. "I feel a bit sorry for him actually, but I suppose it's only what he deserves."

Jasmine snorted. "If you ask me, he'll never get what he deserves, selling out his community like that."

She was probably right, but I couldn't help but feel that Malcolm merited a little compassion. After all, he spent so much of his life hiding who he was to keep his high-powered career and now he had lost even that.

"I'm glad the charges against you got dropped, though," I commented.

"Yeah, me, too. Everybody arrested at the protest has been let off. Apparently the cops couldn't get their damn stories straight. I'm filing a wrongful arrest suit against the SFPD. Of course, my parents aren't pleased, and they're not offering to pay for a high-powered lawyer for that!" She threw her head back and laughed.

I shook my head. Sometimes I couldn't help but feel just a tinge of sympathy for Jasmine's parents. I doubted that they had ever anticipated having such a strong-minded, outspoken, and lively lesbian daughter. I supposed they were just going to have to get used to it.

"And latest I heard," Jasmine continued, "is that conspiracy case against the Coalition leaders is falling apart. Stevie said he wouldn't be surprised if they end up throwing it out of court. That's good news, huh?" She grinned, clasping her clipboard to her chest. "Hey, and I heard that they caught that guy who was making the threatening phone calls, that's great!"

"Yeah, it's such a relief not to have to deal with those bloody horrible calls any more."

"Didn't he gay bash someone as well? What was his name?"

"Frank Frederickson," I answered. The information provided to the Hate Crimes Unit about Frederickson by Alex, combined with Jeff Easton's article in *The Reporter,* had put pressure on the cops to more thoroughly investigate his activities. And though it did indeed turn out that he had solid alibis for the murders, a careful examination of his phone records and the information available through the phone trap at The Project revealed that it was Frederickson who had made the hate calls. Hopefully, this time the system would succeed in holding him accountable for his actions. Who knew, maybe he'd even spend a little time in jail.

When I arrived at The Project there were a three men in overalls waiting outside. Each held a Styrofoam cup of coffee in one hand and a cigarette in the other. "You Lou Spencer?" one of them asked, flicking his ash across the pavement.

"Yes, that's me."

"Joey sent us. We're starting the work today, been waiting almost half an hour for you. He said you'd be here earlier." He gave a disgruntled glance at his watch. The other two sucked hard on their cigarettes and gave me steely-eyed stares.

I apologized profusely. It had entirely slipped my mind that renovations on the building were scheduled to begin today. After the extensive press coverage of Amanda's shooting and the role that the bad wiring had played in those events, the city's Building Inspector had begun looking into the conditions of the buildings owned by our landlord, Joey Pepper. They had come up with some none too favorable findings and with the threat of a city-backed lawsuit against him, Joey had finally been forced to initiate repairs on his properties. The renovations at The Project were scheduled to take six weeks, and during that time, since we didn't have anywhere else to go, we were going to have to put up with the construction.

I unlocked the door. The three men slugged back the remains of their coffee and puffed greedily on their burned-down cigarettes. As I turned to let them in a man naked to the waist, wearing high black boots and leather chaps, walked by. All three workmen gaped after him. "Hey, what kind of neighborhood is this anyway?" one of the men asked, giving me a wary glance. "There's been some pretty weird people walking round here."

"It's the Castro," I answered, cheerily, "you know, the gay capital of the world." Horror and panic rippled alternately across their faces. And as we tramped together up the stairs I couldn't help but think that this was going to be a rather interesting six weeks. By the time Mario arrived, the workmen had already adjourned for their second cigarette break and I was beginning to wonder if the six week time frame might have been more than a little optimistic.

Every morning that Mario's steps sounded on the stairs and his face appeared at the door, I found myself so grateful he was no longer in jail that I just wanted to run over and hug him. And sometimes I did. He was doing well, although now that he no longer had to deal with a murder charge, he had really started to grieve over Peter's death. I knew that in the long-run he would get over it and eventually get back to being his old self. In the meantime, he just seemed sad a lot of the time. In the last couple of days, however, after much nagging from me, he had signed up for a quit smoking program. I considered that a good sign.

Since Amanda's departure things at The Project changed dramatically. The Board of Directors, desperate to create some stability for the agency, invited me to step into her shoes. I had refused. Despite the notoriety I had achieved after Amanda's arrest, I wasn't cut out to take up such a public position; behind-the-scenes administration work was much more my cup of tea. And besides, whoever took charge of all the post-Amanda mopping up had their job cut out for them. Mario had also declined to take the job. He didn't feel like he was in any shape right now to take on the responsibility, and we had started a search for a new Executive Director in earnest. But it would be a while before someone was appointed. In the meantime the rest of us carried the extra load. Peter's replacement, a woman named Rachel Wang, had started work only a week ago but seemed to have adapted well. And after Donna handed in her notice, we were able to find someone with a lot of relevant experience who would join us in just a couple of days.

In the meantime, the three of us remaining had to pull together to deal with the extra work and help out clients. Only the other day I had spent almost an hour with Natalie Featherstone, talking over her case. She seemed a lot better and the work she was doing with her therapist had really helped her get over some of the trauma. I was certain that in time she really would heal. Patrick Tanner, on the other hand, was still dealing with some serious psychological problems and stubbornly refused to seek professional help. After another violent outburst he had been banned from the office but we continued to counsel him over the phone. Recently there had been some positive developments in his case. A sympathetic city supervisor had been putting pressure on MUNI to fire the driver, and a lawyer who had worked before with Gay Legal Advocates had taken up a civil case on Tanner's behalf. It was my feeling that if Patrick continued to see some action and results, he might yet develop faith in the system and agree to get psychiatric help.

Despite the problems and the overwhelming workload, I continued to love my job, though it wasn't easy. Some days I felt like I was still reeling from all the changes, and all the shocking revelations I had uncovered in the course of my investigation. To have dealt with murder, violence, corruption and so many lies in such a short period of time was a little disorienting to say the least. And after the construction at the office was done, and a new director appointed, I promised myself I would take a vacation. In fact, I had begun considering taking a trip home.

Ever since I had fled the relationship with Justine, I had been too afraid to return, worried that she would find out I was visiting and track me down, or that we would just bump into one another in the street. Out of necessity I had ignored the dull ache of homesickness, told myself there was nothing back in England that I missed. Now, after the events of the last few weeks, the longing to go home emerged bolder and stronger, no longer something I could resist. I yearned to walk meandering London streets, take a double decker bus over Waterloo bridge and gaze into the dark murky waters of the Thames. I wanted to eat Indian food in a shabby cafe along Brick Lane, and go with friends to a play in the West End. I wanted to take a train up to Cumbria, press my face against the window and watch the lush green fields flash by. And I longed to stride carelessly over the fells near where I grew up and look down on quiet stone-hewn villages and still, deep blue lakes. But most of all I wanted to put to rest the ghost of fear and pry myself free from the past. And now, for the first time in five years, that seemed like a real possibility.

1997 MYSTERIES FROM NEW VICTORIA PUBLISHERS
PO BOX 27 NORWICH VERMONT 05055
OR CALL 1-800 326 5297   EMAIL newvic@aol.com
Home page http://www.opendoor.com/NewVic/

CEMETERY MURDERS   A mystery by Jean Marcy $10.95
Meg Darcy, single, has the hots for Sarah Lindstrom the attractive but aloof city police detective. Conflict and competition dominate their interactions, particularly their erotic entanglement, as both Meg and Sarah strive to be the first to find the killer.

NO DAUGHTER OF THE SOUTH   A mystery by Cynthia Webb $10.95
Brash, humorous and chilling—Laurie Coldwater, a New York journalist, returns to her Florida hometown and the white southern roots she has soundly rejected.

TORRID ZONE   A mystery novel by ReBecca Béguin $10.95
Ida Muret reluctantly agrees to shelter one of her lover's students who is being harassed on campus.A well-layered story of a country dyke reclaiming life, love and labors lost.

SIX STONER MCTAVISH MYSTERIES BY SARAH DREHER

BAD COMPANY $10.95 paper $19.95 hardcover   Stoner and Gwen investigate mysterious accidents, sabotage and menacing notes that threaten members of a feminist theater company."Sarah Dreher's endearing creation, Stoner McTavish, is on every list of beloved lesbian detectives."

STONER MCTAVISH $9.95 The first Stoner mystery introduces us to travel agent Stoner McTavish. On a trip to the Tetons, Stoner meets and falls in love with her dream lover, Gwen, whom she must rescue from danger and almost certain death.

SOMETHING SHADY $8.95 Investigating the mysterious disappearance of a nurse at a suspicious rest home on the coast of Maine, Stoner finds herself an inmate, trapped in the clutches of the evil psychiatrist Dr. Milicent Tunes. Can Gwen and Aunt Hermione charge to the rescue before it's too late?

GRAY MAGIC $9.95   After telling Gwen's grandmother that they are lovers, Stoner and Gwen set off to Arizona to escape the fallout. But a peaceful vacation turns frightening when Stoner finds herself an unwitting combatant in a struggle between the Hopi spirits of Good and Evil.

A CAPTIVE IN TIME $9.95   Stoner finds herself inexplicably transported to a town in Colorado Territory, time 1871. There she encounters Dot, the saloon keeper, Blue Mary, a local witch/healer, and an enigmatic teenage runaway named Billy.

OTHERWORLD $10.95   All your favorite characters—business partner Marylou, eccentric Aunt Hermione, psychiatrist, Edith Kesselbaum, and of course, devoted lover, Gwen, on vacation at Disney World. In a case of mistaken identity, Marylou is kidnapped and held hostage in an underground tunnel.